DEADFALL

CreateSpace ISBN: 15-0086-045-X
www.bluespikepublishing.com
Printed in the United States of America

To All My Old Friends

OTHER BOOKS FROM DAVID LENNON

The Quarter Boys

Echoes
Lambda Literary Award Winner

Second Chance

Blue's Bayou
Lambda Literary Award Finalist

Reckoning

Fierce
Lambda Literary Award Finalist

INTRODUCTION

As I've gotten older, it's become increasingly apparent that perception is fluid. It varies not just from person to person, but from one point in our lives to another. Looking back on my childhood, I see things very differently than I did at the time (and presumably than I will in another thirty years). While my control freak side finds the mutability of perception unsettling, the writer side finds it intriguing. It inspired me to ask the essential question behind most mysteries: What if?

DeadFall is set in my home town and takes place largely in and around my old neighborhood, but it's not autobiographical (though I *may* have had a stash of magazines hidden in the basement ceiling). That's just the area of town I knew best. Though Weston doesn't have a lot of people, it has a lot of space, with neighborhoods separated by miles of narrow, twisting roads. Until I could drive, my life outside school was limited to just the places I could reach by bike without taking my life in my hands. A lot of time, especially in my early teens, was spent with my friends Eric and Kent in the woods and fields belonging to the Campion Center, a former theological college, abutting our neighborhood.

I'm occasionally prone to nostalgia, and if there were any time I'd want to revisit, it would be the summer of 1975, when I was thirteen. It was one of the most intense periods in my life because I was experiencing so much for the first time. My hormones had kickstarted, I was madly in love with my second girlfriend and harboring a huge crush on one of my best friends (I won't say which), I was experiencing music and books in a personal way I never had before, and we'd begun experimenting with substances that heightened it all. It was when I stopped feeling like a little kid and took a few tentative steps toward being a sullen teen. This book is in part a love letter to those days when everything felt new, yet we thought we already knew it all.

Each book has had a unique playlist I've returned to again and again for inspiration or to capture mood as I write. As always, there was a lot of classic rock for this one, but the primary soundtrack was the singer-songwriters of the late 60s and early 70s: Gilbert O'Sullivan, Cat Stevens, Joni Mitchell, Gordon Lightfoot, Carole King, Phoebe Snow, Simon & Garfunkel, and especially Janis Ian and Carly Simon.

I'm not sure what it says about me, but the two songs that most profoundly shaped my expectations about love and relationships were *At Seventeen* and *That's the Way I've Always Heard It Should Be* (though it was already four years old by the time I remember first hearing it). Kind of bleak, and it certainly explains a lot about my early relationships, but whenever I got stuck or felt I was losing the tone of the story, I turned to those two songs to get back on track. So thank you, Janis and Carly!

In the process of writing, I discovered that memory is as fluid as perception. I'm grateful to my Weston friends—especially Ed Coburn and Lisa Govan—who helped fill in the gaps, and to whoever thought it might be useful to put TV schedules, record and movie charts, fashion trends, and ads from 1975 and 1988 on the Internet.

I owe a huge debt of gratitude to Drewey Wayne Gunn who read the first draft and (among many insightful comments) made the audacious suggestion that I cut the scenes set in the past from the beginning and gradually reveal them as memory later. Though I ultimately went only halfway, his suggestion illuminated a major structural and narrative flaw.

I'm also thankful to the people who encourage me to keep writing—Bob Mitchell, Vion DeCew, Ernie Gaudreau, Esme McTighe, all my family, and especially Brian and Blue, who also give me the physical and mental space and provide me with a happy real world to come back to when I'm done.

D.L.

DEADFALL

DAVID LENNON

CHAPTER 1

August 1975

"Tyler residence."

"Tyler residence," Joey Gardner's mocking voice repeated, followed by a staccato burst of high-pitched laughter. "Hey, dork. How come Caroline didn't pick up?"

"She's at Grace's 'playing canasta' or whatever they supposedly do while they get hammered," Danny Tyler replied. It had become a private thing between them that summer, referring to their parents and their parents' friends by first names. "You just get back from your grandparents'?"

"Like an hour ago."

"How was it?"

"Lame. What are you doing?"

"Nothing." Danny absently tried to unkink the phone cord. "Just hanging out, listening to music."

"What?"

"*Dark Side of the Moon.*"

"Dude, give it a rest. That album is like two years old. *Captain Fantastic* is ten times better."

"Elton John is for fags," Danny replied.

"Then Jerry must love him," Joey cracked.

Danny laughed despite the mild sting. "Yeah, probably," he said. He'd stopped feeling an obligation to defend his father around the time Jerry had stopped feeling an obligation to be a husband and father and had followed his boyfriend, "Karl...with a K," to Manhattan. Danny picked up the phone and flopped onto the black bean bag next to his desk.

"So you alone?" Joey asked.

Danny smiled at the flutter of excitement in his voice. "Yeah, but not for much longer."

"Does that mean I can come over?"

"No, it means Caroline's going to be home in like twenty minutes."

There was a brief pause, then, "So? We've done it faster than that before." There was a hint of pleading in Joey's voice now. "I'm wicked horny."

"Try using your hand."

"But you feel so much better."

Danny felt his penis suddenly twitch to life. "No way," he said quickly, trying to ignore it. "The last time she almost caught us."

"Well, what about after she goes to bed?" Joey pressed.

"Too risky. She hasn't been sleeping well lately. She keeps getting up and walking around the house."

"But you said she never comes into your room because she's afraid she'll catch you jerking off."

"That was before those kids got killed. Now she checks up on me like every hour." It was half of the truth. He decided to leave out her drunken tears and that it had been going on since long before the first murder.

"Come on," Joey whined. "It's been almost a week." He paused, then added, "We can do *whatever* you want."

Danny unconsciously adjusted the crotch of his tan corduroys as he checked the glowing dial of the clock on his dresser. It was almost 9:30 PM. He did a quick mental calculation. "Okay, but let's meet up instead."

"Isn't she going to notice you're gone?"

"Probably, but not until after she has her night cap. I figure I have at least an hour before she calls the cops."

And if I'm lucky, she'll pass out in front of the TV as soon as she gets home.

"You sure?" Joey asked with uncharacteristic worry.

"Yeah. I'll meet you behind your house."

"Why don't we just meet at Lovers' Rock? It'll be faster."

"I don't want you in the woods by yourself," Danny replied, surprising himself with the urgency of his tone.

"Why not?"

"Duh. Because four kids have been killed, including one who lived three houses from you."

Joey laughed. "Right. Like the killer's just happens to be in the woods behind my house right now. Don't be such a pussy."

"I'm serious," Danny replied more insistently.

"What about you?" Joey argued. "You could get killed on the way here."

"No, because I'm much less of a pussy than you are, and I'm a much faster runner."

"Whatever."

"So are you going to wait?" Danny asked, but all he heard was loud chewing. "Promise, or I'm not coming."

Joey sighed resignation. "Fine."

The tension in Danny's shoulders loosened slightly. "Cool. I'm on my way. Meet me behind your garage in ten minutes."

* * * * *

Joey collapsed against Danny's back. Usually one of them would have made a joke about the farting sound, but now Joey just kissed the back of Danny's damp neck.

"Thanks. I so needed that," he said, his voice barely a whisper.

"Me, too," Danny sighed.

Joey's arms slipped under his chest and hugged him tightly.

"I wish we could stay here like this all night," Joey said.

Danny had fooled around with a few other guys from school in the past, but it had always been awkward and fumbling, followed by guilty silence and weeks of avoidance. With Joey it was different. Though Joey could be aggressive, bordering on violent, as he worked toward orgasm, after he was always gentle and affectionate, and seemed almost desperate to remain together, as if he needed assurance that their connection was more than

3

just sexual. Danny was always surprised by how soft and yielding Joey's body became in those moments.

"Yeah, that would be awesome," he deadpanned. "Especially when the cops found us in the morning."

For a moment Joey didn't respond, then he yanked his hands from under Danny and rolled onto his back. "Don't be a dick."

"Sorry," Danny said. He'd always understood the physical and friendship parts of their relationship, but was still learning to navigate the new terrain that seemed beyond both of those.

He rolled to face Joey and draped his left arm across Joey's chest. Joey didn't react, just stared hard at the sky.

"I really am sorry," Danny tried again, kissing Joey on the cheek. "I wish we could stay here, too."

"Like that's ever going to happen," Joey said.

Danny sensed he was talking about something more than just spending the night together, but didn't know how to articulate the thought. He settled for, "Why not?" then felt stupid.

"Because 'love was meant for beauty queens,'" Joey said.

"What's that supposed to mean?" Danny asked. He studied Joey's profile. Even in the dim light of the half moon he could see Joey's eyes start to shine.

Joey sighed, wiped the back of his right hand across his face, and tried a smile. "Nothing," he said. "It's just a stupid song." He sat up and grabbed his shirt from the blanket. "We should get going before Caroline loses her shit."

Danny frowned, but nodded. "Yeah, you're probably right."

CHAPTER 2

February 1987

He was falling, his heart banging. He could see his arms flailing and his hands clawing at the air, but beyond them was just blackness. He closed his eyes, waiting for the impact.

Suddenly he felt warm gentle pressure moving in a slow circle across his chest.

"Enough with Jane Fonda already," a flat nasal voice said. "Yes, she's talented, but do they have to give her an Oscar every year? And I like that Sissy Spacek, but she's already won, too."

Danny knew the voice, but couldn't remember how.

"Time to give someone else a chance, I say, though I'm not so sure about Sigourney Weaver. I mean, all she had to do the whole movie was look determined but hot. I could do that. Well, I could look determined, anyway." The woman paused for a moment, then continued thoughtfully, "Actually I might just look constipated." She chuckled. "Personally, I'd vote for Kathleen Turner. I thought she was adorable in those little sweaters. But you know me, I'll probably change my mind a hundred times before the ceremony."

Abby, Danny thought.

The hand stopped and the voice came back, much closer, urgently. "Danny, honey, did you say something? Danny? Stay with me, honey. Stay with me!"

* * * * *

Danny opened his eyes. The lights were off but the sunlight filtering through the curtains told him it was long past morning. He wondered if he'd been asleep for hours or days this time.

5

It had taken him the better part of two days to break through the haze for a few minutes. He'd been conscious of the buzz of activity around him, of people coming and going, but hadn't been able to react. Finally he'd managed to open his right eye for a short while. It wouldn't have caused more excitement if he'd shit a gold brick.

He'd drifted off again quickly, but it had been a different level of unconsciousness. He'd still felt connected to his surroundings, and had awoken remembering fragments of dreams. At one point he thought he heard Jerry and Caroline arguing, though after he wasn't sure if it had been real or just a memory.

On Monday afternoon he'd finally been able to respond to questions, though his throat began to hurt almost immediately and he had trouble finding and forming words. Hearing his own voice for the first time had been a shock. It wasn't just the raspiness or lack of clarity and modulation, but that it was the voice of a man.

He'd been told he was at Shady Meadows, a long-term nursing facility, but not why or for how long. He knew it had been a very long time. He was unable to sit up or lift his head on his own, and he'd seen the wasting of his muscles and the hair on his body that hadn't been there before.

He stared hard at his twisted left arm and willed it to move.

* * * * *

"Ten more seconds, Danny! You're almost there!"

The muscles in Danny's legs, butt, and lower back quivered. Sweat stung his eyes. His t-shirt was plastered to his torso.

"Five, four, three, two...one!"

Danny sagged down into the safety harness and let out a gasping breath. A cramp threatened his left calf for a moment, then the muscle released.

"Good job," the physical therapist said, wheeling the chair in behind Danny. "Next time we'll go for two minutes."

Danny gulped air and shook his head. "One more time."

"Sorry, man. Can't do it. I've got another session."

"Then just let me stay here for another couple of minutes. I'll be fine. Abby can come get me."

"No, that's enough for one day," the therapist said. "You can't expect to undo twelve years of atrophy in a month. You have to pace yourself. Remember, recovery is a marathon, not a sprint."

The sports metaphor set Danny's teeth on edge. He twisted sideways and gave the man a scornful look. "You can either let me stay here where I have this nice harness to keep me from cracking my head open, or I can practice in my room with all the sharp edges. Your choice."

CHAPTER 3

May 1988

Danny gripped the wheel tightly with his left hand while he lit a cigarette, then quickly switched hands again. Though he'd been able to regain most of the strength in his left, the mobility of his arm was still extremely limited, making steering hazardous.

He flipped on the blinker and veered right at the fork in front of St. Peter's Episcopal Church, past the white sign:

Welcome To The
TOWN OF WESTON
MASSACHUSETTS
INCORPORATED 1713

He was both excited and nervous to be going back home. Finally. It had been a long journey back, not just physically, but mentally and emotionally. Typically, Caroline and Jerry had complicated things in their own special ways. Jerry by being an asshole. Caroline by going for a drive after a few too many afternoon cocktails.

He'd been surprised when he found that he'd been moved to an out-of-state facility just a half-hour from Jerry's home. It had seemed uncharacteristically paternal of Jerry to want him nearer, and uncharacteristically selfless of Caroline to let him go. He'd been less surprised when Abby let slip how infrequently Jerry had actually visited, and he'd wondered why Jerry had even bothered. Had it just been a momentary enthusiasm that faded, or had he been trying to impress his friends with his comatose son?

It's the latest thing, darlings. Everyone should have one!

When Caroline lobbied to move him to a facility closer to Boston for his rehabilitation, he'd sided with her, partly because he missed her and partly out of spite. Then she'd gone out for her fateful drive. She'd ended up with a mandatory one-year sentence because of a previous DUI conviction, and he'd ended up staying at Shady Meadows for another nine months, then with Jerry and Karl for three more while he continued outpatient therapy.

When he found out about Caroline's arrest, he'd felt a familiar rush of disappointment. Unfortunately, that was one of the memories he hadn't lost. He didn't think Caroline was going to hell, but he was pretty sure she'd paved the road there at least a few times over.

As her release approached, she'd floated the idea of his moving back home.

"It will be just like the old days. Me looking after my baby."

He'd almost laughed, wondering whose childhood she was remembering. Still he'd agreed. Though her maternal impulses usually died before she acted on them, he knew she needed him. Her license would still be suspended for another six months after she got out.

Jerry had predictably opposed the move.

"I just don't think it's a smart idea, Dan. You need to move forward with your life, not go backward. She can have her friends drive her or take a taxi."

"Leaving things behind is your specialty, Jerry. And stop calling me Dan."

But the truth was that he wasn't moving back just to help Caroline. He had his own reason for wanting to return.

"You and Bryce were attacked in the woods behind his house and Bryce was killed. You were pushed or fell off a 35-foot cliff while trying to escape and were found by Tom Parker the next morning while he was walking his dog. The man responsible for the attack, Tim Walczak, was arrested a few months later and convicted on five counts of homicide and one count of attempted homicide. He's serving consecutive life sentences at MCI-Cedar Junction."

That was what he knew. That was what he'd been told. Again and again. By Jerry and Karl. By Caroline. By the doctors and nurses. Always in that order with just minor variation, never with any more detail. Always clinical and dispassionate. The defining moment of his life had been reduced to a police blotter entry.

It wasn't enough. He needed to know the details. He needed to remember it all. He needed to find that part of his past.

He passed the library, parked alongside the town green, and got out of the truck. On the far side of the grassy bowl, the white columns and cupola of town hall glowed in the late-morning sun. The sweet smell of freshly cut grass drifted on the warm air. He closed his eyes and inhaled deeply, trying to imagine what it would have been like to march across the green with the rest of his class at graduation. Had it been sunny that day? Had they been excited? Anxious? Stoned? Had any of them thought about him?

He opened his eyes and turned toward the center of town. From a distance it seemed untouched by time. He smiled, wondering if Caroline had ever turned his bedroom into the shoe closet she'd always threatened.

CHAPTER 4

He'd spent the afternoon cleaning and vacuuming. Other than a different floral wallpaper and "brick" linoleum in the kitchen, and shortened drapes in the living room and study, the house hadn't changed in the thirteen years since he'd been there. He opened a window over the kitchen sink and pressed his right hand against the screen, savoring the feel of the cool evening air against his skin for a moment.

A knock startled him and he spun around. Through the screen door he could see the shoulder of a dark blue shirt and a badge. His heart did an unexpected quickstep as he moved cautiously to the door.

The officer looked to be in his late thirties, though the soft belly swallowing the top of his belt buckle suggested older. His face was unremarkable, his receding hair faded blond. Only his eyes were interesting. They were pale green, watchful.

"Can I help you?" Danny asked.

The officer just stared back. Danny licked his lips and stole a quick glance at the silver nameplate pinned above the right breast pocket: Holtz. An image of mirrored sunglasses and a thick blond mustache flashed in his mind. "Dick Hole," he whispered involuntarily, then tried to cover it with a cough.

"Nice to see you, too, Danny," Weston Police Lieutenant Rick Holtz said dryly, then gave a tight smile. "Or is it Dan now?"

"Danny's fine," Danny replied. "Sorry about that."

"It's okay," Holtz said. "As I recall, I may have earned the name a few times. I heard you were back in town and just wanted to stop by to say hello. All right if I come in for a minute?"

Danny immediately felt wary, but pushed the door open. Holtz stepped stiffly past him into the hallway, then turned right

11

into the kitchen. He took a look around before turning back to Danny. Danny leaned against the door frame, cradling his left arm across his stomach with his right hand.

"Settling in okay?" Holtz asked.

"Yeah, I guess so." Danny's mouth suddenly felt dry. "You want something to drink?"

"Do you have any coffee?"

Danny shook his head. "Sorry, I don't drink it." He felt oddly embarrassed. "I guess I just never acquired the taste."

"Mommy has a headache. Make mommy some coffee, just the way I showed you."

"Probably just as well," Holtz said. "Stains your teeth and rots your gut." He nodded toward the family room. "Shall we?"

"Yeah, sure," Danny said uneasily.

Holtz sat on the plaid couch, while Danny took the orange twill recliner by the fireplace. He shook a Marlboro from a pack on the side table, then looked up. "You mind?"

"It's your house," Holtz shrugged.

Danny clamped the cigarette between his lips and lit it.

"So is your left arm paralyzed?" Holtz asked. It came across as detached curiosity rather than intrusive.

"No," Danny replied. "The nerves are okay, but it got busted up pretty badly and the bones fused in this position. By the time I was stable enough for surgery, they would have had to re-break them all. Didn't seem worth it since no one expected me to wake up." He looked down and wiggled his fingers. "Maybe some day I'll get it fixed, but right now I don't want to see the inside of another hospital for a long time."

"I'm sure," Holtz nodded. "So are you planning to stick around for a while?"

"Yeah. Seems like a good place for me right now."

"Emotionally comfortable," Holtz offered.

Danny considered it, smirked. "Well, let's just leave it at emotionally familiar. Plus my mom's going to need me to cart her around for six months until she gets her license back."

"When does she get out?"

"Monday."

Holtz nodded. "I'm sure it'll be good for her to have you here. I think she got lonely out here by herself."

The words hung there for a moment, and Danny wondered if he'd imagined a note of blame. He decided to change the subject. "So how long has the Gardners' house been empty?"

"It's not," Holtz said. "Joey lives there."

Danny blinked back. "It looked abandoned when I drove by."

"Yeah, he hasn't exactly kept the place up. I don't know if anyone told you, but his mother committed suicide a few months after Bryce was killed. Pills. His father has some sort of degenerative brain disease. Joey moved back to take care of him about five years ago but had to put him into a home last year."

Danny nodded, only half-listening. It hadn't occurred to him that he might see Joey again, at least not so soon. "Is he married?" he asked. "Any kids?"

Holtz frowned. "I don't think he's exactly the marrying kind. He pretty much stays to himself at the house. We see him in town once in a while, though never for long."

So he's some kind of freaky homo hermit now?

The neurologist told Danny "the voice" was just unconscious thought bubbling up from a part of his brain that hadn't reintegrated with the whole yet. He preferred to think of it as a remnant of his fifteen-year-old self lurking in some corner of his brain. He found the idea comforting.

"You should stop by and visit," Holtz said. "I'm sure Joey would appreciate seeing you. And it might be good for both of you." He looked at a grouping of family photos on the wall above the mantel for a moment, then pushed to his feet with a grunt. "I should get going. I'm sure you still have a lot of unpacking to do, and my wife's holding dinner for me. Like I said, I just wanted to stop by to say hi." He paused for a half-second before adding, "Though I would like to sit down and talk with you at some point."

Danny's stomach clenched. "Why?"

"I'd like to hear what happened the night you and Bryce were attacked."

Danny considered just telling the truth—that he didn't remember anything from that night or the weeks leading up to it—but something in Holtz's tone struck him as odd. "Why? What does it matter?" he asked. "Tim Walczak's already in jail."

Holtz shrugged casually. "You never know. You might remember something that didn't come out during the original investigation."

"Like what?" Danny pressed, beginning to feel annoyed.

Holtz smiled as though he'd just discovered Danny was slow. "If I already knew, then there wouldn't be any reason to talk to you, would there?" Before Danny could reply, Holtz took out his wallet, removed a card, and handed it to him. "Give me a call when you have some time. I'm not on patrol anymore, so I'm usually at the station." He patted his stomach and offered up a grin that seemed intended as self-effacing. "Or grabbing a bite at Ye Olde Cottage."

Danny felt the old dislike come rushing back.

CHAPTER 5

Danny watched the taillights disappear down Cherry Brook, then went back inside and locked the door. He grabbed a Coke from the fridge and lit a cigarette.

He wasn't sure what to make of Holtz's visit. Clearly it had been more than just a social call. How had Holtz even known he was back? He'd been in town for less than nine hours and had made only a quick stop at the boutique grocery store that replaced the Triple A Market.

The Holtz he remembered had been petty, insecure, and desperate to have his authority respected. He'd been like a substitute teacher who starts class by warning the kids not to test him or they'll be sorry. It might have made him dangerous if he hadn't also been predictable. Danny had always gotten off with a slap on the wrist because it had been so easy to push Holtz's buttons and get him to undermine his own credibility.

This Holtz seemed outwardly different. More direct, at ease with himself, maybe even thoughtful. Yet Danny had still sensed the old Holtz lurking behind the not-so-shiny new facade, and the visit had definitely felt like a warning shot.

But for what, and why did he need to stop by so soon? It's been thirteen years. What difference would another few days make?

His thoughts began to move faster.

Or another few years? Walczak's already in jail, so what does it matter? Why does he want to talk with me at all? I don't know anything. I didn't have anything to do with the murders. I was almost killed. But what if he doesn't believe that? What if he's been waiting all this time to prove that I was the killer, and...

Danny caught himself and laughed. He took a drag on the cigarette to slow his racing pulse, and shook his head. Or maybe he's just missed me because he hasn't had anyone to hassle since I've been gone. He cracked the tab on the Coke, took a sip, and headed upstairs.

* * * * *

Though he'd expected to be immersed in his past when he moved back, he hadn't realized it would be quite so literal. His room was a virtual time capsule. Marantz receiver and Technics turntable still on a low stand under one window, albums neatly arranged beneath. Bookshelves lined with classic adventure and mass market paperbacks. Walls a who's who of stoner rock— Pink Floyd, Hendrix, the Dead, Jefferson Airplane, Aerosmith, the Allman Brothers, Cream, Skynyrd, Marley. Paint and a new mattress were definitely in the near future, he decided.

He looked at the lone poster over the bed, a stark black and white shot of Robert Plant and Jimmy Page from a 1973 show at the Boston Garden. Plant's shirt was open, his hips thrust forward, his cock and balls gaudily outlined against his upper thigh. Danny smiled, remembering Caroline staring at the poster with a combination of disapproval and curiosity. How did she not know? he wondered. I hardly ever listened to Led Zeppelin.

She was married to Jerry for seventeen years.

He knelt in front of the stereo and pressed the ON button. After a few seconds the tuner glowed blue. He set the function to FM and slowly turned up the volume. A station promo— "WBCN Boston. The more you listen, the longer it gets."— segued into the frenetic marimba organ loop of *Baba O'Riley*.

Guess that hasn't changed either, he thought. He opened a box and began sorting clothes into the dresser.

The idea of seeing Joey scared him. It wasn't just the disturbing picture Holtz had painted. What if things between them were too different? Though he knew it would be ridiculous to assume they could pick up like no time had passed, what if there was no connection at all?

16

He pushed the drawer shut, opened another, and began filling it with socks and underwear. He had a vision of Karl giving him an exasperated look and straightened up the underwear.

He'd never been one of the popular kids or even part of a clique, but he'd always felt like he belonged. It wasn't just pieces of his memory that were missing. He'd lost that sense of belonging. The world he'd been part of had moved on without him, but he didn't feel part of this one yet either. Something was missing. He'd hoped he could find it by coming home. Maybe Joey would be part of that.

He pushed the drawer shut and reached into the bottom of the box for the porn magazines Abby had slipped into his bag as a going-away present from Shady Meadows. He already had them pretty much memorized, but couldn't bear to part with them. He crossed to the nightstand and opened the top drawer. All thoughts of Joey faded.

The drawer was empty save for an oversized white book with horizontal bands of both bright and dark green above blocky hand-drawn type: WESTON 78. It was the yearbook of what should have been his graduating class.

He laid the magazines on the nightstand, sat on the edge of the bed, and took the book out, resting it on his lap. He stared at it for a moment, then ran his fingers over the cover. He felt a tingle run through his body, raising the hair on his arms. He took a deep breath and flipped it open.

The inside cover and fly leaf were covered top to bottom with scrawls of blue and black ink. Danny leaned closer and studied them. There were a few short notes, but mostly signatures. He recognized nearly all the names, and felt a lump form in his throat. He looked self-consciously into the hallway as though Caroline might be watching.

He turned the page. On the right was a photo from his last Christmas morning, proudly modeling the fleece-collared Levi jacket Caroline had gotten him. His long sandy hair was disheveled and his eyes still a little puffy with sleep, but he looked genuinely happy. He was sure it was the only choice Caroline had given the yearbook committee. She'd told him it was her favorite photo of him because he was always sweetest in the morning, before he remembered to be a teenage boy.

Across the top of the page it read *DEDICATION*, and just above the photo, *To Our Friend Danny Tyler*. Below it, *We Miss You. Love, The Class of 1978*.

Danny began to cry.

CHAPTER 6

Danny nervously checked his reflection in a dirty pane of glass, smoothed a few hairs, and knocked on the back door, listening reflexively for the reply of scampering paws. Silence. He leaned closer, shielding the glass with his right hand.

The low bench still stood against the back wall of the hallway, but the planks were bowed now by stacks of yellow-brown newspapers. A pair of winter boots lay in a ghost puddle of sand and dried salt underneath. A ratty orange parka, a red rain slicker, and a blue down vest hung on hooks to the right, a snow shovel propped beside the parka. The swinging door separating the hall from the kitchen was closed. Danny wondered if it had been opened since winter.

He straightened up and poked the doorbell. Muffled chimes sounded deep within the house. He waited. No response.

"Fuck," he whispered. Of the dozen scenarios he'd imagined playing out that afternoon, none had included not seeing Joey at all. He sighed and backed off the porch, craning his neck to see the upstairs windows. The shades were drawn. Maybe Holtz was wrong, he thought.

A soft metallic *plink* from behind the house brought a sudden rush of fragmented memory.

Reaching toward a flat stone, holding a dented Coke can. A small zip of air, then something hitting the stone and ricocheting, ripping the can from his hand. Stinging fingertips, turning to numbness. Bryce's stuttering bray.

Another *plink* brought him back to the moment. He crossed the driveway and started around the garage. As he neared the back corner, he heard the familiar discharge of a CO_2 cartridge but no impact, followed by a grunt of discontent.

He moved along the chain link fence surrounding the dog run behind the garage. For as long as he could remember, there'd always been at least two chocolate labs living at the house. The weeds and grass covering most of the gravel suggested there hadn't been any in a long while.

The yard sloped away from the house toward the woods. Typical of the region, the two were separated by a low stone wall. There were a few gaps where stones were missing now, and one section where a soft blanket of moss had claimed almost the entire wall, but even after two hundred years the boundary was clear. Danny noticed that the opening to the path had been covered by a large tangle of branches.

He stepped away from the dog run and saw a thin younger man sitting on a folding chair in the middle of the patio, facing toward the wall. He was wearing a faded blackwatch plaid bathrobe and cradling a pistol in his right hand. He stared at a lone battered Budweiser can atop the wall for a moment, then lifted the gun and fired a quick shot. A loud *ping* echoed off the back of the house as the can sailed into the trees.

Danny took a few cautious steps toward the center of the yard. The man appeared to be about his own age, though his face was drawn, his cheeks hollow. His dark bushy hair was matted, and he had at least a week's scruff on his face and neck. Danny guessed he might not have bathed in at least as long.

"This is private property," the man said without looking at Danny. His tone was reedy, the pitch fluttery. He turned his head and angled the pistol toward Danny, but didn't raise it. Danny recognized the Daisy Power Line BB Pistol that Bryce had gotten for his thirteenth birthday. "I said this is private property," the man said, more anxiously than hostile. He watched Danny with wary cornflower blue eyes. Now Danny was sure.

"Geez, give a guy your cherry and you'd think he'd at least remember you," he said. "Typical man."

Confusion clouded Joey's face, and Danny wondered if Joey had even known he'd come out of the coma. He tried a smile.

Joey jumped up, knocking the chair over, and took a few tentative steps. His eyes were wide and his mouth worked soundlessly for a moment. "Danny?" he managed finally.

Danny nodded and Joey let out a small cry. He began a shuffling run toward Danny. His robe flapped open, revealing only stained blue boxer shorts underneath. Danny could almost count his ribs.

"Holy fuck!" Joey cried as he wrapped Danny in a tight bony hug, the butt of the pistol digging into Danny's right shoulder blade. Danny returned the hug as best he could with his right arm, but had to turn his face away to escape the miasma of stale smoke and body odor that enveloped him.

After nearly a minute Joey took a step back. His eyes darted from Danny's face to his feet several times, lingering only briefly on his left arm.

"I can't believe it," he said, wiping tears on the right cuff of his robe, seemingly oblivious to the pistol he was waving around. He swallowed and gave a goofy grin. "Your hair is short. I like it."

It sounded both ridiculous and entirely genuine. He and Danny both laughed.

"Thanks," Danny said, searching for a return compliment but failing.

"I know," Joey said. He shrugged in embarrassment. "I didn't think I was going to see anybody today so I didn't bother getting cleaned up."

And the other six days this week?

"It's cool," Danny said. "I understand."

Joey stared at him for a moment longer, a childlike grin plastered to his face, then waved toward the house. "Come on, let's go inside."

He started toward the door without waiting for a reply. Danny reluctantly followed.

* * * * *

The inside of the house wasn't as bad as Danny had anticipated. The family room wasn't clean, but there wasn't much clutter either. Just some newspapers and magazines on the floor, a dozen mugs on the coffee table, and an ashtray on the mantel. The air was stale, but not rank.

"When did you get back?" Joey asked, eyes shining with excitement. They faced one another from opposite ends of the worn tan corduroy couch.

They were lying at opposite ends of the couch, knees bent, feet almost touching, staring at the TV while Aerosmith blasted from the stereo. It was a Saturday night, spring of his freshman year. Bryce's parents and sister were out. Bryce was home from school for the weekend but had snuck out to a party in Wellesley, leaving him to make sure Joey didn't do anything that would make it obvious Bryce hadn't been watching him. It wasn't the first time it had happened, but he didn't really mind. Sometimes hanging out with Bryce was too much work, especially when he was with his prep school buddies.

Joey had been restless all night, bouncing up every few minutes to dance around the room or poke him, trying to provoke a reaction. Joey had just settled down again when the blues boogie intro of the next song kicked in. Joey jerked into a sitting position and locked eyes with him, a strange half-smile playing on Joey's lips.

"Got me a strange woman..." Joey mouthed along. "Believe me, this chick's no cinch."

He felt a charge building in the air.

"But I really get her going..." Joey begin to extend his right leg, slowly, deliberately. "When I whip out my big ten inch..."

He closed his eyes and let out a small gasp as Joey's foot pressed into his crotch. He was afraid to speak or move, afraid he was misinterpreting what was happening. He no longer heard the music or smelled the popcorn on the coffee table. He was aware only of the still, gentle pressure and warmth of Joey's foot. It was the most exciting and excruciating moment of his life.

Then suddenly Joey's foot was gone. He slowly opened his eyes. Joey was lying back watching TV like nothing had happened.

He turned and stared at it, too, not really seeing what was on. Had he imagined it all? Had it just been a mistake, or a joke? Had Joey felt him getting hard?

Danny came back to the moment. Joey's legs were pulled up against his narrow chest, the robe wrapping his whole body like a cocoon. Danny looked at the bruised skin under his eyes and the fine lines bracketing his mouth, and felt guiltily grateful for the distance between them. "Just yesterday," he replied.

"Caroline called when you woke up," Joey said. "I couldn't believe it. She said they'd be moving you someplace closer in a few months, then you'd be coming home."

And yet she never mentioned you to me.

"But then she had a liquid lunch and went for a drive, and I ended up staying at Shady Meadows and living with Jerry and Karl," Danny finished.

"I still should have come to visit," Joey said, frowning. "I'm really sorry."

Something about it struck Danny as disingenuous, though he wasn't sure why. "It's okay," he said.

"So are you back for good?" Joey asked.

"For a while, anyway. I don't want to be the pathetic old guy who still lives with his mom, but it works for now. Caroline's going to need me to play chauffeur for a while when she gets out, and I need a place to live until I can get a job."

"What are you going to do?"

Danny gave a dispirited laugh. "Flip burgers at Dairy Joy? People aren't exactly busting down doors to hire twenty-eight-year-old high school dropouts with no experience."

"It's not like you chose to leave school."

"Yeah, well I still don't have a diploma. I'll study for my GED this summer, then maybe take some college courses to see if I'm good at anything."

"You should take art," Joey said. "You always did those cool drawings on your notebooks."

It came across as sweet and naive, and again Danny had the

sense it wasn't entirely genuine. "Yeah, maybe," he said. "What about you? What do you do?"

The sudden tight press of Joey's lips made it clear it was something he didn't want to talk about. "I'm not working right now," he said softly.

So much for small talk.

"I was sorry to hear about your mom," Danny tried.

"Thanks," Joey replied, "but I think it was inevitable, even without Bryce being killed, don't you?"

Danny gave him a curious look. "Why?"

"Because she was always so unhappy."

"Was she? I don't remember that. I mean, she was pretty quiet most of the time, but I didn't think she was depressed or anything."

Joey shrugged impassively. "I guess she saved all the good stuff for us."

Danny studied him, trying to decide if he was supposed to pursue it. He decided he wasn't. "How's your dad?" he asked.

"Still alive," Joey said. "If you want to call it that."

He shifted suddenly and pushed to his feet, wavered unsteadily, then straightened and padded to the mantel to grab the ash tray. Danny was surprised by how much smaller he seemed, though he was at least six inches taller than he'd been the last time they'd been together.

Joey dropped back onto the couch, pushed a few mugs out of the way, and set the ashtray down. A silver roach clip rested on the lip. He fished out a half-smoked joint, pinched it with the clip, and lit it. He inhaled deeply, then held it out to Danny. Danny stared at it a moment, then flinched as a wave of anxiety swept over him.

"What's the matter?" Joey asked, exhaling quickly.

Danny closed his eyes and focused on his breathing. He'd had panic attacks since he'd come out of the coma, though the frequency had dropped as he gained more control over his body. Now they seemed to be triggered only by sense memories—

particular sounds, tastes, smells, sensations—though he couldn't always trace the exact memory.

When he opened his eyes, Joey was watching him nervously.

"Are you okay?" he asked.

"Sorry," Danny said. "Yeah, I'm okay." He blinked a few times, then looked at the joint and shook his head. "The doctors told me to avoid drugs that might kill more brain cells," he lied. "It was probably bullshit, but I don't want to chance it."

He took out his cigarettes and lit one. Joey hesitated a moment, then took another hit and stubbed out the joint. His expression changed from concern to curiosity. "So what was it like?"

"The coma?"

Joey nodded.

"Basically nothing. I didn't dream, I wasn't aware of my body, I couldn't feel anything. And I don't remember thinking. But on some level I must have been aware of things happening around me. At least occasionally."

"Why's that?"

"I had a nurse named Abby. When I woke up, I recognized her voice and knew her name. I also have a surprising grasp of mid-80s pop culture."

Joey laughed.

"No, seriously. She used to read *People* magazine to me. Some of it must have filtered through."

"That's weird," Joey said, then pursed his lips reflectively. "So you weren't aware that time was passing?"

Danny shook his head. "That was the hardest part. One day I was fifteen and the next I was twenty-seven. It was a total mind fuck. And not only did I have to relearn how to do the things I could do before like walk and feed myself and wipe my ass, I had to learn to do the shit that adults need to do like drive, cook, clean, pay bills, balance a checkbook."

Joey looked around the room and gave an impish grin that almost managed to turn him into the boy Danny remembered. "Clearly I'd disagree that all of those skills are necessary."

"Clearly," Danny deadpanned, then more seriously, "I also had to learn how to relate to other people like an adult. I mean, I spent half my life just trying to get away with shit, so it took like a month before I realized the doctors were asking questions because they wanted to help, not because they thought I'd done something. It was weird. Still is sometimes. I feel like I'm pretending to be grown up, and I keep waiting for someone to call me on it."

"I can see that," Joey replied. He stared at his hands for a moment and his index fingers began worrying the raw skin along the sides of his thumbnails. When he looked up, his expression was somber. "How much do you remember about that night?"

"Almost nothing," Danny sighed, "and not just from that night. Like the whole summer. I remember finishing school and the party at Cat Ellis's house, but only bits and pieces after that. The only things I remember from that night were sensations. Being so scared that I almost puked, and then falling. But I don't remember why I was scared or actually hitting the ground." He shook his head in frustration. "It was this huge life-altering event, and I don't remember it. How can that be? I don't even know why I was in the woods or what I was doing. Or even why I fell."

"You were pushed or slipped when Walczak was chasing you," Joey said.

"So everyone keeps telling me, but how do they know? Is that what he said?"

"No. He said he wasn't there."

"So then how does anyone know what really happened? I mean, what if Bryce being killed and my fall didn't have anything to do with one another?"

Joey suddenly looked uncertain. "But they found your blanket near his body."

"What blanket?"

"The one with the peace sign."

Danny frowned. He remembered the blanket, but nothing more. "Why would I have that with me?"

Joey didn't respond.

"Sorry," Danny said, grinding the cigarette in the ashtray. "Sometimes it gets to me. I just want to know what happened." He shook his head. "Maybe I *should* talk to Holtz."

Joey stiffened noticeably. "Holtz?"

Danny gave him a curious look. "Yeah. He stopped by last night. That's how I found out you were here."

Joey pushed back against the arm of the couch and pulled his robe tighter. He studied Danny's face. "So what did he want?" he asked after a moment.

"To 'say hello,'" Danny air-quoted.

"What does that mean?"

"Maybe nothing. It just seemed like he might have a bug up his ass. Or I'm just being paranoid. He wants to talk to me about that night."

Joey's forehead creased. "What are you going to tell him?"

"Like I said, I don't remember anything except sensations, so there's nothing I *can* tell him." Joey's eyes moved to the ashtray and Danny read debate in them. "What's wrong?" he asked.

"Nothing," Joey replied.

"Bullshit. As soon as I mentioned Holtz you tensed up."

Joey hunched his shoulders against a phantom chill. "Look, I'm really happy you're back, but I don't want *it* back."

"*It?*"

"The murders. Being treated like a freak. The whole thing. You have no idea what it was like."

"You're right," Danny replied. "I don't. So tell me."

Joey looked skeptical for a moment, then surprised. He nodded at Danny's cigarettes. Danny tossed him the pack. Joey took one out and lit it, tossed the pack back, and settled into the corner of the couch.

"At first," he said, an almost-wistful smile spreading across his face, "everyone was really nice. Kids who'd treated me like shit before were suddenly my friends. Even the teachers treated me differently. It was like I was some kind of celebrity. The boy whose brother was murdered."

"Kind of perverse."

"Then after a few months it all changed." Joey's smile faded and his voice grew quieter. "It was like everyone got tired of it. Tired of me. It wasn't like I ever asked for special treatment. They just gave it to me. But then they began to resent me for it." He took a drag and watched the smoke curl toward the ceiling. "Most kids just stopped talking to me, but a few took it further. The teachers saw what was going on but didn't do anything about it. It was like they thought I deserved to be punished, too."

"I'm sorry," Danny said.

Joey shrugged. "Eventually they got tired of punching me and sticking my face in the urinal. Then I pretty much just stopped existing. That was fine. Being ignored was much better than the alternative."

Cue the violins. Let the melodrama begin.

"When I moved back, I became a freak all over again," Joey went on. "Everyone in town staring at me and whispering."

"Are you sure it wasn't just your imagination?" Danny asked.

"No, I heard them," Joey replied sharply, then seemed to catch himself and rearranged his face, his lower lip threatening a pout. It happened so quickly that Danny questioned whether he'd imagined it. "It finally died down," Joey sighed, "but now you're back and it's going to start again."

Danny knew it was pointless to argue. Joey either really believed what he was saying or he was looking for pity. "Look, Holtz just wants to talk to me," he said. "It's not like he's planning to re-open the case. You don't have to worry about anything. I promise." He waited for Joey to meet his gaze. "Okay?"

Joey gave a small nod and a fragile smile. Danny was sure it was the most he'd get. He decided it was a good time to leave.

"I need to get going," he said, "but I'll give you a call."

"You still remember the number?" Joey asked.

"*That* I remember," Danny said. "It's just the last decade or so that's a bit fuzzy." He picked up his cigarettes and stood, but Joey didn't move. Danny raised his eyebrows.

"So have you outgrown it?" Joey asked, his eyes darting down nervously.

"What?"

"Fooling around with guys."

"Why would I outgrow it?" Danny asked.

"Because everyone else did. Except me."

Danny sat back down. "No, I haven't outgrown it. I haven't done anything since the coma, but I definitely didn't outgrow it."

But I watched two of Jerry's and Karl's friends waste away and die in one month, and now sex scares the shit out of me.

He caught the hope and yearning in Joey's eyes too late.

"So do you want to?" Joey asked.

Danny could hear blood pulsing in his ears as he fumbled for a plausible excuse. He didn't want to hurt Joey's feelings, but he didn't want to leave the possibility open either.

"I'm not able to yet," he said finally, "and it's going to be a while before I can."

The vulnerability in Joey's eyes vanished. "Oh, so your dick broke in the fall?" he snorted derisively. "Isn't that convenient?" He jumped up. "Go fuck yourself, Chicken Wing."

He was through the kitchen door before Danny could react. Danny felt heat spreading across his cheeks.

CHAPTER 7

Danny tried to slam the refrigerator door with his elbow. It closed with an unsatisfying *thunk*. He opened the can of Dr. Pepper, took a sip, and banged it down more satisfyingly on the counter. Foam erupted and cascaded over his hand and onto the harvest gold Formica.

"Motherfucker!" he shouted, jumping back.

He fumed at the spreading puddle for a moment, then grabbed a handful of paper towels and headed it off before it reached the edge of the counter. He put the can in the sink, rinsed his hand, and took a calming breath.

So much for connection, he thought, but am I pissed at him or myself? He stared out the back window without seeing for a moment. Or am I even pissed? Not really. Then why am I slamming shit around? Frustration? Yeah, maybe. Because it was weird and I don't understand what happened? Definitely.

Because you're a drama queen?

Joey had always been prone to mood shifts, though he'd usually just alternated between silly-gentle and manic-obnoxious. This shift had been different. It was abrupt, angry.

He shook his head. There was more to it than that, and it wasn't just that Joey seemed damaged. Something hadn't been right all along. Joey had been acting strange.

Compared to when he was fourteen, or compared to your average pot head shut-in?

The initial wrong notes, the self-pity. It had felt... He had a sense of the word but couldn't pinpoint it. Something to do with math. Run the alphabet, try to capture the feel. It was a trick one therapist had taught him so he wouldn't just get frustrated when he lost words.

A...abacus, algorithm, arithmetic. B...boring. C...calculus. Almost right. Calculator...

Rhymes with ejaculated, sweetie.

Calculated! It had all felt calculated.

But for what? A sympathy fuck? Could Joey be so desperate that all he'd care about after thirteen years was getting laid?

A "Chicken Wing" or a ride down Norumbega Road and a write up in The Town Crier for "open, gross, lewd, and lascivious behavior." Hustlers don't travel west of Newton.

His head hurt. He took an ice cube from the freezer and pressed it against the back of his neck. The bead of cool water rolling down his back felt good.

He looked at the stove clock. Almost time for *General Hospital.* It was an addiction he'd picked up at Shady Meadows. He grabbed another Dr. Pepper, poured it into a glass, and walked down the hall. He opened the basement door, flipped on the light, and smiled at the orange shag carpet covering the stairs.

* * * * *

Another time capsule, this one dustier. Caroline had had the basement finished in 1970 with the idea of throwing regular parties. They managed one that year before Jerry realized the fatal flaw of hosting: he couldn't drag Caroline home before she embarrassed them both. When Jerry moved out, Danny had usurped both the space and Jerry's beloved Bang & Olufsen stereo. At the time, he'd bitchily wondered if he'd been allowed to do the latter out of guilt or because the components clashed with Karl's drapes.

He'd wanted to move his bed to the basement, but Caroline vetoed the idea. She didn't want to make it easier for him to sneak out of the house. He'd settled for transforming it into Haight-Ashbury by way of Spencer Gifts: adding posters, candles, incense holders, a lava lamp, some black lights, a dozen oversized floor pillows, and a rainbow tie-dyed blanket with a purple peace sign to cover Caroline's plaid nightmare of a couch.

31

As he looked around, he realized that the only thing that appeared to be missing was the blanket. He wondered if Caroline even been down to the basement since the attack?

He walked to the bar beside the stairs and squatted down. Southern Comfort, Seagram's Seven, Black Velvet, Johnny Walker Red, V.O., Crown Royal, Wild Turkey, most nearly full, all older than him. Caroline had always been a gin and vodka drinker. Obviously that hadn't changed. He briefly considered emptying or hiding the bottles just in case, but decided against it. If she really wanted to drink, it wouldn't be that hard. Though the town was dry, her friends weren't.

He put down his glass, grabbed the bottle of Wild Turkey, opened it, sniffed, and put it back. The idea of having a drink to relax was appealing, but the reality had never worked for him. At fourteen and fifteen alcohol had made him edgy and aggressive. Now it turned him brooding, bitter, and angry.

And one of those in the house is enough.

He crossed to the TV, hooked the knob, and pulled it out. As the tube warmed it emitted a high-pitched whine, then a few pops and hisses. After ten seconds the screen suddenly brightened, and excited game show voices boomed from the speakers. Danny lowered the volume and changed the channel. Clint was still time-warping in the old west town of Buchanan on *One Life to Live*.

He pushed a few pillows into a pile with his right foot and settled down against them. He sipped Dr. Pepper as he waited for *General Hospital*.

He almost wished he'd taken Joey up on the offer of the joint. Getting stoned had always relaxed him and cleared his mind. But why had he reacted that way when Joey offered it? They'd gotten high together literally hundreds of times and nothing bad had ever happened. Why the sudden apprehensiveness?

An image of a silver pipe flashed in his mind and he sat up. "I wonder," he whispered.

* * * * *

The stepladder was still propped on the left, just inside the storage closet. Danny opened it, pushed it against the wall, and climbed to the top. He reached into gap between the second and third joists above the basement ceiling. Bingo, he thought, as his fingers found the corner of a box. He slid it out and stared at the Philly Blunt logo for a moment, savoring the memory of how the cigar smoke mingled with the smells of leather and Old Spice in his grandfather's Cadillac, then flipped the lid. A rolled up baggie the size and shape of a cigar lay in the middle, a nickel-plated brass pipe beside it.

He stepped down and placed the box on the top step, took out the baggie and unrolled it. An inch of what looked like fine gray sawdust rested on the bottom. He peeled open the flap and inhaled deeply through his nose. Only a faint aroma, more sweet than sharp. So much for that, he thought, dropping the baggie back in the box. He put it on the floor, and stepped up again.

He reached farther back into the space until he found the stash he'd been most concerned about keeping hidden, and slid the magazines out. Vincent Van Patten, Tony DeFranco, Donny Osmond, Linda Blair, Michael Gray, and Brett Hudson looked back at him from the cover of a November 1974 *Tiger Beat*. The latter four offered fresh-faced smiles, the former two their best impressions of smoldering. Danny stepped down again and flipped to the next magazine. A *16* from February 1975. Virtually the same cover, but with Marie Osmond as the token girl.

What the hell was I thinking? he mused as he walked back into the main room.

* * * * *

Danny stared at the Polaroid. It had been stuck in a centerfold poster of Robby Benson holding a sand-crusted acoustic guitar. The guy looked to be eighteen or nineteen. His hair was dark and wavy, his eyes barely visible under long bangs. His body was slim, legs and stomach hairy. He was sitting on a stone wall, his arms braced out to the sides, ankles crossed, a half-smile curling his lips, an erection proudly rising to his naval.

Tim.

CHAPTER 8

Holtz looked up disinterestedly as the outer door swung open, then again quickly when he registered who'd come through it.

Danny walked up to him and tossed the Polaroid down on the dispatch desk. "Tim Walczak?"

Holtz gave it a fast look, flipped it face down, and slid it back. He looked around uneasily though there was no one else in the room. "What the hell are you doing here?"

Danny snorted derisively. "You said you wanted to talk with me, remember?"

"I also told you to call me. I didn't say anything about coming down here."

"Well, you didn't say not to, either," Danny replied angrily.

Holtz gave him a hard look. "So you knew him."

"Obviously, and obviously you already knew that. Why didn't you mention that when you were at the house?"

"Why didn't you?" Holtz challenged.

"Because I didn't realize it at the time."

"But you remember now?" It was more statement than question.

"Not really, but when I found the photo I remembered his first name. I put two-and-two together. But I don't know how I knew him or where I got the photo."

"You're sure about that?"

"Yeah, I'm sure."

Holtz frowned.

Danny gave a helpless look. "Well, what did *he* say?"

A muffled flush was followed by a door opening in the back right corner behind Holtz. An older cop carrying a newspaper stepped into the room and closed the door behind him. He paused to give Danny the once-over, then settled down at a desk and spread the paper across it.

"Outside," Holtz grunted under his breath, adding, "Please," when he saw the hostility in Danny's eyes.

Danny hesitated, then slipped the photo into his shirt pocket, turned and stalked back through the narrow lobby and out to the parking lot. A few minutes later Holtz came around the right corner of the building.

"What the hell was that about?" Danny asked.

"This isn't the place," Holtz replied.

"The place for what?"

"The place to talk about this."

"Why not? This is the police station, right?"

"Right, but the case has been closed for twelve years."

Danny stared back blankly for a few seconds, then confusion turned to irritation. "Then why do you want to talk with me?"

"I think there are still questions about what happened," Holtz said, cutting a quick look toward the entrance, "but I like my job enough that I'm not going to ask them here."

Danny felt blood rushing to his head. "What questions?"

"Just a few things that didn't entirely make sense to me."

"Like what?"

"I'm off duty in an hour," Holtz said firmly. "I'll stop by then."

Though he was both pissed off and suddenly anxious, Danny nodded.

CHAPTER 9

Danny handed Holtz a Coke and sat in the chair by the fireplace. "So what do you mean, you still have questions about what happened?" he asked immediately.

Holtz shook his head. "I have a few questions for you first."

Danny barely suppressed an eye roll. "Fine. Go ahead."

"You said you found the photo. Where?"

"In the rafters above the basement ceiling."

"Any particular reason you were looking there?"

"It's where I used to hide stuff."

"What kind of stuff?"

"Weed."

And jerk-off material.

"Unfortunately, it composted a long time ago."

Holtz gave him an unamused smile. "So you don't remember how you knew him?"

Danny shook his head. "I already told you that."

"Seems kind of convenient, don't you think?" Holtz asked.

"As a matter of fact, no," Danny replied acidly. "I happen to have a great big hole in my memory, and it's not a lot of fun. It starts when school ended in 1975 and ends when I woke up last year. So I assume I must have met him that summer or I'd remember. It's not like I took pictures of dozens of naked guys."

Unfortunately.

Holtz gave a slow nod, as though comparing Danny's statement against what he already knew. "Walczak was usually on the other side of the camera," he said.

Danny caught the implication. "You found pictures of me?"

"Not personally, but I've seen them. About two months after your fall, Walczak approached a sixteen-year-old at Callahan

Park, offered him twenty bucks to pose shirtless. The kid told his parents, they called the Framingham cops, the cops set up surveillance. They caught Walczak propositioning another kid a week later and arrested him. When they searched his house they found photos of you, a few of the two of you together, and a few of another unidentified boy about your age."

"You think he was murdered, the other kid?"

"Doubtful since no other bodies were found. Walczak said they met at Cochituate State Park, that he thought the kid was from Natick, but didn't know his name. The cops checked the high school but couldn't identify him." Holtz paused then added, "It appeared that what happened between you two was consensual."

"Yeah, probably," Danny shrugged. "So what did Walczak say? How did we meet?"

"You were both walking on the road around the pond behind the Campion Center. You chatted, he offered you money to pose, and things progressed from there. You met up two more times, both pre-arranged. He said you never exchanged numbers, last names, etc... It was just a casual sex thing."

Danny closed his eyes and pictured the photo. Walczak was so familiar, yet he couldn't conjure any specific memories of their being together. He looked back at Holtz. "And what about the night of the attack?"

"He said he wasn't there, but he couldn't provide an alibi."

"What do you think?"

"Like I said before, I think there are still questions."

Danny grunted annoyance. "Can we not play games? What kind of questions?"

Holtz shrugged. "It doesn't matter." He took a sip of Coke and looked at the clock on the mantel, then at his watch.

"Funny," Danny said.

Holtz just smiled blandly.

Danny felt heat creeping into his face. "Look, if you don't tell me, we're done. I'm not answering any more questions."

Holtz gave another unconcerned shrug. "You should have

made that threat before you told me you don't remember anything. As far as I'm concerned, we're already done. You're not useful to me any more." He took another sip of Coke.

Danny experienced a quick flash of anger, then something more uncomfortable settled over him, tightening his chest. He breathed slowly, trying to make sense of what he was feeling.

Frustrated?

Yes.

Incompetent?

Mmmm...yeah, kind of.

Impotent?

Maybe.

Like Holtz?

Danny blinked at it. Was that it? Though their relationship had always been mutually antagonistic, he'd usually been the one pushing buttons. Was he feeling what he'd made Holtz feel?

He studied Holtz. Holtz's expression remained neutral, but Danny sensed he was enjoying the moment. He could almost feel Holtz's eyes crawling over his face, watching for a reaction.

Suddenly Holtz lifted his eyebrows in a way that seemed to say, "Your move," and Danny felt the familiar determination to undermine him kick in. He shook a cigarette from his pack and lit it, took a drag, and blew the smoke at Holtz. "That's cool. Then I won't bother calling if I remember anything else."

Holtz's gaze didn't waver. "What makes you think you're going to remember anything?"

"I didn't say I would. I just said it's a possibility."

"According to who?"

"My doctors. They said familiar places and people might trigger memories."

"You've been back for three days. How's that working out?"

"I remembered Tim's first name, didn't I?" Danny replied with a thin smile. "And that you're an asshole."

Holtz chuckled. "Both of which I already knew. Unfortunately, neither one helps me."

"Helps you what?"

Holtz smiled and shook his head.

"Look, I don't really care," Danny said. "If I never have to see you or talk to you again, that's fine, but you're the one who wanted to talk to me, so why the big secret suddenly?"

Holtz seemed to consider it a moment, then nodded at the cigarettes. "My wife's going to kill me if she smells it on me, but can I bum one?"

"Gee, I don't know," Danny replied. "I wouldn't want to be a bad influence." He waited a beat, then tossed the pack and lighter.

"Thanks," Holtz said. "She made me quit a few years ago. Said I could either smoke or be fat, not both."

Fascinating.

"She didn't want to be a widowed mother of two at forty. I chose food, but I still sneak one from time to time." He pulled out a cigarette and lit it, inhaling like he was taking a cool drink after a week in the desert. He exhaled and smiled contentedly.

"So?" Danny prompted. "Or did you just want to steal my smokes?"

Holtz's smile turned patronizing. "All right, I suppose it won't hurt to tell you, but it has to stay between us."

Danny fought the urge to flick his cigarette at Holtz's face.

"What do you know about the trial and the evidence against Walczak?" Holtz asked.

"Nothing. Just that he was convicted and sentenced to consecutive life sentences. Why?"

Holtz leaned forward. "At the time of the investigation, I was low man on the totem pole. Basically I got donuts and made coffee for the detectives. But I studied the file later, and a few things struck me as peculiar."

"Such as?"

"Such as the evidence against Walczak was pretty thin. Actually, that's being charitable. There wasn't any physical evidence linking him to any of the murders. No weapon, no blood on his clothing or in his car or apartment. He also didn't have any apparent connection to any of the other victims." He took a quick drag, exhaled. "Basically it came down to three things: he knew you, he had the right blood type, and he was gay."

"Blood type?"

"Things were a lot worse than the public was ever told. A lot was kept out of the papers because the victims were all minors. The other boys were sodomized and tortured before they were killed. Blood type can be determined from semen. All of you except Bryce were sexually assaulted by someone with O-positive blood. Of course that only narrows it down to about forty-five percent of the population."

Danny looked at him blankly for a second until the words hit. "Wait, you're saying I was raped?"

Holtz's throat made an uncomfortable clicking sound and he exhaled loudly. "You weren't told?" He ran his fingers through his thinning hair. "Shit. I'm sorry. I assumed you'd know."

"Yeah, you'd think," Danny said more to himself. He felt slightly nauseated.

"We should stop," Holtz said.

Danny stared dumbly at the rug for a moment, then looked back up and shook his head. "No, go ahead."

"You're sure?"

Danny found the sympathy aggravating. He shook his head again more vigorously. "Go ahead."

Holtz hesitated another moment before going on. "The most damning evidence was the fact that he knew you and you'd been intimate, but that raised red flags for me. From everything I'd read, serial killers usually have patterns. Based on Walczak's behavior with you, his pattern presumably would have been to cultivate a sexual relationship, document it with photos, then kill—or try, anyway—keeping the photos as trophies. But there were no photos of the other victims, and nothing to suggest he'd ever even met them."

Danny gave a questioning look. "Are you saying you think he's not guilty?"

"No, I'm just saying I don't think he should have been convicted on the basis of the evidence. I'm still not sure if he's guilty or not."

"Then why was he?"

"He was convenient and there were no killings after he was arrested. It wasn't quite so blunt in the reports, but it seems as though former-Chief Cronin, the DA, and the state police decided there couldn't possibly be more than one quote, unquote sexual deviant in the area, and the fact that the killings had stopped was proof that they had the right guy in custody."

"And the jury went along with that?"

"Juries are just regular people, and regular people get scared by things like child murder. I don't think it was too hard to convince them, especially since the public defender mounted only a token defense. It seems he might have agreed that it was in everyone's best interest for his client to spend the rest of his life in jail."

"You're serious?" Danny asked incredulously.

Holtz turned his palms up.

Danny took a moment to let it all sink in, then cocked a critical eyebrow. "So let me get this straight. You think Walczak might not be guilty, and your big plan was to run a one-man undercover investigation in hopes that I might possibly remember something useful?"

"Well, when you put it that way it sounds kind of stupid."

"How would you put it?" Danny asked. He enjoyed seeing the discomfort in Holtz's eyes.

"Pretty much like that, I guess," Holtz replied finally.

Danny was surprised by the lack of defensiveness. It made him suspicious. "Why the secrecy?" he asked.

Holtz's eyes dropped self-consciously. "Self-preservation, mainly. Though Chief Cronin is gone, a lot of the guys who worked the case are still around, and they've risen through the ranks. They wouldn't be happy to know I'm poking around. If it came out that the Weston PD, the State Police, the DA, and the Public Defender were all in bed together and railroaded the wrong guy, it would make a lot of people, including our current Attorney General and Lieutenant Governor, look very bad. I'll risk the fallout if it turns out Walczak is innocent, but I'm not willing to put my career on the line needlessly."

Danny nodded, took a drag on his cigarette, then shot Holtz a troubled look. "Why wait until now to do anything about it? I mean, I get that you were hoping I'd be able to tell you something, but what if I'd never woken up? He's been in jail a long time."

"When I first read the reports, I didn't know my ass from my elbow. Serial killers, patterns, that's not the sort of thing they teach in the basic academy courses. It wasn't until I took a criminal psych course a few years later that I started to have questions. At that point I talked to one of the detectives who'd worked the case, and the next thing I knew, Cronin hauled me into his office and made it abundantly clear that the powers-that-be were very happy with the resolution of the case."

"You could have gotten another job," Danny said.

Irritation flashed in Holtz's eyes. "If I weren't a cop in this town, I wouldn't be able to live here," he said coldly. "One of the guys who retired my rookie year wanted to keep his house so he'd have a place to stay when he comes to visit his kids. He rents it to us for just enough to cover the taxes and maintenance. That's the only reason I can put my kids in one of the best school systems in the country. You don't just walk away from something like that."

"Sorry," Danny replied. He tried a conciliatory smile. "So you really have kids?"

Holtz glowered a second longer, then his face softened. "So my wife claims, anyway. Two boys. Eight and six." He frowned thoughtfully. "I guess maybe that's part of what's motivating me now, too, having kids of my own. If Tim Walczak didn't kill those boys, the real killer could still be out there, maybe in another state, maybe moving from place to place doing the same thing. I'd hate to think I was letting that happen."

"What's the other part?"

"What do you mean?"

43

"You're willing to risk a lot," Danny said. "Why? What's in it for you?"

"Justice."

Danny pulled a face.

"Believe it or not, I became a cop because I believe in quaint notions like that," Holtz replied. He took another drag, then ground the cigarette into the ashtray on the end table.

Danny shook his head. "Even if I bought that, you were practically waiting at the door for me to come home. Why? What's the big hurry?"

"Tim has AIDS," Holtz replied without missing a beat. "He's not doing well."

"You're in touch with him?"

Holtz nodded.

"Jesus, why didn't you just tell me that right away?" Danny asked. "Why the games?"

"Because I didn't want to put that kind of pressure on you."

"I'm sure Joey would appreciate seeing you. And it might be good for both of you."

Danny's eyes widened. "You already knew about my memory loss, didn't you?"

Holtz didn't respond, just showed a sudden interest in some invisible lint on the left leg of his pants.

"What the fuck?" Danny exclaimed. "How?"

Holtz looked up. "Your mother. I ran into her at Post Road Liquors about a month before her last DUI. She'd obviously already had a few at the Red Coach, so I gave her a ride home. She was chatty."

"Chatty, or you pumped her for information?"

"I may have steered the conversation a bit."

"You fucking asshole," Danny said. "The doctors said I'd remember things when I was ready. They said not to force it."

"I know. Your mother told me that, too, but I'm not sure Tim has that much time, so I just gave you a little nudge."

"So much for not putting on the pressure," Danny muttered.

He smoked sulkily for a minute, then fixed Holtz with a hard look. "You used us. Me and Caroline."

Holtz nodded. "Sorry, and sorry for the way I handled things, but I didn't have much choice. If I'd said, 'Hey, Danny, old pal, I think Tim Walczak may be innocent. Wanna help me prove it?' you would have just told me to go fuck myself."

Danny knew it was true. He sighed acquiescence. "Okay, so what do you need from me?"

"Have you seen Joey yet?"

"Yeah, this morning. That went really well."

Holtz cocked his head.

"Long story," Danny said.

"Did it trigger any memories?"

"Not really. Well, kind of at one point, but not anything specific. Just a feeling. That happens a lot."

"Are you going to see him again?"

"Not sure. We didn't leave things at a good place. I hope so."

Holtz nodded, pursed him lips for a few seconds. "How would you feel about visiting Tim?" It took Danny off-guard, but before he could respond, Holtz held up his hand. "Don't decide right now. Take a day. I know you're already dealing with a lot on your own, and with your mother coming home..." He let the thought finish itself.

"All right," Danny said. "I'll think about it."

* * * * *

Danny laid the steak on the grill, closed the lid, and sat on the edge of the wicker couch. He lit a cigarette.

Nothing Holtz said had felt like a lie, but it hadn't felt like the whole truth either. Something was missing. Why had Holtz been reviewing the case files in the first place? Was he looking for something specific? Maybe something related to another case, or something personal? Personal would explain his willingness to risk so much, but what could it be?

45

He took a contemplative drag.

And why the abrupt attitude shift? One minute Holtz had been his usual asshole self, and the next he'd come clean about everything, and even shown compassion. True, Holtz needed his help, but it had felt...that word again...calculated.

All the mentions of his wife and kids had seemed calculated, too. Was it just an attempt at image rehab? "Hey, look at me, I'm a dad. Of course you can trust me." Or had Holtz been trying to make him aware of how much was at stake? Either way, it seemed intentional.

He rolled his neck slowly and leaned forward to release the tension in his lower back. A light breeze carried the buttery smell of the searing steak across the patio. He closed his eyes and tried to savor it, but a sudden vision of Tim Walczak lying in a hospital bed intruded. Danny opened his eyes and sat up.

Though he obviously didn't want to admit it, Holtz had to believe Walczak was innocent or he wouldn't be willing to put so much on the line. Danny sighed. He wanted to help, and on some level even felt he owed it to Walczak to try to find the truth, but he wasn't sure he was ready to see him yet. It felt like too much too soon.

CHAPTER 10

Danny shuffled into the kitchen and poured water into the coffee maker. He'd woken with an unexpected conviction that it was time to start drinking coffee. He took the bag of French Roast he'd bought for Caroline out of the freezer, pressed a filter into the basket, and dumped grounds into it. He flipped the top down and hit the ON button. The actions still felt completely familiar, though emotionally different. There was no dread or sadness.

As the pot began to fill, he stepped into his Nikes and went out on the side porch. The sun was just visible though the tall pines, and dew glistened in stripes of pale light across the lawn. He closed his eyes and inhaled. The cool air was already rich with the earthiness of spring. He lit a cigarette and headed down the driveway to see if the paper had been delivered.

As he reached to retrieve *The Boston Globe* from under an azalea, a figure rounded the curve from Cherry Brook Road. The man's head was down and he appeared lost in thought.

Danny straightened up. "Mr. Parker?" he said gently, reflexively dropping the cigarette and stepping it out in the mulch.

Tom Parker stopped, looked up, blinked.

"It's me, Danny Tyler."

Parker stared blankly for a few seconds longer, then his eyes cleared and he gave a wan smile. "Danny. Of course. Your mother told me you were coming back." His voice was thin, raspy. He narrowed his eyes and looked into the middle distance, then nodded. "But that was a while ago."

Parker had always seemed old to Danny. Danny guessed he'd been over fifty when his son Andy was born, close to sixty when Andy was murdered. Parker still had the same thinning, carroty red hair, though now there was a half-inch of dull gray at the roots. The bags under his bloodhound eyes had sagged lower, revealing half-moons of pink below the irises.

"Yeah, things got delayed a bit," Danny said. He looked toward Cherry Brook, expecting to see a black Labrador retriever emerge from the brush along the edge. Parker and the dog had passed the house coming and going every morning and evening for as long as he could remember. "Lily?" he asked.

"She died five years ago," Parker said. "I thought about getting another dog, but just never got around to it. I still like to walk, though." His tone was flat, distracted.

"I'm sorry," Danny said. "I was going to stop by. I wanted to thank you for finding me. You probably saved my life."

Parker nodded slowly. "It was Lily. We didn't normally go that far into the woods, but she was on a mission that morning. I think she knew something was wrong."

"She was a great dog," Danny said.

Parker gave another bland smile.

"How's Mrs. Parker?" Danny asked.

"Fine, last I heard," Parker replied, "but her name is Saltzman now and she lives in Connecticut." For the first time his voice held a trace of emotion. Perhaps regret, perhaps something darker.

"I'm sorry."

"Those things happen," Parker replied with seemingly practiced stoicism. "It was already rocky between us, and once Andy was gone there was nothing to keep us together. Unfortunately it took us a while to figure that out. One day I came home and she was gone. Said she couldn't take being reminded of Andy every day." He gave a melancholy smile. "I've always found it comforting."

Thanks for oversharing.

Danny was at a loss.

"Well, I should probably get going," Parker said abruptly. He gave an awkward nod and started on his way.

Wow, there are way too many damaged people in this neighborhood, Danny thought.

* * * * *

He flattened the paper on the counter and scanned the headlines: an earthquake in Costa Rica, a mobile missile deal expected with the Soviet Union, Vice President Bush branded a "quintessential elitist establishment Republican country-clubber" by the chairman of the Democratic National Committee.

He yawned, stretched, scratched his stomach, and took a mug from the cabinet. He blew the dust out, then rinsed it, making a mental note to wash all the dishes over the weekend. A car door slammed in the driveway. He turned and leaned across the counter. Joey was coming up the walk.

Crap, Danny thought. He ran his fingers through his sleep-matted hair and walked to the door. Joey was standing on the other side of the screen, staring at his feet and having a spirited but silent conversation with himself. Danny tried to read the words but couldn't.

The bell, or knock? The bell, or knock? The bell, or...

"Hey," Danny said.

Joey started, his eyes darted up. "I didn't realize the door was open," he said. He licked his lips. "Guess I looked pretty stupid."

Danny shrugged noncommittally. "I talk to myself a lot."

Though I don't move my lips.

Joey grinned anxiously. "Nice ride." His left hand fluttered at the shiny black pickup in front of the garage.

"Karl let me borrow it," Danny replied, keeping his tone neutral.

"I wouldn't have pegged him as the butch truck type based on what you told me," Joey said.

"He's not, but they have a summer place in the Hamptons and he doesn't like to get dirt in his Jag when he picks up pansies at the local nursery."

Joey smiled more easily, then frowned. "Can we talk?"

"Sure."

CHAPTER 11

Joey was wearing wrinkled baggy khakis, a frayed pink Oxford shirt that looked like it had been pulled from the bottom of a pile, and flattened Sperry Topsiders he hadn't bothered to pull up over the heels of his sockless feet. Still, Danny thought, it was a big improvement over the previous day. It looked like he'd even made an attempt to tame his hair, with a suggestion of a part on the left.

"I'm sorry I called you that," Joey said immediately.

"It's okay," Danny replied.

"I thought you didn't want to fool around with me because you assumed I was sick," Joey said. "I know a lot of people do, but I'm not. I just can't sleep. I used to go out to bars in Boston sometimes, but I stopped because I could see the way guys looked at me when I tried talking to them. They were afraid. Not that I blamed them. Whenever someone who looked sick came up to me, I felt the same way." He paused. "Sad, huh? That we react with fear instead of compassion?"

Danny didn't sense the same self-pity he had the day before. "I'm sorry, too," he said. He wasn't sure what more to say. Sorry that happened to you? Sorry people are assholes? Sorry for making you feel that way? Sorry that I *did* think you had AIDS? He decided to leave it alone. "You want some coffee?"

Joey relaxed noticeably. "Sure." He jumped up on the counter the way he'd always done when they were younger.

Danny rinsed another mug and filled it. "Milk or sugar?"

"Black is fine."

Danny handed the mug to Joey and picked up his own. They each took a sip.

"Wow," Joey said, making a sour face.

"Too strong?"

Joey nodded vigorously.

"Good," Danny said. "I was afraid it always tastes like ass."

Joey gave him a perplexed look.

"I've never had it before."

"Why not?"

Danny shrugged. He wasn't sure other than that coffee had been a "Caroline thing." He took another sip, then dumped it in the sink. "I felt like it was time to give it a try. That's the way Caroline taught me to make it."

Joey pushed off the counter. "Then you need another lesson. Where's the coffee?"

Danny took the bag out of the freezer and handed it to him, then turned on the water to wash the pot.

"I can do that," Joey offered.

"So can I," Danny replied.

"Yeah, I know, but I'd like my coffee today," Joey cracked.

It felt natural, like old times. Danny smiled and backed away from the sink. He hopped up on the counter.

"So what have you been up to?" Joey asked.

Danny decided there was no point in delaying the inevitable. "I went to see Holtz."

Joey stopped washing and looked back at him. "Why?"

"I found a photo of Tim Walczak. Naked."

Joey's eyes widened.

"So I never mentioned him to you?" Danny asked.

Joey's face flushed as his expression grew defensive.

"It's not a trick question," Danny said quickly. "I don't remember him. I mean, he looked familiar and I remembered his first name when I saw it, but I don't remember actually being with him. I thought maybe I'd mentioned him."

Joey shook his head, then frowned. "So it was you."

"What was me?"

"The papers said Walczak had a connection to one of the victims. That was how the police linked him to the murders. But they never said who it was or how they were connected."

Danny nodded. "Holtz said that a lot of details were kept from the public because we were all minors. I guess that was one of them." He suddenly wondered if the town library kept copies of the *Globe*, *Herald* and *Town Crier* from that far back. He decided it would be worth checking out to see how the trial had been covered.

Joey didn't respond for a minute, just finished washing and filling the pot. "So does that mean you had sex with him?" he asked finally.

"Apparently a couple of times," Danny replied. He saw Joey's shoulders stiffen. "What's wrong?"

"Nothing," Joey said, keeping his back to Danny. "I just...I didn't realize you were having sex with anyone else. I mean, I knew you had before...but I didn't know you still were...by then."

"I'm sorry..."

"Yeah, no, it's cool," Joey murmured hastily. "Don't worry about it. It just took me by surprise. I guess I shouldn't have... whatever." He looked over his shoulder and forced a smile, then poured the water into the coffee maker and put a fresh filter and grounds in the basket. "One tablespoon per cup," he said. He hit the ON button.

For a minute the only sound in the room was the coffee gurgling down into the pot, then Joey turned to face Danny. "It really is okay," he said, smiling more convincingly. "So did you and Holtz talk about anything else?"

"Not really," Danny replied.

"You want to try that again?"

"Huh?"

"Remember how you always said you were a such great liar because no one could read your face?"

Danny nodded.

"You were wrong. I've always known."

Danny felt an unexpected twinge of embarrassment about all the unremembered lies he might have told Joey. "He told me Walczak is dying," he said.

Joey raised his eyebrows. "And?"

"And he thinks Walczak might be innocent."

A fleeting glimmer of something Danny couldn't name crossed Joey's face. "Who does he think did it then?" Joey asked.

It wasn't the question Danny had been expecting. "He doesn't have a theory. At least not that he shared with me."

Joey's eyes locked on a spot on the floor and he began softly chewing his lower lip. Danny felt the same erratic energy building he'd felt the day before. "Are you okay?" he asked.

Joey didn't respond.

"Joey?" Danny said more sharply.

Joey's head snapped up and his eyes cleared. "Sorry."

"What's the matter?"

"Nothing. I just spaced out."

Right, and I'm the bad liar.

"So why does Holtz think he might be innocent?" Joey asked.

It was the question Danny had been expecting first. "Let's pour some coffee and sit down," he said.

* * * * *

"He said I was sexually assaulted by someone with the same blood type as Walczak, but almost half the population is O-positive," Danny finished. He took another sip. The taste was growing on him.

Joey stared down at his hands for a few seconds, then looked back up at Danny with a pained expression. "I wouldn't call it assault exactly."

"What?"

"You really don't remember anything, do you?" Joey sighed. "You were with me. That's why you were in the woods and why you had the blanket."

For a few seconds Danny just stared at Joey, then numbness gave way to disbelief, anger, and confusion. "What about Bryce?" he managed.

"I don't know," Joey replied weakly. "I never saw him, but they said he was killed about the same time I went in the house, so you must have run into him right afterward." He swallowed hard, wiped the tears welling in his eyes.

Danny took shallow breaths, waiting for the anger to pass. "Why didn't you tell the cops you were with me?" he asked finally.

"I was afraid," Joey replied. He took a few ragged breaths. "If I'd seen anything, I swear I would have, but I didn't. I waved goodbye, went inside, and went to bed. That was it."

"But still..."

"What would have been the point?" Joey cried helplessly. "My brother had just been murdered. Can you imagine how my parents would have felt if they found out we'd been fucking in the woods just before it happened?"

Danny couldn't argue it, though he sensed compassion hadn't been Joey's only motivation. "Joey, you're going to have to tell Holtz," he said.

"Why?" Joey whined. "I told you I didn't see anything."

"Because the only physical evidence against Walczak was the semen. If it belonged to you, there's no evidence."

"But maybe he raped you afterward," Joey argued, his tone verging on desperate. "He raped all those other kids, didn't he?"

Danny opened his mouth, but Joey cut him off.

"Why would they put him in jail if they didn't really think he did it? Not everybody is a homophobic asshole."

"No, but juries can be..." Danny searched for the word Holtz had used but couldn't find it. "But the judge and jury only saw what was presented. If the two lawyers agreed he should be convicted, they could have skewed the evidence."

He could see Joey shutting down and realized that reason wasn't going to have any effect.

"Look, I'm sorry," he said, "but Holtz has to know. You can tell or I will."

"It's all going to start again," Joey moaned.

"No, it won't," Danny said, keeping his own tone measured.

"Holtz is doing this on his own. Unless he can prove that Walczak is innocent, no one else is ever going to know about it."

Joey's whole body began to shake as tears spilled down his cheeks. "You promised," he sobbed.

Yeah, well I guess we both lied, Danny thought.

CHAPTER 12

"I suspected Joey knew more than he let on at the time," Holtz said, pushing what remained of his lunch away, then immediately snatching a soggy fry from the plate.

They were seated at a booth in the back corner of the Prime Deli, just off the Brandeis University campus. The lunch rush had passed and the other booths and tables were empty.

"Why's that?" Danny asked.

"Because I knew you two were close," Holtz replied in a way that left no doubt about the meaning.

Danny's face grew warm. "How?"

"I saw you behind the practice wall by the main tennis courts at the Campion Center. I thought you were going to get high and followed. I was wrong. Fortunately you didn't see me."

"And you didn't bust us?"

"I wasn't that much of an asshole," Holtz said. "You weren't hurting anyone." He paused to chew the fry. "And I knew what kind of hell your lives would be if I did. I had a cousin, Steve, who was gay. We were close."

"Were?"

Holtz looked down at his plate. "High school was too much for him."

"I'm sorry," Danny said. "And thank you."

Holtz nodded acknowledgment. "No problem."

Danny took a small sip of vanilla Coke and swirled the straw for a few seconds, then his eyes turned troubled. "Can I ask you a question?"

Holtz nodded for him to go on.

"Why did it seem like you were always around whenever I did anything wrong?"

Holtz smiled humorlessly. "Why do you think?"

Danny felt the heat returning to his face. "Please tell me you didn't have a crush on me."

Holtz made a face. "Hardly. I hated you."

"Wow, that's kind of harsh, don't you think?" Danny asked. "I mean, I was just a kid."

"Yeah, a kid with an attitude," Holtz said. "You have to understand something, Danny. I grew up in a blue collar family in Medford. To us, people who lived in towns like Weston and Wellesley and Newton were all assholes who thought their shit didn't stink, so I was already coming in with a chip on my shoulder. Then on my second day, I busted a kid..." He shot a finger at Danny, "...who didn't even show me the courtesy of pretending to be scared, and who made me look like I had my head up my ass in front of my new boss. After that, I just wanted to make your life miserable."

Danny let out an uncomfortable laugh. "Well, I guess it's good to know I wasn't just imagining that part." He frowned. "I'm sorry I did that, but it wasn't because I thought I was better than you." He reconsidered, realized it was a lie. "Okay, maybe I thought I was smarter, but there was also shit going on that made me kind of hostile toward anyone who thought they could tell me what to do."

"That's called being a teenager."

"I suppose," Danny shrugged, knowing there was more to it.

They sat in awkward silence for a minute before Danny pushed up straighter on the banquette. "Maybe this is a stupid question, but can't you run tests to see whether the semen belonged to Joey or Walczak? On *Unsolved Mysteries* last week they were talking about DNA testing."

"Sure, if the samples were still around," Holtz replied, "but DNA profiling has only been around for a few years. Nowadays all evidence gets stored in case they want to run tests down the line, but back then it was up to the discretion of the individual police department. The physical evidence from the case is long gone. Presumably they decided they didn't need it once Walczak was convicted. At least that's the explanation I'd like to believe."

Danny slouched back down.

Holtz picked up another fry, chewed it slowly. "Have you given any thought to visiting him?"

"I'll do it," Danny said. He hadn't made up his mind until that moment, and waited for regret to settle in. None came.

Yet.

"Is tomorrow too soon?" Holtz asked. "I already cleared it with the wife, just in case."

"Yeah, I guess," Danny replied. "May as well get it over with." He paused, then smirked. "I have to meet this wife some day. Make sure she's not just a figment of your imagination."

"What, you don't think I could find a woman who'd marry me?" Holtz asked.

"Not with that pornstache you used to have."

CHAPTER 13

Danny looked out at the driveway, then at the stove clock again. How is that possible? he wondered. He turned to the microwave. Only 9:55 AM there, too.

He paced back to the family room and checked himself in the mirror. Again. He had to admit that the high-waisted Guess jeans Karl had bought him were a big step up from the Toughskins Caroline had forced him to wear all through elementary school, though not quite as comfortable as his Levi's. He wondered if he should change.

You know, some shoulder pads and leggings would really dress up that outfit.

Like he's going to give a shit how I look, he thought. He stalked to the chair and forced himself to sit. His legs immediately began jittering.

He'd managed only a few hours of fitful sleep before giving up and going down to the basement to watch a marathon of late-60s TV: *Land of the Giants, Lost in Space, Star Trek* and *Wild Wild West.* The last at least had featured a surprisingly homoerotic scene of Robert Conrad being chained up by Pernell Roberts while wearing just skintight lavender pants, boots, and leather chaps.

At 7 AM he'd headed upstairs to take a shower and get dressed. He'd been restlessly chainsmoking and drinking coffee since.

I should pee, he thought, jumping up again, then immediately forgot about it as he saw a boxy blue minivan with faux-wood paneling coming up the driveway. He did a quick check to make sure everything was turned off and was out the door before Holtz had closed the driver's door.

"Is that yours?" Danny asked.

Holtz turned, surrender already obvious on his face. "This?

No, it's just a loaner while my Porsche is in the shop."

"It's...um...spacious," Danny said.

"My wife thought it was more stylish than a station wagon."

Danny moved around the vehicle, pretending to study it from various angles. "Yeah, I can see that," he said. He stopped and looked at Holtz. "I've seen them from a distance before, but never thought I'd get to ride in one."

"You're not," Holtz replied flatly.

"Why not?"

"Can you make it through the entire trip without smoking?"

Danny frowned doubtfully.

"That's why."

Danny took out his keys, then gave the minivan another appraising look. "So does it come with a matching sweater vest?"

"Are those your mom's jeans?" Holtz shot back.

* * * * *

Danny had imagined an imposing stone fortress set on a high precipice far from civilization. The reality was that MCI-Cedar Junction, one of the state's maximum security prisons, was located just off a rural two-lane highway, only a mile from a shopping plaza and three miles from Walpole's town center. The simple white-walled compound was set back a hundred yards, barely visible through the trees. Until they took the first curve up the driveway, Danny couldn't even see the guard towers.

Holtz pointed to the visitor parking area and Danny pulled the truck into a space and killed the engine.

"You ready for this?" Holtz asked.

Danny's mouth was dry and he suddenly needed to pee. He wished he'd stopped for water and had had a little less coffee. "Can I smoke inside?" he asked.

"In the infirmary?" Holtz arched his eyebrows.

"Then I'm going to need a few more minutes," Danny said.

* * * * *

It had taken almost fifteen minutes to sign in, check their personal belongings, and go through screening, another ten until their number was called. By the time they'd been led through a maze of stark corridors and locked gates and handed off to another armed corrections officer outside the door to the infirmary, Danny's nerves were so tightly wound he thought he might hyperventilate.

The guard picked up the phone on the wall, made a quick call, then unlocked the door and ushered them in. "Wait there," he said, then locked the door behind them.

The room was long, narrow, and nicotine yellow, with a dozen beds along the right wall. Dozing patients occupied five of them. A wired glass window ran the length of the left wall, interrupted only by an open door in the middle. A pudgy balding man in white peered at them quickly through the glass, then went back to whatever he'd been doing.

"Which one is he?" Danny whispered anxiously.

Holtz nodded at the white curtain stretching across the back of the room. "They keep the AIDS patients segregated."

Just then the curtain parted and a man stepped through and started toward them. He was small and slight, young, Latino, more pretty than handsome. His wavy black hair had been molded into a high pompadour, the sides and back tightly wrapped by a bright orange do-rag. Though he was dressed in scrubs, Danny sensed he was a prisoner.

As he got close, the man broke into a dazzling smile. "Officer Holtz, how are you?" His voice was soft, musical, lightly accented.

Holtz clapped him on the shoulder. "Fine, thanks, Angel. How about you?"

"No complaints."

Holtz nodded at Danny. "This is Danny Tyler."

Angel took a step forward and stuck out his right hand. His fingers were surprisingly delicate, the nails long but neatly trimmed and coated with clear polish. "A pleasure to meet you, Danny," he said. "Timmy's been talking about you non-stop for the past week."

Danny took Angel's hand and tried a smile, knowing it didn't look right. Angel didn't seem to notice. He began leading them toward the back of the room, still lightly holding Danny's hand. The smell of disinfectant grew stronger as they approached the curtain. Danny's stomach clenched in response.

"I bathed and shaved him, just in case," Angel said.

Danny gave Holtz a questioning look.

"I called yesterday and told him we might be coming," Holtz said, then to Angel. "How's he doing?"

Angel rocked his left hand. "Maybe a little better this morning. Hard to say."

Danny had a sudden vision of Jerry's friend Kelly shortly before he died, and faltered. Angel stopped, his expressive brown eyes full of concern. "You okay, mijo?"

"Uh, yeah...fine. Just a little anxious," Danny replied.

Angel squeezed his hand. "Don't worry. It's going to be fine." He pushed the right side of the curtain back to reveal three more beds. Only the back right was occupied. Tim Walczak's eyes were closed, his head tilted slightly toward the back wall. A surgical mask covered his mouth and nose.

Danny's heart beat quicker. Angel gave him a gentle smile, and whispered, "His immune system is pretty much gone. He should really be in an isolation tent, but we make do with what we have around here."

He let go of Danny's hand and guided him through the curtain, waited until Holtz followed, then came in behind and closed the curtain.

"Company, Timmecito!" he trilled in a falsetto.

Walczak's eyes popped open and he slowly turned his face toward them. "Oh, Miss Delgado, what's that mess on your head?" he rasped.

Angel made a face and wagged a finger. "You just remember who wipes your ass." He walked to the bed, pulled latex gloves from the box next to it, slipped them on, and pressed the back of his hand against Walczak's forehead. "Your fever's going down," he said, suddenly all business.

Walczak looked past Angel's shoulder and the corners of his eyes crinkled. "Hey, Rick. How's it going?"

"Good, thanks, Tim." Holtz moved to the side of the bed. "How about you?"

Walczak grunted, his whole body seemed to shrug. "Rough night, but better now." His eyes shifted to Danny hovering just inside the curtain. "Hey, Danny. Still handsome, I see."

Angel turned and raised his eyebrows expectantly, then subtly motioned Danny closer when he still didn't move. Danny hesitated a half second before approaching.

"Thanks," he said, only briefly glancing at Walczak's face.

"Well, shall we give them a few minutes to get reacquainted?" Angel said as an awkward silence threatened to settle in. "How about some truly nasty coffee from the nurses' station?"

"How can I refuse an offer like that?" Holtz replied.

"Just hit that button if you need anything," Angel said. He saw the apprehension on Danny's face, smiled reassuringly, and nodded at the camera mounted high on the opposite wall. "And no exchanging bodily fluids, you two." He winked. "The guards and I will be watching."

Please don't go, please don't go, please don't go...

"You really do look good," Walczak said as soon as the others were gone. "How do you feel?"

Danny forced himself to look Walczak in the eyes. "Okay. My arm is still fucked up, obviously." He realized how relatively trivial it sounded and quickly added, "But it doesn't hurt."

"It's okay," Walczak replied with a light chuckle. "You're allowed to have physical problems, too."

Danny relaxed just a bit. "How about you?"

"To be honest, most of the time I feel like shit, but Angel hooked me up with a nice new morphine drip right before you got here. At the moment, I'm feeling pretty good."

Danny nodded numbly, disconcerted by Walczak's eyes. They were haunting, clear, green, and unblinking. They reminded him of the eyes of Holocaust survivors he'd seen in photos, seeming to hold all the suffering and wisdom of the world.

"Don't tell Nurse Ratched I did this," Walczak said, pushing up against his pillows. He lowered the mask to his chin.

Danny felt a spike of panic. "Are you sure you should be doing that?"

"I'll be fine for a few minutes. Just don't sneeze on me." Walczak smiled at his joke. "Besides, I know it's kind of creepy talking to just a pair of eyes. Especially when they look like mine."

This time Danny was able to smile back. Walczak's face wasn't as wasted as he'd expected, though it was still hard to see any of the younger man from the photo. The cheekbones and jaw were too prominent, the lips too thin, the skin too drawn.

"Could you pour me some water?" Walczak asked.

"Um, sure."

Danny started to reach for the pitcher but Walczak held up a warning hand. "Gloves, please."

"Sorry." Danny took a pair from the box and struggled into them, amazed at how quickly Angel had managed it.

"You don't want to know what happens when I get any kind of bug in my intestines," Walczak said.

Danny filled the styrofoam cup on the tray table and stepped back. Walczak picked it up in his trembling hand and slopped water onto the edge of the bed

"I've got it," Danny said. He took the cup and carefully lifted it to Walczak's pale cracked lips. Walczak sipped, smiled gratefully, lay back.

"So, here we are," he said.

Danny shifted uncomfortably. "Yeah."

Walczak studied him a moment, then looked down and frowned. "You still don't remember me, do you?"

"No. I'm trying, but... I'm really sorry."

"It's okay. Rick told me it was a long shot." Walczak sighed, seemingly more frustrated than self-pitying. "I just wish you did because you'd know I couldn't have hurt you. You know, I never forced you to do anything." His gaze was almost imploring.

"I believe you," Danny said, "and I'm sorry." He wasn't sure what else he could say. "Maybe it would help if you told me about how we met. Holtz said it was behind the Campion Center."

Walczak nodded and smiled wistfully. "It was on the dirt road by the pond, next to the soccer field. I was just coming out of the woods on my way to the parking lot, and you were heading the other way carrying a basketball. You asked me why I had a camera and I gave you a story about taking pictures of birds, but I think you knew the truth right away."

"Why?"

"Because you told me you knew where some really cool birds had built a nest."

Danny laughed. "I can't believe you fell for that old one."

"I would have followed you if you told me you'd seen a pink condor," Walczak replied almost flirtateously.

To his surprise, it didn't make Danny uncomfortable.

"You took me to a place in the woods," Walczak continued. "A cluster of big rocks."

"Stonehenge," Danny said. "That's what we always called it."

Walczak nodded. "Of course there weren't any birds or nests there, so then you suggested I take some pictures of you. I took a few of you climbing around on the rocks." His eyes grew distant. "You stood so close to me as we watched them develop." He paused and licked his lips. Danny held the cup close again and he took another sip. "Finally, I got up the nerve to ask if you'd pose shirtless for twenty dollars."

"And?"

Walczak let out a rattling chuckle. "You said you'd pose naked for free if I did the same."

Danny's eyes widened in theatrical horror. "Oh my God, I was such a little whore."

"But a cute whore."

"So then what?"

"Then we took some pictures and fooled around."

Danny closed his eyes. For just a moment he caught the scent of a memory—warm grass, something both sweet and spicy. When he opened his eyes, a tear was rolling down Walczak's cheek.

"You know what I remember most about you?" Walczak asked, his voice cracking. "How fun you were, how uninhibited. You never seemed ashamed of what we were doing." He took a labored breath. "I wished I could have been more like you."

"I'm sorry," Danny said, not entirely sure why.

"Don't be. Those were some of the best moments of my life."

"I'm sorry," Danny repeated, meaning it in a different way. He sensed the curtain move behind him and took a half step back.

"Is everything all right?" Angel asked, coming up alongside him. He slipped on a glove and wiped away the trace of Walczak's tear with his thumb, then caressed his cheek.

Walczak swallowed, gave a shaky smile. "Yes, mother. Just reliving some memories. You know how maudlin I get when I take my morphine."

"We should probably let you get some rest," Holtz said, coming up between Danny and Angel.

"Would it be okay if I came to visit again?" Danny asked.

"That would be nice," Walczak said, then added playfully, "There's a rumor Mother Teresa might come visit us next month. Maybe she can work a miracle on your arm."

"Or brain," Danny said.

* * * * *

"Was he hallucinating?" Holtz asked as they reached the door. "That part about Mother Teresa?"

Angel shook his head. "There have been whispers." He held both hands palms up and see-sawed them a few times. "Calcutta. Cedar Junction. She should feel right at home."

Holtz grinned. "By the way, how's your sister doing?"

"Great. Loving the job."

"You know his sister?" Danny asked.

"No, but she graduated the academy last year," Holtz replied. "She's a rookie in Brockton."

"Isn't that kind of a rough area?" Danny asked. "Or did that change while I was Rip Van Winkling?"

"No, it's still rough," Angel replied. "That's where we grew up. But Pepper's a badass. She can take care of herself."

* * * * *

"So?" Holtz asked.

Danny squinted against the smoke from his cigarette as he turned the key in the ignition. He sat back, turned to face Holtz. "For just a second I had a sense memory. Grass and something else I recognized but couldn't quite place. Sweet, but also kind of spicy or peppery." He shook his head dejectedly. "But nothing about him. Sorry."

Disappointment clouded Holtz's eyes for a second, then his expression softened. "Don't be. We knew it was a crap shoot. And maybe you'll remember something later."

Danny gave a half-hearted shrug. "Maybe." He frowned. "Angel is a prisoner, right?"

Holtz nodded.

"He's pretty flamboyant."

Holtz nodded again.

"And he doesn't get beat up by the other prisoners?"

"Everyone knows he takes care of the AIDS prisoners," Holtz replied. "They're probably afraid to hurt him. Worried he might bleed on them."

"Does he have it, too?"

Holtz shrugged. "I don't know, but it doesn't really matter. It's all about perception. Besides, believe it or not, Angel is pretty badass, himself."

"Yeah, right. He can't weigh more than a buck-twenty-five soaking wet."

"When he was fifteen, he was working the block near Copley Square in Boston. A trick picked him up and drove to a park near Washington Street in the South End. Two other guys were waiting and they all jumped Angel, set on him with tire irons. Two of them ended up in critical condition, the other dead. Angel got away with just a few broken ribs and a busted nose."

"Seriously?"

"Oh, yeah."

"Is that why he's here?"

"That's why. Should have been self-defense, but they nailed him for manslaughter. He's got another two years till he's eligible for parole."

"That's sad."

"Yup."

Danny cocked a curious eyebrow. "I noticed you're really nice to them."

"I'm nice to everybody."

"You've never been nice to me."

"Because you're an asshole."

"Only to you."

Holtz turned his head toward the window. "Then I guess it's just a vicious cycle."

Danny put the truck into gear and backed out of the parking space, drove to the end of the winding drive, and turned left.

* * * * *

"It's just so weird," Danny said as they reached the merge onto Interstate 95. His tone suggested they'd been having a conversation for the previous ten minutes rather than driving in silence. "Tim and I are almost the same age, but I'm essentially just starting my life and his is almost over. How can that happen?"

"Are you asking me if I think there's some sort of grand design or moral principle guiding the universe?" Holtz asked. His left hand snaked out for Danny's Marlboros on the dashboard.

DEADFALL

Danny stared at him a moment, then laughed. "Fuck no. I don't think I even understood your question." He sighed. "It just doesn't make sense to me."

Holtz punched in the lighter and took out a cigarette. "No, it doesn't," he said. "A lot of things don't make sense, but they still happen." The lighter popped and he pressed the glowing coil to the tip of the cigarette and took a few short puffs until it caught.

Danny blinked at him. "That's it? 'Shit happens' is your great existential observation? Gee, maybe you should put that on a t-shirt or something."

"Hey, you said you didn't want to hear about grand design and moral principles," Holtz replied. "Besides, what do you want from me? I'm just a small town cop. And I'm only eight years older than you are."

Danny grunted dissatisfaction and they lapsed back into silence for another mile.

"When do you start to feel like an adult?" Danny asked finally.

"Some people seem to be born feeling that way. Some never do," Holtz replied, then chuckled when he saw the flash of annoyance on Danny's face. "I guess for most it starts off as pretending," he said. "Then when enough other people buy it, it begins to feel real, though I'm still a little surprised sometimes that anyone lets me carry a gun."

"That's very comforting," Danny replied dryly.

"I guess I really started to feel it when my first one was born. Suddenly I had responsibility for another human being. It forced me to grow up fast."

So if I don't have kids, I might be able to skate by?

"But you'd already been a cop for a few years by then."

"And we saw how well I handled that," Holtz replied with a wry smirk. "Yes, I had an inferiority complex because I wasn't from Weston, and yes, you made me look like an asshole the first time I busted you, but I was also immature, plain and simple. And I was so afraid that someone would realize what a fraud I was that I overcompensated by throwing my dick around. Figuratively."

He took a drag on his cigarette. "Once Ricky was born and I began to understand what being an adult was really about, I was able to let the petty bullshit go. I didn't feel the need to constantly convince people I was credible, so I was able to focus on actually becoming a good cop."

Danny wasn't sure how the last part was relevant for him, but realized he felt more relaxed. "Thanks," he said.

"Sure," Holtz replied. "And since we're getting all touchy-feely confessional, can I ask you something?"

Danny shot him a wary glance. "I don't guarantee I'll answer."

"Fair enough. Are you nervous about your mother?"

Danny had expected something related to his sexuality. "Yeah, a little bit, I suppose." It was a cautious understatement.

"Why?" Holtz asked.

Have you got a month?

"It's just going to be weird," Danny replied. "We don't really even know each other anymore, but we're going to go back to playing mother and son." He was surprised by his own candor. It was a thought he hadn't even articulated to himself yet.

Holtz nodded. "I'm sure there's going to be an adjustment period. On both sides." He stared out the window and took another long drag on his cigarette. "Even though my boys are still young, I catch myself worrying sometimes. As a parent it's my job to prepare them to go out into the world, but when I see them asserting their independence, it already hurts a little. I'm not ready for them to grow up just yet." He turned back to Danny. "Just be patient. The last time you and your mom lived together, you were just a teenager. Now you're a man." He paused to give Danny an exaggerated once over. "More or less. It's going to take her a while to get used to that, especially since she's going to be dependent on you for a while."

So what's changed?

"Yeah, I suppose you're right," Danny replied. He suddenly felt anxious and wanted to change the subject. "You want to stop and get some coffee?"

"I thought you didn't drink it."

"I just started."

"Have you tried Dunkin Donuts yet?"

Danny shook his head.

"Then you're in for a real treat," Holtz said. He licked his right thumb, stuck his hand out the window, and moved it slowly back and forth.

"What the fuck are you doing?" Danny asked.

Holtz gave a sly grin. "Cop radar. We can always sense when there's a donut in the area. Take the next right."

CHAPTER 14

He ground his erection against Tim's, teased Tim's lips with his tongue. "Do you want to make love?" He cringed inwardly at the sound of it, wishing he'd gone with "fuck." Fucking was masculine, sexy. "Making love" was what the simpering bitches in the romances Caroline devoured always said.

Tim's clear green eyes looked into his for a moment, then dropped. Tim bit his lower lip head and shook his head almost imperceptibly. "I can't."

"Why not?"

"I'm just not ready for that yet. It's too...intimate."

"Like kissing and sucking each other's dicks isn't intimate?"

"Not the same way," Tim said, hesitated. "It just...it just seems like something you should do with someone you love." Tim's eyes flitted searchingly across his face, then Tim frowned.

"Why?" he asked. "Why can't it just be fun, just because it feels good?"

"It can," Tim replied, "but not for me. I need something more than that. At least the first time."

CHAPTER 15

"Oh, great, I'll call the DA right up," Holtz said caustically. "How could they *not* let Tim out now?" He let out a groan. "How can you even be sure it was a memory and not just a wet dream?"

"I'm sure," Danny snapped. The positive feelings toward Holtz that had been generated during their trip the previous day evaporated. He trapped the phone with his right shoulder while he lit his first cigarette of the day. "Remember I told you that I had a sense memory when I was talking with him? I smelled the exact same thing during the dream. It was grass and cologne. Jovan's *Musk for Men*, I think."

"How do you know that?"

"My father used to wear it back in the day."

Holtz exhaled loudly. "And you don't think that makes the memory a little suspect? Maybe you were just mixing random bits and pieces from the past."

"I guarantee my father was not part of that particular memory," Danny replied coldly.

I hope.

"Can you just contact him and find out if he ever wore it?"

"Yeah, I'll get right on that," Holtz deadpanned. He yawned. "What would it prove?"

"That he wasn't capable of molesting anyone."

During the long silence that followed, Danny wondered if Mrs. Holtz and the boys were nearby, waiting impatiently for Holtz so they could all sit down for a family breakfast. He listened closely but didn't hear any noise in the background.

"Look, I'm just trying to help," he said, trying to keep his tone even. "You asked me to let you know if I remembered anything. That's what I'm doing."

"All right," Holtz said. Another extended silence, then another yawn. "I've got a shrink friend in the State Police sexual and domestic violence unit. I'll run it by him and see what, if anything, he thinks it could mean, assuming it actually happened."

"Thank you," Danny replied.

"Anything else?"

"No, that's it."

"Okay," Holtz said. "Just do me a favor, Danny."

"What?"

"Don't ever call me before nine on a Sunday morning again."

"Sorry," Danny said to the dial tone.

He hung up and looked out the window. Tom Parker was standing at the bottom of the driveway, his arms dangling at his sides, staring farther down the road. Suddenly his head swiveled toward the house and Danny took a step back from the window. Parker looked at the house for almost a minute, then slowly continued on his way.

Freak.

CHAPTER 16

Danny rinsed his plate and glass and put them in the drainer. He rolled his head in a slow circle, then bounced up and down a few times and shook out his right arm. As the day had gone on, he'd been feeling more and more restless, tension settling into his neck and shoulders.

I need to get out of here, he thought. He tucked his cigarettes into his right front pocket.

* * * * *

The neighborhood abutted ninety acres of pine and oak forest and overgrown fields owned by the Campion Center, a Jesuit retreat that had once been a theological college. Danny, Bryce, and later Joey, had considered "the college" to be their own private playground, racing motorbikes along the dirt roads, swimming in the pond in the early summer before the surface became clotted with algae, playing tennis and basketball on the cracked courts.

A stockade fence had been erected across the end of the street since Danny had last been there. One section lay on the ground. The mangled pickets suggested it had been driven through. The Virginia Creeper covering half suggested it had happened years earlier. Danny stepped through the opening, closed his eyes, and inhaled deeply.

Home.

The contours of the ground and a few stubborn bald patches still hinted at the dirt road that had looped from the main building on the hill down to the pond, though most of it was overgrown. Danny followed it through a small grove of crab apple, willow, and bittersweet, into the fields where he and Bryce had dug pits and packed the dirt into ramps for jumping their bikes. Any sign that they'd ever been there had been swallowed by sweet vernal grass and bristly blackberry.

He crested a small rise and started down. Ahead, a narrower foot path snaked off into the woods. To the left, another path skirted the edge of the field for two hundred yards, then turned right into the woods behind Joey's house. He knew it was where Bryce's body had been found. He turned right and continued along the road.

As he reached the edge of woods separating the wild fields from the sports fields maintained by the town, he stopped and looked back. Someone was walking up the road, heading back the way he'd come. He shielded his eyes and squinted, then took a step into the shadows in case Parker looked his way.

He took the left fork toward the spillway at the eastern point of the pond. The road around the pond hadn't succumbed to the encroachment of nature. The packed reddish-brown soil was raised against the wetlands on the right, and heavily rutted. It was cooler and damper under the canopy, the air earthier and filled with the chorusing, trills, and whistles of horny frogs.

As he broke back into the sunlight, he stopped and looked out across the pond. On the right, a family of mallards swam lazily in the shallows near the skating shed. Across from them, Lovers' Rock jutted out from the shore. Joey sat crosslegged on top of it, facing the ducks.

For a second Danny wondered if he was having a flashback, but it wasn't the Joey of his memories. It was the damaged creature he'd become. As if hearing his thoughts, Joey suddenly turned his head and waved wanly.

Too late to run?

Danny waved back and continued on.

Either by fluke of nature or design of some long ago conservationist with an eye for order and symmetry, the pines along the southeast shore grew in two neat rows, their trunks rising almost fifty feet before the first branches came together in a soft arch. Walking there had always reminded Danny of being in a cathedral.

He stopped and stared at a faded trail marker a few yards ahead. There was something important about it, he was sure.

I have only one burning desire...

He felt a wave of both anger and sadness pass through him.

Rhymes with...

Either tell me or shut the fuck up.

Silence. The moment passed.

* * * * *

Joey looked over his right shoulder as Danny approached. "Hey." His voice was flat, his expression neutral.

"Hey," Danny replied. "How's it going?"

Joey just shrugged.

"You come out here a lot?" Danny asked.

"Once in a while. When I need to think. It's peaceful."

Danny clambered gracelessly onto the rock and walked to the edge. He noticed the pipe lying in front of Joey, pulled out his cigarettes, lit one. The smoke floated out over the pond. "Do you remember why we started calling this Lovers' Rock?" he asked.

Joey shrugged. "You and Bryce called it that long before I started coming here." He cut a sharp look at Danny. "Maybe you two fucked here."

Danny shook his head, ignoring the challenging tone. He lowered himself onto the warm granite, his feet dangling above the murky green water. "Bryce and I never fooled around. We didn't even jerk off together." He stared pensively at the reflection on the water for a few seconds, then said, "I'm pretty sure he made it up when we brought Diane Costello and Nancy Gorman here in seventh grade. I think he told them they had to kiss us because this was Lovers' Rock, and if they didn't, we'd all have bad luck." It felt right. "At least I think that's where it came from. You'd think I'd know since it was a few years before my fall."

"But it was also a long time ago."

"Not for me."

Joey stared at the pipe for a moment. "Yeah, me neither." He looked away toward the spillway. "We came here that night," he said almost dreamily.

"We did?"

A short nod. "I wanted to just meet you here, but you made me wait at my house because of the murders. You didn't want me walking around by myself. You walked me home, too." He looked back at Danny. "Kind of ironic, huh?"

Not the word I would have chosen.

"Yeah," Danny agreed, anyway.

"We came out here and went up into the orchard."

Danny closed his eyes. Though he could easily summon memories of the orchard at night—the trees transformed into sinister creatures by the moonlight, the light sweetness of damp grass, the cloying sweetness of rotting fruit on the ground—and the feel of Joey's body, he knew they weren't from that night.

"Do you miss him?" Joey asked suddenly.

Danny's eyes popped open. "Bryce?"

Joey nodded, his eyes searching Danny's face.

"Not so much," Danny said, surprising himself. He watched for a reaction, saw none. "I mean, he was my best friend for most of my life, but we'd been growing apart for a while. Once your folks shipped him off to Fessenden, we barely saw each other anymore. Even that first summer. He had his new friends." He felt unexpectedly relieved. It was a truth he'd been unable to realize at the time, and unable to admit later because it felt like a betrayal of the friendship they'd once shared.

"We'd grown apart, too," Joey said, "except it started before he went away to school." Danny saw traces of guilt, anger, fear, and sadness on his face. "The truth is that I was actually relieved when he went."

And when he was killed?

"Why?" Danny asked.

"Because he treated me like shit."

It took Danny by surprise. Though Bryce had frequently been an asshole to other people, he'd always been surprisingly protective of his younger siblings. "Since when?" he asked.

A cloud passed over Joey's face. "I don't remember exactly."

Danny was sure it was a lie. "What about Amy?"

Joey appeared to give it serious thought. "I guess he treated her the same until just before he ran away. Afterward he treated us both like shit, like he didn't care about us anymore. Actually more like he hated us."

"You know that's not true," Danny said.

"You weren't there," Joey replied tersely.

I sense a refrain!

"I guess I wasn't," Danny said, though he knew it wasn't true. Before and after Bryce ran away they'd been inseparable, right until Bryce transferred to The Fessenden School for eighth grade. Danny took a long drag on his cigarette, looked at Joey. "Did he ever tell you why he took off?" Though Bryce had eagerly shared every detail of his adventures on the road, he'd never been willing to explain why he'd left.

Joey abruptly picked up the pipe, lit it, and inhaled, holding the smoke in his lungs for a full ten seconds before exhaling explosively. "Like I said, we weren't close by then." He took another hit and looked at Danny with glassy but resolute eyes.

Danny didn't know where to go with it. He contented himself with watching the ducks paddle around in the reeds.

"Do you know why I like to come here?" Joey asked after a few minutes. The tension was gone from his voice.

"Because we were here that last night?"

"Wow, you have quite an ego for someone with a chicken wing." Joey cracked a teasing smile.

"But in your memories, I don't have one," Danny shot back.

"No, you don't," Joey agreed, "but that's not why. It's because I was always happy here."

A dozen well-intentioned platitudes about letting go of the past and searching for new happiness popped into Danny's head.

Most sounded like Jerry. He was sure all of them would sound judgmental. A gust of wind rippled the pond and he shivered.

"It's getting kind of chilly," he said, pushing to his feet. "You want to walk back with me?"

"No, I'm going to stick around for a while," Joey said. "The cold doesn't bother me. I don't really even feel it anymore."

Danny nodded. "Caroline's coming home in the morning."

"That's okay," Joey replied, catching the implication. "Call me or stop by when you can."

* * * * *

As Danny reached the trail marker again, he stopped and looked around. It felt familiar, but not special.

CHAPTER 17

He heard the high whine of a two-stroke engine and stood up. He could see Bryce zipping toward him through the trees. As he reached the clearing, Bryce hit the brakes hard and threw the motorbike sideways, skidding to a stop.

"Where the hell have you been?" he grumbled as soon as Bryce cut the engine. It was the first time they'd gotten together in two months, and Bryce was a half-hour late.

"I told you I was umpiring a Pee Wee game." Bryce shrugged carelessly. "It went into extra innings."

He gave Bryce a sour look. "I don't know why you even do that bullshit. It's lame."

"Because it's funny," Bryce replied. "It's like watching retards play because none of them can catch or throw. Every hit is a home run. Plus I get to piss off their asshole parents by making bad calls."

He rolled his eyes. Though he could see the merits of both, he couldn't see putting up with the screaming brats or the aggravation.

"Come on, don't be such a little bitch," Bryce said. "I have a surprise."

"What?" he asked warily. Sometimes Bryce's surprises were fun for both of them, sometimes just for Bryce.

Bryce reached into the inner pocket of his Levi's jacket and pulled out a round metal tin, holding it up proudly in the palm of his right hand. "I found Sterno in our pantry."

"So?"

"So we can light it."

He whirled his right index finger in the air. "Woo hoo. Fire." He grunted discontentedly. "You're a fucking pyro."

Bryce ignored him and leaped onto Lovers' Rock. He pried the lid off the can with a quarter, set the can down in the center of the rock, and lit it.

He stared at the low blue flame for a moment, then widened his eyes mockingly. "Wow, this is awesome. Glad we got together."

A malicious smile crept across Bryce's face. "You want awesome? How about this?" Bryce stepped forward and kicked the can, sending it spinning into the pine needles below. Scattered globs of jellied alcohol smoldered for a few seconds, then caught.

"You fucking asshole!" he cried.

He jumped down and kicked the still-burning can toward the pond. A trail of flame erupted behind it. Bryce doubled over, his howl of laughter piercing the air.

He stamped out one of the smaller fires, then looked desperately at Bryce. "Help me!" he yelled, fighting panic.

Bryce just smiled at him for a few seconds, then jumped down and rolled his motorbike a safe distance up the trail.

Crackling embers shot into the air and smoke began to sting his eyes as the fire spread. He pulled off his jacket and began frantically beating down the flames.

* * * * *

Danny stared into the shadows on his bedroom ceiling and wiped away real tears. His heart was racing.

I buried it, he thought. Near the trail marker.

Though it hadn't been his fault, he'd known instinctively that Caroline's feelings would be hurt if she knew what had really happened, so he'd buried the jacket she'd given him for Christmas, and told her it had been stolen. She'd been annoyed, but not sullen. She'd just snapped that if he wanted another one he'd have to buy it himself.

Great, a Caroline guilt dream, he thought. Like I won't be getting enough of the real thing. He knew he wouldn't find sleep again and rolled out of bed.

CHAPTER 18

Danny signed the paperwork and settled into a molded green plastic chair to wait.

"It's not like the movies," the woman sitting across from him said. She had a hard Yankee accent. Her long hair was gray and stringy, her skin deeply weathered. "They don't just give 'em a new suit and ten bucks and let them out the front gate. Not anymore."

Please, tell me more about life during the Depression.

Danny gave her a quick nod and smile, and grabbed a very old issue of *Sports Illustrated* from the table to his right.

"What happened to your arm?" the woman asked.

Danny pretended not to have heard her as he thumbed pages.

"I was just trying to be friendly," the woman squawked, her voice rising. "Can't see any reason why we should both be sitting here acting like we don't see one another."

Danny looked up. "Sorry. I'm just a little anxious."

The hardness in the woman's eyes faded and she gave a knowing nod. "It's your boyfriend who's getting out, isn't it? The one who did that to your arm?" She offered a long-suffering sigh of solidarity. "Been there more times than I care to remember."

Danny blinked at her, wondering how she knew he was gay and why she'd assume he was in an abusive relationship.

"No, actually I'm picking up my mother," he said.

"Is she the one who hurt you?"

Yes, but those scars are all on the inside.

"No, it happened in a fall."

The woman made a troubled face. "If you say so."

Danny was about to protest Caroline's innocence when a buzzer sounded and she was escorted into the room. She saw Danny and broke into a trembling smile. Danny stood up.

Caroline dropped her small suitcase, rushed to him, and wrapped him in a crushing embrace. "Oh, honey, it's so good to see you," she gushed breathlessly.

"You, too," Danny said, realizing he actually meant it despite feeling that Caroline had rehearsed their reunion scene many times in her head.

After a moment, she took a step back and wiped a single tear from her cheek with a surprisingly well-manicured nail, then looked around self-consciously. She cast a quick critical look at the old woman, then fixed her gaze on the guard, a blond linebacker in drag. "My son," she said. "Isn't he handsome?"

The guard gave a cursory nod, then looked at Danny. "She's all yours." It sounded to Danny like a threat.

He looked toward the old woman, intending to make introductions, but she was staring at the floor with a hurt expression.

"Shall we?" Caroline said brightly.

* * * * *

Caroline rolled down the window, lit a Benson & Hedges 100, and draped herself into the corner, left arm across the back of the seat, right elbow propped in the open window. Danny wasn't sure he'd ever seen her sitting or standing straight. There'd always been some attitude to her posture.

"So what do you think?" she asked, turning her head slowly from side to side.

The last time Danny had visited, her hair had still been shoulder length and auburn, though the top had been wrapped under a floral scarf. Now all traces of the auburn had been cut away, leaving silver shot through with some dark brown. He wondered why he'd never known auburn wasn't her natural color.

And you call yourself a homo?

Despite the gray, the cut actually made her appear younger than she had a year earlier.

"I like it," he said. "Who cut it?"

"Jasmine, one of the girls in my unit."

"They let prisoners have scissors?"

Caroline dipped her head as though peering at him over imaginary glasses, and gave a small sigh of exasperation. "Of course they let us have scissors. We're drunks and drug addicts, Danny, not killers."

And drunks with sharp objects are a lot less dangerous?

"They even have classes in hair styling, make-up and manicuring to train the girls for jobs when they get out."

"So what did you take?" Danny asked.

Another exasperated sigh. "And why would I need to take anything? Like my life isn't full enough without a job?" She took a long drag on her cigarette, then narrowed her eyes and cocked her head. "You're just teasing me, aren't you?" She shook her cigarette at him and smiled as though she'd just caught a joke.

"Yes, I'm just teasing," Danny agreed, knowing it was the path of least resistance.

God forbid you actually have any practical skills.

"I knew it," Caroline said. "You always liked to tease me."

Danny wondered again whose life she was remembering.

"So we should go out to dinner to celebrate," Caroline said, sitting up excitedly as though the idea had just come to her.

Danny's stomach tensed. "Celebrate" was one of her code words—along with "unwind," "pick-me-up," and "refreshment"— that usually led to a long messy night.

"You don't want to just relax on your first night back?" he tried. "I'll cook."

Caroline waved him off. "I have the rest of my life to relax. I need a little treat after all that God-awful cafeteria food."

CHAPTER 19

Caroline did a dainty sashay across the kitchen, arms out, wrists and fingers poised like a ballet dancer. She was dressed in a fitted pink sleeveless shift with a neon lime island-and-palm-tree motif and Mandarin-inspired collar.

"Can you believe it?" she asked, doing a runway turn. "I haven't been able to fit into any of my Lilly Pulitzers in years."

Despite shunning any exercise beyond a weekly game of doubles tennis, Caroline had always been lanky and managed the appearance of fitness. When she'd come to visit him in the hospital the last time, however, Danny had noticed a pronounced belly and thickening around her waist. Now her waist was narrow again and her lower abdomen protruded only slightly.

"I know it's not summer yet, but I'm in such a good mood I wanted to wear something cheerful."

Your word, not mine.

"Have you been working out?" Danny asked, nodding at the toned muscles in her shoulders and arms.

Caroline gave a falsely modest shrug. "Just some aerobics with my roommate, Sandy. She used to be a competitive bodybuilder until her asshole ex-boyfriend got her hooked on cocaine."

"Aerobics with your bodybuilder roommate?" Danny widened his eyes. "Wait, you didn't go lesbo in there, did you?"

"That's disgusting," Caroline replied flatly.

"Gay does seem to run in the family."

Caroline fixed him with an icy look. "Don't be insipid."

Danny felt suddenly dizzy and gripped the counter for support. A memory taunted him but wouldn't come into focus.

"Besides, how can you be sure *you're* gay?" Caroline went on obliviously. "Have you been with anyone since the coma?"

Danny took a deep breath and felt the dizziness fade a bit. "No," he managed weakly.

"Well, there you go," Caroline crowed as though it were conclusive proof. "A lot of boys have sex with one another when they're young, but then they outgrow it." She stared at Danny, waiting for a reaction, then frowned. "Are you okay?"

"Yeah, fine." He absently touched his cheek, then added more resolutely, "And I'm not going to outgrow it."

Caroline shook her head. "You've always been so stubborn."

Yes, I like dick out of obstinacy.

"So where to?" Danny asked quickly, sensing she was warming up for a longer sermon.

Caroline looked momentarily irritated, but recovered. "One of the girls mentioned an Indian place on Moody Street in Waltham. It sounds intriguing."

"Not the Red Coach?" Danny asked, surprised. It had always been Caroline's "go to" choice, presumably because it was the closest place where she could get a drink.

Caroline gave a coquettish shrug. "What can I say? I'm a whole new me."

* * * * *

Caroline slipped her hand around Danny's right elbow as they walked to the parking lot. "So what did you think?" she asked.

"I think it was as good as the place that Jerry and Karl say has the best Indian food in Manhattan." He saw the sudden interest in Caroline's eyes and knew he'd made a mistake.

"Your father, the expert on everything. He always claimed to know the best restaurant, the best doctor, the best way to do things. He was exhausting."

Danny didn't respond. He knew that in the past he would have egged her on as a show of solidarity, but now he just wanted the topic to die. They'd managed dinner with just innocuous small talk, and he didn't want to give her an excuse to go off on a tirade.

"So was it terrible living with them?" Caroline tried again after half a block of silence.

Danny sighed inwardly. "No, not really." He kept his tone neutral. "They have some nice friends." It felt like safe territory.

He pulled his cigarettes from his right front pocket, transferred the pack to his left hand, worked out a cigarette, put it between his lips, took out his lighter, and lit it. Caroline kept hold of his elbow the whole time. He was aware of her watching him out of the corner of her eye and braced for a comment.

"So does it make you self-conscious?" she asked finally.

Being seen in public with you in that dress?

"What?" Danny played dumb.

"Your arm."

"Not really. Why? Should it?"

"No, of course not," Caroline replied too breezily. She paused to light her own cigarette, then added, "I just remember how you were when you chipped your front tooth. Always on me to get it fixed because you were sure everyone was staring at you."

And yet, seventeen years later...

The tip of Danny's tongue reflexively darted to the triangular notch for a second. "That was a little different," he said. "In this case I'm just happy to be alive. I can live with my little chicken wing. At least for now."

"Oh," Caroline replied, looking vaguely disappointed. She wrinkled her nose. "And don't call it that. That's disgusting."

* * * * *

Caroline came back into the kitchen in a flowing flowered caftan. "Do you want to stay up and watch television with me for a little while? I'm not really tired yet."

It was a common refrain. When he was a small child, Caroline had bribed Danny to stay up late and watch movies with her on the weekends. After Jerry left, it had become an every night occurrence that usually ended with having to help her upstairs to bed. He'd survived junior high and ninth grade on only four or five hours of sleep each night.

"I'm pretty wiped," he said, putting the orange juice back into the refrigerator.

Caroline pushed her lower lip out into an exaggerated pout and batted her eyelashes at him. "Please. Just for a little while? I'm not used to being by myself anymore."

Were you ever?

Danny couldn't help but laugh. Despite her many flaws, Caroline could be charming when she chose. "All right, fine," he said, "but just until midnight."

CHAPTER 20

"Do you want some coffee?" Danny asked. He was surprised to see Caroline up so early and looking so rested.

"No, thanks, honey. I don't do caffeine anymore. It makes me too irritable."

Do? Caffeine is an activity now?

"Plus the coffee in the prison cafeteria was like turpentine." She opened the cabinet to the right of the stove and shuffled cans and boxes until she came out with a box of Lipton tea bags. "Maybe you could pick up some herbal tea for me today?"

"Sure," Danny replied, "but I figured we'd go to the market together. I'm sure you need to pick up some other things, and I don't even know what you like to eat anymore."

"I'm sorry, didn't I tell you?" Caroline said. "Beth is taking me to the Chestnut Hill Mall, then to Wellesley." She grabbed the kettle from the stove and crossed to the sink. "We're going to make a day of it. Shop, lunch, massages, a little more shopping."

"Oh. When did you decide that?"

A hint of annoyance passed over Caroline's face. "Yesterday afternoon. I called her while I was trying to decide what to wear to dinner and told her none of my clothes fit anymore. She suggested we run up some charges on your father's credit cards since he hasn't had to pay for anything in a long time."

Other than this house and my hospital bills, you mean?

Caroline saw the disapproval on Danny's face and sighed. "I'm kidding. He told me to treat myself." She rinsed out the kettle and refilled it. "Guilt...the gift that keeps on giving." She walked back to the stove, set the kettle on the front right burner, turned it on, and faced Danny. "We can go to the grocery store tomorrow if you can just me the tea and some tampons today."

Buying your mom's feminine hygiene products...the embarrassment that keeps on giving.

"Yeah, sure," Danny said, feeling suddenly uneasy. While he was happy not to have to ferry her around, it seemed too soon for her to spend the day out with a friend.

Because you can't keep an eye on her?

At least she'll be with Beth, he thought. On a scale of toxicity, Beth Wallace didn't even register. She wasn't particularly bright and tended toward manic cheerfulness, but at least she wasn't—or hadn't been—one of those ladies who took her lunch in a martini glass. At least she wasn't Grace O'Neill.

"Then I guess I'll stop by the library while I'm in town," he said distractedly.

Caroline gave him a curious look. "The library?"

"I just want to find something to read."

CHAPTER 21

As Danny ascended the stairs from the microfilm archives, the damp mustiness of basement gave way to the acrid mustiness of old books.

Six of one, half a dozen of another.

Shhh. This is a library!

He approached the desk where an older man with a neatly trimmed mustache, badly dyed hair, and a sweater vest perched on a stool reading a paperback of *Valley of the Dolls*. A nameplate identified him as Mr. Lamont.

"Excuse me, is there a pay phone I can use?" Danny asked.

Lamont looked up, gave Danny the once over, and sniffed as though he'd smelled something distasteful. "Out front."

"Thanks," Danny said, then patted his pocket. He pulled out his wallet and took out a dollar bill. "Do you have any change?"

Lamont laid his book down very delicately and fixed Danny with an imperious look. "Do you have a library card?"

Danny had found it still sitting in the middle drawer of his desk and tucked it into his wallet before he left the house. He handed it to Lamont, who stared at it for a moment, then turned it over several times before laying it square on the counter. "I've never seen one like this before," he said.

"I've had it for a while."

Lamont picked it up again and flipped it a few more times. "It doesn't look like it's gotten much use."

"I usually use the library at the high school," Danny replied.

Lamont placed the card on the counter again and pushed it toward Danny. He raised his eyebrows suggestively. "Really?"

"Before I moved, I meant," Danny said quickly. "I can get a new one if you want."

"That won't be necessary," Lamont replied with a self-satisfied smile, apparently content with his demonstration of power. He opened a drawer, counted out ten dimes, and pushed them across the desk.

"Thanks," Danny said.

By the way, Mr. Lamont, how many cats do you have?

* * * * *

Danny dropped a dime in the slot, waited for the tone, then dialed Holtz's direct line. After three rings, a recording of Holtz's voice came on. Danny hung up, unsure whether anyone else had access to Holtz's messages.

Shit, he thought. He checked his watch and looked past the town green toward the center of town. A blue minivan with fake wood paneling was parked in front of Ye Olde Cottage.

* * * * *

The lunch rush had passed and the restaurant was nearly empty. Holtz sat in the back booth, facing the door, his attention on the newspaper spread over his empty plates. Danny walked to the adjacent booth and slid onto the banquette facing him.

"What are you doing here?" Holtz asked without looking up. His tone was neither friendly nor hostile.

"I saw your stylish ride out front," Danny replied, keeping his voice low though there was no one nearby.

"Does that mean you wanted to talk to me?"

"That was the plan."

Holtz looked up. "Then why are you sitting over there?"

Danny felt his face flush. "Hey, you're the one who wanted to be all cloak and dagger, remember?"

Holtz gave him a measured look. "I don't think whispering across the room is going to achieve that, do you?" He smirked and nodded at the banquette on the opposite side of his table.

Danny scowled, got up, and slipped into Holtz's booth. A waitress came over.

"What can I get you, hon?"

"Just some coffee, please."

"You got it."

"So is this just a social visit?" Holtz asked as she walked away.

"No. I was just at the library reading the newspaper coverage of the murders and Tim's trial."

Holtz sat up straighter, folded the paper, and set it aside.

"It got me wondering about a few things," Danny said.

"Such as?"

Danny waited while the waitress brought his coffee and warmed Holtz's cup, then leaned forward. "The papers said the first four boys were all taken from their rooms during the night, but they didn't say how exactly."

"Through their bedroom windows."

"And no one woke up while the guy was jimmying the lock or breaking the glass or whatever?"

"It was summer. The windows were open."

Danny cocked his head. "Doesn't that seem like kind of a big coincidence?"

"Weston is a safe town," Holtz shrugged. "Even safer then. A lot of people sleep with their windows open during the summer."

"But all four just happened to be sleeping with open windows on the night the killer went for them?" Danny lifted a skeptical eyebrow. "And I babysat Andy Parker a few times..."

"Really?" Holtz interrupted. "Isn't that interesting?"

Danny rolled his eyes. "So did Bryce."

"But he'd dead."

"So did half the older kids in the neighborhood."

"Can you prove that?"

"Not funny. I didn't even know the other three victims."

"That you *remember*. Convenient."

Danny glared back. "Fuck you. Do you want to hear what I have to say or not?"

Holtz smiled, clearly pleased with himself. "Dazzle me."

Danny shook his head irritably. "Andy's bedroom was on the second floor, which means he had to be carried down a ladder. He weighed at least sixty pounds, and I'm betting he would have been scared and putting up a fight."

"Unless he was drugged."

"Was he?"

"There weren't any toxicology reports."

"What about the other kids' rooms? First or second floor?"

"I'm not sure about Michael Frazier, but the other two were on the second floor." Holtz nodded for Danny to go on.

"I was also wondering how he found his victims."

"The original investigators assumed Tim staked out schools. Lots of kids to choose from, lots of people picking them up. Easy to blend in."

"But Tim was into the nature thing."

"Like I said in the beginning, I think he was just convenient. They glossed over any facts that didn't fit their theory."

"Even so, schools don't make sense," Danny said. "According to the papers, Andy and Frazier went to Field School, Talbot went to Meadowbrook, and Levitt went to a place called the Maimonides School in Brookline."

"I doubt he would've limited himself to just one school."

"But he happened to pick another Weston kid from a school in Brookline?"

"Yeah, that would have been another big coincidence," Holtz replied. He added some sugar to his coffee and took a few sips. "You've obviously given this a lot of thought already. So do you have a theory, too?"

"Maybe. Sort of."

"My favorite kind."

Danny hesitated a moment, took a quick sip of coffee. "It seems to me that a stranger watching kids would've been noticed, especially in a town like this. I mean, other than school and maybe the grocery store, the only place where you have a lot of kids and adults together is at the town pool, and that wasn't open when Andy and Frazier were killed. I think it had to be someone local. Someone no one noticed because he was supposed to be there."

Holtz rubbed his fleshy cheeks. "When you put it that way, it seems pretty obvious."

Danny braced for the sarcasm shoe to drop. It didn't. "I also think it had to be someone who was around kids a lot," he said. "Someone they'd trust." He sat back and sipped his coffee, watching Holtz carefully over the rim of the cup.

Holtz stared at the table for a moment, slowly rocking his head from side to side as though rolling an idea around, then nodded. "And someone they'd go with willingly."

"That's what I'm thinking. They might even have been expecting him."

"Maybe you should consider becoming a cop," Holtz said.

I don't like donuts that much.

"But there's one thing that still doesn't make sense to me," Danny said. "You said serial killers follow patterns. Bryce and I didn't fit the pattern. We weren't kidnapped or sexually abused. At least I probably wasn't."

"No," Holtz agreed matter-of-factly. "And neither of you matched the victim profile, either."

Danny blinked at him. Holtz flashed a sly smile.

"And I haven't told you anything you didn't already know, have I?" Danny asked.

Holtz shrugged. "You told me you're a little brighter than I thought." He drained his cup and signaled for the check. "Where's your truck?"

"Parked along the green."

"Let's go have a cigarette."

* * * * *

"The others were all under the age of ten and pre-pubescent. You and Bryce were both fifteen and sexually mature."

96

"And that's unusual?" Danny asked.

"Depends on the type of serial killer. Richard Ramirez's victims were physically dissimilar and they were killed in a variety of ways, but these were what are called lust killings because the killer derives sexual pleasure from torture and killing. Lust killing victims tend to fit a specific physical profile, like middle-aged women who resemble the killer's mother, that sort of thing. And the killings usually follow a specific ritual. The lack of consistency was the reason I decided to go back and review the case files in the first place. I wanted to see if anyone had addressed those issues during the investigation."

"And did they?"

Holtz shook his head. "Of course, it's possible you were all picked on the basis of something other than appearance, like the way you acted or something specific you did, but that still leaves the change in the ritual unexplained."

"Maybe he had to stop to chase me after he stabbed Bryce, then was afraid to go back and finish."

"I considered that, but in every other case, the sexual assault and torture happened prior to the killings. The order theoretically shouldn't have varied. And Bryce was the only one who was stabbed, and the only one whose throat was cut post-mortem. In fact, the only thing that was consistent across the board was the type of knife used."

Danny frowned uneasily. "So what are you saying?"

"I'm saying I think it's possible you and Bryce were attacked by a different person."

Danny waited for a smile that didn't come, then for the dizziness to pass. "Jesus, Holtz!" he exclaimed finally. "When the fuck were you planning to tell me?"

"When it stopped sounding crazy in my head." Holtz replied. "That hasn't happened yet, but what the hell."

Danny eyed him doubtfully. "You're really serious?"

"That's what the evidence suggests, though I could be wrong."

"But that would mean two killers still running around."

"Maybe. It's been thirteen years. A lot could have happened in that time. And it's still possible that Tim was one of them."

"But you don't really believe that."

"It seems unlikely, but I can't completely rule him out yet. Until I do, I'm trying to keep an open mind."

Danny took a drag on his cigarette, watching the smoke curl out the top of the window for a moment. "It's a lot to take in," he said.

"Yeah, I've had a while to get used to the idea, and I'm still having some trouble with it."

"How long have you actually been working on it?"

"A little over three years now. It's been slow going since I can't use official channels, but little by little I've been retracing the steps of the original investigation to see if there's anyone obvious who should have been a suspect but never made the list."

"Like who?"

"I've been focusing on the school angle. Even though they went to three different middle schools, all four boys started out at Woodland Elementary together."

"So did Bryce and I," Danny said. He tried to remember if there had been any teachers or staff who seemed at all threatening. No one came immediately to mind. "But if it was someone who worked at Woodlawn, that would mean he'd probably picked them while they were still going there, right?"

"Presumably."

"That means at least a year before the killings. You really think someone would have waited that long?"

"Sure, if the boys had to be or look a certain age for him to get off on it."

Danny curled his upper lip. "That's even more disturbing."

Holtz nodded. "But that would have given him plenty of time to cultivate the relationships and learn the families' habits." He abruptly stubbed his cigarette in the ashtray and cracked the passenger door open. "Well, I need to get back to work."

"Wait," Danny said. "What am I supposed to be doing?"

98

"Nothing," Holtz replied casually. "Just give me a call if you remember anything. And don't get any ideas about playing Nancy Drew or anything stupid like that." He stepped out of the truck and stretched, then frowned at Danny. "By the way, didn't your mother come home yesterday?"

Danny nodded, didn't say anything.

"Are you sure it was smart to leave her alone so soon?"

"She's out shopping with a friend."

"Which one?"

"Beth Wallace."

Holtz considered it, nodded. "She should be safe enough." He closed the door and gave Danny a perfunctory smile through the open window.

"I still feel like you haven't told me the truth about why you're doing this," Danny said.

"Does it matter?"

"Probably not, but I'd still like to know."

"Maybe some day." Holtz said. He turned and started back toward the parking lot. Danny scowled at his back.

Nancy Drew?

CHAPTER 22

Danny topped the rise in the driveway, braked the truck, and muttered, "Fuck." A vintage black Mercedes fintail was parked in the turnaround. He suddenly wished he'd hidden all the liquor after all. He parked, got out, and walked to the porch. The back door was open and he could hear laughter coming down the hall from the living room.

"Grace...you should have seen...the look...on her face," Caroline pushed the words out between fits of giggles, "when I asked...what time...the maid came."

Grace O'Neill's howl was followed by a near-breathless, "Oh no, you didn't!"

"I swear. Then I asked...if I could get room service."

Another explosion of laughter while Danny let himself in and walked down the hall and through the foyer. Grace O'Neill was sitting on the near end of the couch, her back to the doorway, wearing one of her signature sporty casual ensembles as though she'd just stepped off a yacht. Caroline sat on the far end, wearing another colorful Lilly Pulitzer outfit, this time Capri slacks with a matching short jacket. When she noticed Danny standing in the doorway, she waved him in with a fluttery hand.

"Danny, honey, you remember Grace, of course." Her voice was too loud, manic.

"Of course." Danny forced a smile and kissed the overly tanned and tucked ash blond on both cheeks. "Nice to see you again." He looked at the bottle of Moët and two half-empty champagne flutes on the coffee table. "Where's Mrs. Wallace?"

"She had to cancel at the last minute so I called Grace. She brought over some champagne to celebrate my return," Caroline gushed. Her eyes were already becoming unfocused.

"How nice," Danny said, wondering if Beth Wallace had ever really been part of the day's plans.

He threw Caroline a quick warning look. She looked startled, then checked to make sure Grace wasn't looking before mouthing, "Just one."

"There are two more bottles in the fridge," Grace said, turning the promise into a long shot. "Why don't you join us?"

"No thanks," Danny replied tightly. He locked eyes with Caroline. "In fact, I think I'm going to go out."

As he walked down the hall, he heard Grace's spectacular fail at sotto voce, "Such a handsome boy. You'd never know what happened from looking at his face, but you have to do something about that arm."

* * * * *

Danny made it to Framingham in time for a 4:15 PM showing of *Dead Heat*, a zombie-cop movie starring Treat Williams, then had a hot pastrami, onion rings, and cream soda at Joan & Ed's Deli. By the time he crossed back over the Wayland/Weston town line, his anger had been replaced by determination.

It was just getting dark as he turned into the driveway. Grace's Mercedes was gone. The only lights in the house were in the kitchen and family room. That's a good sign, right? he thought.

Unless she's swilling martinis at the Red Coach.

He checked the garage to make sure Caroline's silver BMW convertible was still there, then unlocked the back door and went in. The house was quiet. Though he'd spent the whole drive psyching himself up for a confrontation, he was relieved.

We live to fight another day.

He did a quick tour of the first floor. The coffee table in the living room was clear, the accent pillows on the couch fluffed and straightened. Either Caroline had gotten tidier in prison or Grace had cleaned up before she left. The only evidence of their evening was two empty Moët bottles by the kitchen sink.

101

Danny grabbed a Coke and went down to the basement. He was about to turn on the TV when he noticed the faint rush of water through the pipes in the ceiling. He put the Coke down, walked back upstairs and into the front foyer, and flipped on the light in the upstairs hallway. The door to the master bedroom suite was open.

"Mom?" he called.

He climbed the stairs. Caroline's bedroom was dark, but a sliver of light shone under her bathroom door. He stepped into the inner hallway and gave a tentative knock. No response. He leaned closer and knocked again, harder.

"Mom, are you all right?"

All he heard was water splashing. An image suddenly flashed in his mind of Caroline lying in the tub, blood swirling into the water from gashes in her wrists. He grabbed the knob, twisted it, and anxiously pushed the door open.

Caroline was slumped on the toilet to the left, her arms dangling at her sides. There was no blood on the floor, and her back rose and fell rhythmically. He exhaled, then gagged as he took another breath. The room reeked of stale alcohol and vomit.

He skirted Caroline and turned off the spigot. The water had almost reached the top of the tub, and chunks of partially digested food floated on the surface. He fought back a dry heave and reached into it to free Caroline's Capri pants from the drain. The water began to go down. This is so not what I need, he thought, shaking his arm off with a shudder.

He washed his hand and forearm in the sink, then turned to Caroline. Her head was almost on her knees, her face hidden by her short bangs. She wore only a white t-shirt and pink panties, the latter down around her ankles.

He moved closer and nudged her right shoulder. "Wake up!" he said sharply. Caroline let out a groan, but slumped lower. "Caroline!" he barked. "You need to get up and go to bed!" It was all too familiar, but infinitely worse. "Caroline!" he tried again, desperation creeping into his voice.

He squatted in front of her, averting his eyes. Her rank hot breath was making him queasier. He gently slapped her twice on the left side of the face. "Caroline, wake the fuck..."

Caroline's right arm flailed up, her loose fist catching him just below the left eye and knocking him off-balance. He toppled backwards, instinctively trying to break his fall with his left hand. As his head slammed into the radiator below the window, a vivid memory flashed in his mind.

"Don't be insipid."

"Do you even know what that word means?"

Caroline blinked at him.

"No, you don't," he said with a smirk, "because you've been using it wrong for at least fifteen years. Insipid means dull and flavorless. The word you want is insolent."

Caroline's hand came up fast and hard. He staggered back, unsure what had happened until he felt the sting in his right cheek.

"And don't be an asshole, either, Danny."

Danny opened his eyes. Caroline was shuffling toward him, her panties still around her ankles. "I'm so sorry," she cried, hands flapping uselessly at the air. "I didn't realize it was you. I was dreaming that someone was attacking me."

Danny scuttled back against the wall as she started to bend toward him. "Get the fuck away from me," he said, trying to keep from crying. "Pull up your panties, wash the puke out of your mouth, and just go to bed."

Caroline took another step, tutting and whimpering. Danny caught a glimpse of graying pubic hair and pushed his right hand at her, holding up a warning finger. "Don't!" he screamed. "Just fucking leave me alone!"

Caroline fell back as though he'd pushed her. Danny scrambled painfully to his feet, and rushed out the door and down the hall to his room. He slammed the door and locked it behind him.

CHAPTER 23

Danny heard Caroline's heavy steps coming down the hallway and looked up from the paper as she stopped in the doorway. Her hair was matted, her skin pale and puffy, her eyes pink and glassy. He guessed they'd had about the same amount of sleep.

She eyed the mug in his hand. "Is there any more coffee?" Her voice was hushed, hoarse.

"Mommy has a headache. Make mommy some coffee, just the way I showed you."

"I thought you didn't 'do caffeine' anymore," Danny said. The hurt and confusion that had roiled him most of the night had hardened into anger just before dawn, then soured to petulance.

"Don't be insipid," Caroline snapped.

Danny felt a phantom slap to his cheek and stepped away from the counter. Caroline took a mug out of the cabinet, filled it, drank half, and said, "Weak," then refilled it and added cream and sugar. She took a longer sip and closed her eyes.

"Just like old times," Danny said.

Except today I'm not in the mood to placate mommy's bad mood.

Caroline slowly opened her eyes. She leaned against the counter, took her cigarettes from her robe pocket, and lit one. Her expression was unreadable. She took a drag, sipped more coffee.

"So?" Danny asked.

Caroline returned a blank stare.

He shook his head. "You're not even going to apologize?"

"I told you I was sorry last night, but you didn't want to hear it," Caroline replied dispassionately. "What more can I say? You know I didn't mean to do it. I was asleep and had a nightmare."

"You weren't asleep," Danny said coldly. "Let's be clear about that. You were passed out."

Caroline took another long drag, never taking her eyes off him. "I'm really not sure where all this hostility is coming from," she said finally.

Danny laughed humorlessly. "How about just this once, you let me be the victim, okay?" Caroline blinked at him through the smoke, and he could see her calculating her next move. "Just stop," he said. "I don't want to hear it. You promised me you'd only have one drink."

"But I couldn't be rude when Grace was so nice to bring over champagne," Caroline replied as though it were an inviolable truth.

"If Grace were really nice, she would have brought a bundt cake and taken you to an AA meeting," Danny shot back, and immediately felt guilty.

Caroline drew herself up, her eyes sparking. Danny braced himself as her mouth began working. Then the fight seemed to leave her. Her body sagged back against the counter and she lowered her eyes. "I'm sorry I'm such a disappointment to you," she said, her voice barely a whisper.

It took Danny off-guard, and he felt an unwanted stab of sympathy. "You're not *a* disappointment," he said quickly. "You just disappoint me sometimes." He felt his anger fading.

Caroline wiped away a tear. "Not nearly as much as I disappoint myself." She took a wet breath.

Danny felt an urge to hug her. He'd seen her shed a lot tears over the years—some false, most real, never any of remorse that he could remember. He wondered if she'd actually done some soul searching during her time in prison.

Or taken acting classes.

"I know I've been a shitty mother," she continued. "I've been selfish. I'm sorry for that." She paused to get a paper towel and blow her nose. "For all his faults, Jerry was a good father. He was always there for you."

Until he wasn't.

"You weren't a shitty mother," Danny said. "You just..."

"Yes, I was, Danny," Caroline said more passionately. She paused and shook her head sadly. "And apparently I still am. I hurt you." She stared at the floor for another minute, then pushed away from the counter and straightened her robe. "I made a mistake. Many mistakes. And I'm sorry. All I can promise is that I'll try to be better." She wiped away more tears and gave a contrite smile.

Danny nodded. "I'm sorry, too, but you can't do that again. If you do, I'll leave."

I'll see your ineffectual threat, and raise you one "wait till your father gets home."

"I understand, honey," Caroline replied, "and thank you for giving me another chance." She topped off her mug. "I'm going up and clean my bathroom now, then take a shower. Would you mind taking me into town later?"

"Yeah, sure," Danny said.

CHAPTER 24

Caroline had been subdued all day, but as the afternoon crept toward cocktail hour, Danny could see her growing anxious. He suggested a walk before dinner, but she opted for a nap instead. He went out to the screened porch with the well-thumbed paperback of *Jaws* he'd found in his room, stretched out on the couch, lit a cigarette, and stared at the wall.

As he'd replayed the morning again and again in his head, Caroline's words had begun to sound like dialogue from an old movie. Had she really meant what she'd said, or had she just been telling him what she thought he wanted to hear?

Magic 8 Ball says, "Reply hazy, try again."

He took a slow drag on his cigarette and tried to blow the doubt away.

Oddly, the one thing she'd said that still felt completely honest was that Jerry had been a good father. Maybe she'd been trying to show how much she could change that she could give him credit, or maybe she was just so hung over that she let her anger slip for a moment, but Danny sensed that she'd really meant it.

He also realized it was substantively true. Jerry had always been emotionally reserved and a self-involved prick in some ways, but he'd also been steady and reliable, and until he left, he'd never backed away from his responsibilities as a parent.

If only he hadn't left.

Caroline had always been the opposite. She was emotionally intense if unpredictable, and had an instinct for instigating fun, though it sometimes went awry. And though it was clear that being a parent had never been a comfortable fit, she'd always had the ability to make him feel truly special.

Occasionally.

He gave a wry smile. What does that say about me that my best friend was essentially my mother in drag?

* * * * *

Danny closed the study door while he waited for the receptionist to put the call through. He sat on the edge of Jerry's old desk, immediately got up and paced toward the window until the cord pulled tight, then turned and went back but didn't sit.

"Danny?" Jerry came on after a few seconds, his voice tight with anxiety. "Is everything all right?"

Danny smiled, imagining Jerry's shock at hearing he was on the line. "Yeah, fine," he said. "I just wanted to say hi."

"Oh." Jerry's surprise was palpable. "Well, good. I was going to try you later tonight. I called yesterday afternoon but I guess you weren't home."

"I was at the movies."

"With your mother?"

"No, just me."

A brief pause. "Are things going okay with her?"

"Well, we made it through a whole dinner on Monday without her ordering a drink."

"I'm hearing a 'but.'"

Danny hesitated. "But Grace came over yesterday afternoon." Jerry's sigh told him he didn't need to fill in the blanks.

"Danny, I know you love her," Jerry said, "but you don't owe her anything. You don't have to stay there."

"But she won't be able to drive until November."

"She has plenty of friends who can chauffeur her around. Or she could move in with Grace until then."

Danny frowned. "No offense, but I don't want to move back with you and Karl, either."

"Those aren't your only options," Jerry replied. "You could get an apartment. I can help out until you get a job."

Danny felt a flash of irritation. It seemed that Jerry's response to too many problems over the years had been to throw money at them. "I need to be here a while longer," he said. "For myself. Besides, we had it out this morning and I'm pretty sure she heard me. I think she may be ready to turn a corner."

Jerry didn't respond for a moment, then said, "Just remember, if you turn enough corners, you wind up back where you started."

And how was the food that came with that fortune cookie?

"Your mother has been all the way around that block a few times already."

"I think she really means it," Danny said. "I think that being in prison changed her. She seems more humble."

"You always think she really means it, and she always disappoints you." Jerry's voice had taken on an edge of impatience. "Come on, Dan, you're not fifteen anymore."

"That's not true," Danny replied sharply. "She doesn't always disappoint me, and I know I'm not fifteen anymore." He suddenly wished he hadn't called.

"Just don't get your hopes up," Jerry said, his tone moderately more conciliatory.

Danny didn't respond, just lit a cigarette.

"Was there something else?" Jerry asked after a few seconds of uncomfortable silence.

Danny walked toward the window again. He hadn't planned on bringing up the past, but realized he wanted to now. "If you hadn't met Karl, would you have stuck around?" he asked.

"Can I ask where this is coming from?" Jerry asked in typically cautious fashion.

"I've been spending some time thinking about the past since I got back, and I've realized that maybe some things weren't exactly the way I thought at the time."

There was a long pause. Danny began pacing again.

"That was the plan, yeah," Jerry said. "Things were bad with your mother, but I thought I could stick it out until you were out of the house. Then I fell in love with Karl."

"Why didn't you take me with you?" Danny cringed at how whiny he sounded.

"Is that really what you would have wanted? To leave your friends and move to the city where the only people you knew were Karl and me?" Jerry didn't wait for a reply. "Besides, no judge was going to grant custody to your father and his boyfriend. I would have to have proven she was a danger to you, and even then I probably would have lost. The courts usually favor the mother."

It was sensible, but unsatisfying. "Then how were you able to get me moved to Shady Meadows?" Danny asked.

"She allowed it. Of course, only after I agreed to continue child support. To be honest, I think it was actually a relief to her."

Danny knew it should have made him think less of Caroline, but it didn't. He stopped pacing and closed his eyes. "Why did you bother if you weren't going to visit me?" he asked. It felt like he'd just stepped over the edge of his dream cliff.

The silence seemed to stretch for minutes before Jerry broke it. "Who told you I didn't?" he asked evenly.

"Abby."

Jerry sighed loudly. Danny wondered whether it was anger, frustration, or surrender.

"She was right," Jerry said quietly, "but she wasn't there in the beginning." A pause. "Look, I'm not saying I've always been a great father, but I do love you, and for the first two years, I was there every Wednesday and every weekend." His voice broke slightly. "Then it got too hard. Seeing you wasting away like that."

"It's okay," Danny said, trying to remember the last time he'd felt any sympathy for his father. "I get it."

"No, you don't," Jerry replied. "I essentially ran away from you because I was afraid. I justified it to myself that you didn't even know I was there, that it was healthier for me to get some distance, a lot of other self-help bullshit. I could almost feel okay about it sometimes. But the truth was that I was just too scared to face what was happening."

Danny felt unexpected lightness. "Thanks," he said

"For what?"

"For being honest about it. I'm okay with that."

Baby steps.

* * * * *

Caroline was a bit chattier during dinner, though still less animated than usual. Danny decided not to tell her about his call with Jerry.

"So do you want to see if we can find an old movie?" he asked, an olive branch motivated by vague guilt.

"That's sweet, honey, but I'm still feeling a bit worn out from last night," Caroline replied. "I'm just going to make a cup of tea and go upstairs to watch."

"You have a TV in your bedroom? Since when?"

Caroline shrugged. "Six or seven years, I guess. I finally realized that if I was going to fall asleep watching it every night, I might as well do it in my bed."

"Oh," Danny replied. He looked at the floor and frowned, realizing he didn't want to be alone. "Then maybe I'll see if Joey wants to come over, if that's okay."

Caroline smiled indulgently. "You don't have to ask my permission or babysit me. I lived here all by myself for twelve years. I promise I won't raid the liquor cabinet."

"I know," Danny said, "but it's more comfortable here."

Caroline nodded tiredly, gave him a kiss on the cheek, turned to leave, then turned back. "I was thinking the house needs to be freshened up a bit. What do you think?"

You mean the 70s can finally end?

"Yeah, sure. I can help paint."

Caroline looked around. "It's strange, but when you see something every day you stop noticing it. I guess after being away I'm seeing everything with fresh eyes." She looked back at Danny and sighed contentedly. "I just want to brighten it up, get rid of all the clutter. Make a clean start."

CHAPTER 25

Joey was wearing his khakis and pink Oxford again, though they were noticeably less wrinkled than the last time. He'd also shaved and made another attempt to subdue his hair. When Danny hugged him, it gave off a subtle mix of citrus and mint.

"So where's your mom?" Joey asked, looking around the kitchen and family room expectantly.

"Sorry," Danny said, realizing the grooming effort had been made on Caroline's behalf. "I should have told you. She's already gone to bed."

A cloud of disappointment passed quickly over Joey's face. "Then I guess I'll just look pretty for you," he said with a passably boyish smile.

"You want something to drink?" Danny asked.

"You have any beer?"

"Just brown liquor. Lots and lots of brown liquor."

"Maybe just a Coke then."

Danny grabbed two cans from the refrigerator. "Want a glass?"

Joey took a step closer and studied Danny's face, frowning. "What happened?"

Though Danny had covered the bruising with some of Caroline's foundation, the skin over his left cheekbone was still swollen. "I tripped into a door frame," he lied, not entirely sure why. He looked down at his withered arm. "It happens sometimes. I just lose my balance and can't catch myself."

Joey gave him a doubtful look. "But you're allowed to drive?"

Danny smiled. "Yeah. It doesn't happen when I'm sitting. Come on, let's go downstairs."

* * * * *

112

"Wow, flashback," Joey said, turning in a slow circle. He sang an off-key chorus of *Sugar Magnolia*. "I can't believe Caroline never changed it."

"She hardly changed anything. You should see my room."

Joey arched his eyebrows suggestively, then laughed at the discomfort on Danny's face. "Relax. I get it, we're just friends." He dropped onto one of the couches, poured some Coke into his glass, and took a sip. "So how is it having her home?"

Danny felt an unexpected stab of anxiety. He poured his own Coke, but just watched the bubbles work their way up around the ice for a minute. "That hasn't changed really, either," he said finally. "In both good ways and bad." He smiled wistfully. "I just thought maybe it would be different."

Joey gave him a questioning look.

"There was stuff going on before that I never told you about," Danny said. "She's great in a lot of ways and I love her to death, but there's another side, too."

"I knew she drank."

"But there was a lot of drama that came with that." The anxiety was suddenly joined by guilt.

"I'm sorry," Joey said. "Why didn't you ever tell me?"

"Because I thought I'd be betraying her. And because I was embarrassed."

"About what?"

Danny considered it for a few seconds. "I guess I felt like I should have been able to do something about it, make her feel better. Like I was supposed to be the man of the house and a man would know what to do." It felt right, but incomplete.

"But you were just a kid."

"I was supposed to be, anyway," Danny took a sip of Coke and lit a cigarette. "But Caroline was..."

Erratic? Volatile? Unstable?

"...unpredictable." He resisted the urge to touch his cheek. "I guess I was hoping that part might have changed, but it hasn't. Monday she was fine. Then yesterday afternoon she and Grace got

113

hammered. And last night she passed out on the toilet and almost flooded the house because she left the tub running." He paused. "And she hit me." Another pang of guilt. "But it was an accident."

Joey's brow creased. "Are you okay?"

"Yeah, just a bump on the back of my head, some humiliation, and..." Danny pointed to his face. "She said she was having a nightmare and didn't realize it was me."

"Why did you lie before?"

Danny shrugged half-heartedly.

"And you're really okay? I mean emotionally?"

"Yeah." Danny forced a smile. "It may actually have been a good thing. We talked about it this morning, and she promised she'd try to be better." He saw the dubious look on Joey's face, realized how weak it had sounded, and quickly added, "I also called Jerry and sort of made peace. At least the start of it."

Joey raised his eyebrows.

"I think that maybe I misjudged him sometimes," Danny replied. "Or maybe judged him too quickly."

"I'm just surprised you guys didn't work it out while you were living with him," Joey said.

Danny felt his ears burning. "I hardly ever saw him."

Because you were avoiding him?

Joey nodded thoughtfully. "To be honest, I never really understood why you were so pissed at him."

"I'm not really sure, anymore. I'm starting to think that my memories even before that last summer were a little hazy."

"Maybe we shouldn't have smoked so much pot," Joey said, with a lopsided grin.

"Yeah, maybe," Danny agreed, though he knew that wasn't it.

"It seemed like he was actually a pretty cool guy," Joey said. "Bryce thought so, anyway."

"He did?"

"Yeah," Joey nodded. "He loved your dad because he took you guys places."

"So did your dad."

"Yeah, the symphony and the Museum of Fine Arts. Not any places Bryce wanted to go. Your dad took you guys to see Pink Floyd and to Sox games and camping and amusement parks. I actually felt kind of ripped off that he'd moved out by the time we became friends."

Danny gave a small laugh, then grew reflective. "I guess we did do some pretty cool stuff when he still lived here. I kind of forgot about that."

"Come on, Danny. We're going camping for the night."

"What about mom?"

"She's going to stay home. She's not feeling well."

"Can Bryce come?"

"Sure."

He pushed the memory away. "Kind of pathetic that I've been pissed at him for all these years and I'm not even sure why. I'm not even sure there ever was a reason."

Because you always knew...

For a moment he sensed a thought forming and closed his eyes. He could feel it dancing just beyond his reach but couldn't quite grasp it. He opened his eyes and let out a small sigh of frustration. "I wonder if we ever put our parent shit behind us?" A pause. "Maybe when they're dead."

"Maybe when *we're* dead," Joey replied with a strange smile. He stared at Danny for a few seconds, then blinked self-consciously. "Sorry, kind of dark. You want to watch some TV? *Growing Pains* is coming on. Kirk Cameron is kind of fuckable in a twinky way."

There was an undercurrent to the last part that made Danny uneasy. "Yeah, sure, I guess," he said.

* * * * *

These Boots Are Made for Walking was playing. Danny felt something softly stroking the stubble on his left cheek. He started awake. Joey was kneeling in front of the couch, staring at him intently.

"What the fuck are you doing?" Danny exclaimed, jerking back from Joey's hand.

Joey sat back on his heels and smiled soothingly. "You just looked so peaceful. I thought maybe if I touched you I could feel that way for just a few seconds."

The song ended and exuberant cheering erupted from the TV. Danny's eyes jumped to the screen. Nancy Sinatra stood in front of a USO sign, wearing a red, white, and blue minidress and red go-go boots, but her face was too old and her hair wrong for the time period. He wondered if he was dreaming.

"We're friends, right?" Joey asked, snapping Danny's attention back. "Still?"

"Yeah, sure," Danny replied uncertainly. He pushed up to a sitting position and tried to shake his head clear.

"Can I tell you a secret?"

Danny felt a chill pass over him. "I guess. If you want."

"When I was nine, my daddy started fucking me." Joey's voice was matter-of-fact, emotionless. "He fucked Bryce and Amy, too, but Bryce tried to run away even though daddy was done with him by then, and Amy left for college and only came back once. She's a total fucking mess now, but she got away. Not me. I came back again and again, hoping I could make him love me again. How's that for pathetic?"

Danny gaped in stunned silence. Joey seemed on the verge of saying more, then abruptly stood and walked up the stairs. Danny heard the back door open and close.

CHAPTER 26

Caroline was filling a mug from the tea kettle when Danny walked into the kitchen. "Good morning, honey," she said. "I made coffee for you." She looked up at him and a crease appeared between her eyebrows. "Are you feeling okay? You look like hell."

Thanks.

"Yeah, I just didn't sleep well."

Again.

Caroline studied him as she bobbed a tea bag up and down. "Problems with Joey last night?"

"No, just restless. Lots on my mind," Danny lied.

"Well, I slept like a baby," Caroline declared, her maternal instincts apparently exhausted for the moment. She tasted her tea, made a small grimace, added some sugar.

"Good for you," Danny said without enthusiasm. "So what's the plan for today? Do you need me to drive you anywhere or run any errands?"

"No. Beth and I are going shopping. Finally." Caroline exhaled dramatically as though she'd been waiting for months.

Danny sighed inwardly. Joey's revelation had left him feeling deeply unsettled, and he'd been dreading having to spend the day making small talk and pretending everything was normal. It felt like something dangerous had happened.

"Then I guess I'm on my own," he said.

* * * * *

He watched Beth Wallace's baby blue Volvo turn left out of the driveway, then picked up the phone and tried Holtz. He hung up when the recording came on, glancing at the clock. How many breakfasts can you eat, fat ass? he thought sourly. The phone rang and he flinched before snatching it from the cradle.

"Tyler residence."

"It's me," Holtz replied. "I just wanted to let you know I'm at home today."

"Oh, hey, I just tried you."

"Why, what's up?"

Danny noticed Holtz sounded more subdued than usual. "Is everything okay?"

"I just got off the phone with Cedar Junction. Tim's pneumonia is back. They put him on a respirator."

Danny's felt his already-troubled mood take a darker turn. "Is he going to be okay?"

"Too soon to tell."

"I'm sorry," Danny said. "I wish I could remember something."

"It's not on you," Holtz replied. "Even if you did, I'd still need concrete evidence to convince the DA to reopen the case. I don't know what I was thinking. I should have just left the whole thing alone, or at least not gotten Tim's hopes up." He blew out frustration. "So what did you need?"

Danny took a cigarette from his pack but just stared at it for a few seconds while guilt, confusion, and exhaustion fought it out. "Are you free for lunch?" he asked finally. "I need to talk with you about something."

"Sounds serious."

"Yeah. Here at noon?"

"Sure. I'll see you then."

* * * * *

"It was disturbing on so many levels," Danny finished. He took a bite of cold grilled cheese and lost what little appetite he had.

"I wish I could say it's a surprise," Holtz said, "but I always knew something wasn't right with that family, though I had my money on the wife being abused. At least emotionally."

"Why?"

Holtz shrugged. "It's a small town, people talk. I'd heard she was on a lot of prescription meds and figured there had to be a reason. Plus he struck me as the type with a bad temper."

"You never checked into it?"

"You do remember this is Weston, right? People here don't exactly welcome inquiries into their private lives, especially not from the local Barney Fife. Besides, it was a different time."

"Meaning?"

"Back then a lot of people figured it was a man's own business if he wanted to browbeat his wife or slap her around a little. Especially where I grew up."

"That's fucked," Danny said. "Do you think she knew what was really going on?"

"Maybe. She was a tough one to read. The few times I spoke to her, she just seemed...vacant, I guess."

Danny remembered Bobbi Gardner's pale blue eyes. Even when she seemed dazed, there was always something anxious in them. "Maybe that's why she killed herself," he said.

"Could be, but having a child murdered would be enough to drive some people to it."

Danny frowned. "The first time I visited Joey, he said he thought it was inevitable even without Bryce being killed."

"Did he say why?"

"That she was always miserable. He implied that she took it out on them, but I never saw that side of her. I just thought she was quiet and kind of sad."

Holtz considered it for a moment. "Abuse creates complicated dynamics. If an abuser has a strong enough psychological hold, the victim will find excuses for what's happening. For example, a mother might blame her kids for ruining her body, reasoning that's why her husband has to hit her."

"That makes no sense," Danny said.

"No, not logically, but there's nothing logical in that situation. Everything revolves around the whims and moods of the abuser. The only reality is his reality." Holtz paused, sighed. "It's even possible she lashed out at the kids because she knew they were being molested."

Danny sat back hard. "You can't be serious."

"It's not uncommon for people to blame the victims."

"But they were her kids."

"And he was her husband. She chose to marry him. She chose to have children with him. Whether he was actually abusing her or not, it seems pretty clear that emotionally she was troubled. It might have been easier for her to blame the kids rather than admit she married a monster."

"And I thought there was messed up shit in my house."

Holtz nodded. "Of course, this is all speculation."

Danny stared at his plate for a minute, then shook his head. "How could he go back?" he asked, searching Holtz's face as if he might actually find the answer there.

Pot calling kettle...

"Like I said, abuse creates complicated dynamics," Holtz replied. "Joey was only nine when it started. Depending on what his father told him, what happened was either punishment for being a bad son or an expression of love. Emotionally, Joey probably hasn't moved beyond that point. He's still seeking approval, trying to please his father."

Danny squirmed uncomfortably in his seat.

Holtz furrowed his brow. "So do you think you could get him to talk with me?"

Danny shrugged. "Maybe, but what does it matter now? His father's in a nursing home. He'll be dead soon enough." He caught Holtz's clumsy eye shift and sat up straighter. "What?"

Holtz picked at a thread on his place mat before meeting Danny's gaze. "There's usually a history of sexual abuse."

"What are you talking about?"

"For serial killers who commit lust killings. There's usually sexual abuse during childhood."

Danny felt his face grow warm. "You think Joey might have been the killer?" he asked incredulously.

"If I had to guess, I'd say no," Holtz replied evenly, "but he's local, he could easily have known the boys, and now this. I have to at least consider the possibility."

"No way," Danny said with more certainty than he felt, remembering Joey's aggression during sex. "What about his dad? He was the child molester."

"Also a possibility," Holtz agreed, "and maybe Joey could shed some light on that. At the very least, I'd like to hear what he remembers from the night you and Bryce were attacked. We already know he didn't tell everything at the time. Maybe there's more. He owes that much to you and Tim."

Danny knew the last part was pure manipulation, but also realized Holtz was right. "I'll see what I can do," he said, "but who knows what he'll be like with me after last night."

Holtz nodded and sat back. He studied Danny's face for a moment. "By the way, what happened to your face? It looks a little swollen?"

"I tripped into a door frame," Danny said hastily. "He looked down at his withered arm. "It happens sometimes. I just lose my balance and can't catch myself."

CHAPTER 27

Danny let the phone ring ten times before hanging up. He imagined Joey sitting in the kitchen staring blankly at it, and considered going over. A flash of light caught his eye and he looked out to see Beth Wallace's Volvo coming up the driveway.

Great, he thought. I hope she doesn't pour out of it.

He walked out on the porch and waved. Wallace's round cheery face popped out the driver's window and she waved enthusiastically. "Hi, Danny. Sorry I can't come in, but I'm running late." She smiled so hard her eyes narrowed to slits, then added, "By the way, you look terrific."

"Thanks," Danny called back. Wallace was the only one of Caroline's friends he'd ever really liked. He'd never understood why she put up with the others.

As Wallace backed into the turnaround, Caroline came around the corner of the garage toting a half dozen large colorful bags. "Hi, honey."

"Hey," Danny said, giving her a cautious once-over. Her gait was steady, her eyes clear. "Did you have fun?"

Caroline turned as Wallace tooted the horn twice, then they both smiled and waved as she went down the driveway, fingers waggling over the top of the car.

Caroline turned back, half her smile gone. "You know how it can be with Beth. After a while she gets to be a bit much." She recovered part of the smile. "But she's a dear woman."

Danny thought it sounded like, "She's a tiresome bore." He opened the screen door and let Caroline pass.

"So what have you been up to all day?" Caroline asked, heaving her bags onto the kitchen counter.

"Nothing. Just hanging out."

Caroline stared at him for a moment, then pressed her lips together disapprovingly and sighed. "You've always been so secretive."

And you've always been so intrusive.

"What are you talking about?"

"Danny, there are two plates and two glasses in the drainer. Clearly you weren't up to 'nothing.' I don't care if you have people over, but please don't lie to me. I'm not stupid." Caroline arched her eyebrows expectantly.

Danny cursed silently. Ever since Karl had given him a ten-minute tutorial on the proper way to load and unload a dishwasher, he'd had an aversion to using one.

"It was just Joey," he said.

Caroline smiled with satisfaction. "Good, so you made up."

"I told you we didn't have a problem."

"Pardon me for caring," Caroline said, hands up, fingers splayed in theatrical defensiveness.

Danny rolled his eyes. "So what'd you buy?"

Caroline's face immediately brightened and she reached into the first bag.

* * * * *

Danny wiped the counters and table while Caroline loaded the dishwasher. "Is Friday still trash day?" he asked.

Caroline stopped and tilted her head thoughtfully. "You know, I was never quite sure. Whenever the barrel got full I'd put it at the bottom of the driveway and eventually it would get emptied. Finally I got a second one so there'd always be one in the garage."

Danny had to admit there was a lazy logic to it. "I'm pretty sure I heard the truck last Friday morning," he said. "I'm going to take it down."

He pulled the nearly-full bag out of the trash can, twist-tied it, went out to the garage, and dropped it into the closest barrel. He hit the button to raise the door in front of the empty garage space, hefted the barrel behind his right shoulder, and carried it down the driveway. As he lowered it clumsily to the pavement, he heard a familiar sound.

"I'm not trying to hide them, Danny, but I don't like mixing them in with the rest of the trash."

"Why not?"

"I know those men at the dump go through the bags, and I don't want them spreading rumors. If the bottles are separate, they can't tell where they came from."

"So then you are trying to hide them."

"Don't be insipid."

He looked up at the house and saw Caroline walk past the kitchen window and into the family room. He opened the barrel and took out the two bags. In the bottom lay three empty one-pint Smirnoff bottles.

Fuck, he thought.

CHAPTER 28

Caroline breezed into the kitchen in white tights, a purple and white striped leotard, and teal leggings. "Morning, honey." She laid a cassette tape on the counter, filled the kettle, and set it on the burner. Her movements were crisp, energetic. Danny wondered if the three bottles had all come from Tuesday night, or if they'd already been in the barrel when she went to prison and he just hadn't noticed. He hadn't seen any other evidence that she was drinking on the sly, and she didn't seem to be suffering the aftereffects now.

"Are you going somewhere?" he asked.

"Just down to the basement to do some aerobics."

"Don't you have to do that in a class or something?"

"By this point I could teach a class," Caroline declared with a boastful smile. "I just need space and music."

Danny picked up the cassette. "Exposé?"

"It's a band. Or maybe more like a girl group. I don't know if they actually play instruments. But they're very danceable."

"Yeah, I know," Danny said. Thanks to Karl, a one-time DJ who still reviewed music for a gay weekly, he'd developed an unexpected fondness for dance music, George Michael, and Stevie Nicks during his recovery. "I'm just a little surprised you do."

Caroline's nose wrinkled almost imperceptibly. "One of the younger girls turned me on to them. She said they're very hot in the clubs right now."

Okay, Downtown Caroline Brown.

"You want to join me?"

Danny looked deliberately at his left arm, then back at her. "I'll pass."

"Suit yourself. A little exercise never hurt anyone." Caroline opened the refrigerator and took out a cup of vanilla yogurt. "Look at me. I'm fifty and I'm in the best shape of my life."

Fifty-four, but who's counting?

Danny lit a cigarette. "I think I'll go over to Joey's. I called a few times yesterday but he didn't answer. I want to make sure he's all right."

Caroline looked at him quizzically. "I thought he was here for lunch yesterday."

Shit!

"He was. I meant after."

"Is there any reason why he wouldn't be all right?" Caroline asked, studying him closely. "Did you have another fight?"

"I already told you we didn't have a fight. I just meant it was unusual for him not to answer."

Caroline shook her head. "You and your secrets."

Look who's talking.

* * * * *

The back door and most of the windows were open, the left garage door up. Newspapers were stacked inside against the back wall. The screen door opened and Joey came out carrying another bundle. He was barefoot, in loose jeans and a dirty white t-shirt, but clean-shaven, and his hair was short and neat. When he saw Danny, he broke into a wide, easy grin. "Hey."

"Hey. Spring cleaning?"

"Yeah, for like the last five springs." Joey continued into the garage and heaved the papers on top of a stack. He turned back and wiped his hands on his thighs. "The last few years my dad became obsessed with the newspaper. He wouldn't let me throw them away in case he wanted to read an article again." His expression turned wistful, admiring. "Thing is, he actually did. He couldn't remember who I was from day to day, but he'd suddenly remember an article from months before and always knew exactly where to find it."

"Oh, I assumed they were yours," Danny said uneasily, unsure what else to say. Joey's seemingly warm remembrance took him by surprise.

Joey shook his head. "No, the news is for adults. It's too depressing." It came off as playful rather than precious or pathetic. He surveyed the papers for a few seconds, then looked at Danny. "But I guess we all have to let go of the past at some point. Especially when it becomes a fire hazard." He smiled lazily. "And one of these days I may even take them to the dump. You thirsty?"

"I tried calling yesterday," Danny said as he followed Joey through the side door into the kitchen.

Joey opened the refrigerator and stared into it for a moment as though waiting for something different to appear, then shut the door. "Water?"

"Sure."

Joey filled two glasses at the sink, handed one to Danny, and nearly drained the other in a single swallow. He refilled it. "I went to the nursing home to visit my dad," he said. "Then I stopped to get a haircut on my way home. I think the haircut inspired me to start cleaning. Or maybe I got the haircut because I was already feeling like everything was getting out of control."

Metaphorically?

He shrugged casually. "Who knows?"

Danny studied him a moment, trying to get a read on his mood. "Are you okay?" he asked.

"Yeah, great. Why?"

"Because of the other night."

Joey nodded. "Sorry about that. I didn't want to wake you because you looked so peaceful. Actually you looked kind of kissable, but I know that's not on the menu, so I just left."

Danny made a face. "What are you talking about? I was awake when you left."

"You were?"

"Yeah. Remember, we had a conversation?"

"About what?"

127

Danny couldn't tell if it was just a game or if Joey was signaling that he didn't want to talk about it. "About what your dad did," he said, watching carefully for a reaction.

Joey stared back blankly.

"About him molesting you."

Revulsion rippled across Joey's face. "Danny, that's not even a little funny."

"I know it's not," Danny replied, "but that's what you told me. You said he molested you and Bryce and Amy."

"Stop!" Joey cried, throwing his left hand up in front of his face. His shoulders convulsed like he might vomit. He took a few deep breaths and swallowed hard. "Please, don't say any more. That's disgusting. Why would you make something like that up?"

"But..." Danny faltered. Joey's reaction seemed genuine. "Joey, I swear I'm not screwing with you," he tried.

"Then you have some fucked-up dreams," Joey said sharply.

For a split second Danny wondered if it was possible, then he saw something behind the anger in Joey's eyes, something more like fear. "Maybe," he said, "but it seemed pretty real to me."

"Sometimes dreams do," Joey replied pointedly. "Sometimes I can't even tell them from reality."

So you're not sure if you were really molested now?

Danny cocked his head at the tone. It sounded like a negotiation. He decided to play along and see where it led. "I suppose you're right," he said. "Sometimes."

Joey's expression softened and he showed a hint of a smile. "You must have been pretty freaked out when you woke up. "

"Yeah," Danny replied carefully. "I'm really sorry." Joey visibly relaxed, and Danny wondered what he could get in return. "I hate to ask, but I need a big favor," he said.

Joey's eyes turned wary, but he nodded to go on.

"Tim Walczak isn't doing well. It looks like he doesn't have much time left. I know I promised you wouldn't get dragged into it, but Holtz would really like to talk to you."

To Danny's surprise, Joey nodded. "Sure. I've been thinking

about it. I don't know why I've been so afraid. Maybe I'll remember something that could help. But I really want you there, too."

Way too easy.

CHAPTER 29

Two flats of a dozen plants each lay next to a bag of soil at the end of the walkway. Danny regarded it curiously. He couldn't remember Caroline ever showing any interest in gardening or any other form of manual labor.

He walked up the flagstone path and into the house. Caroline was back in the kitchen. She'd traded Jane Fonda for cropped-leg jeans, a pale pink tank top, and straw sun hat.

"Did you see Joey?" she asked. "Is he all right?"

"Yeah, he just went to visit his dad yesterday afternoon," Danny replied. He jerked a thumb toward the driveway. "What's with the green stuff and dirt?"

"They're for my herb garden."

"Since when do you have an herb garden?"

"Oh, for years now. It's wonderful. And sometimes I plant tomatoes. Not that those are herbs." She pursed her lips. "I think they may actually be fruit." She took a quick sip from her mug.

"Where'd they come from?" Danny asked.

"Grace dropped them off. Wasn't that sweet?"

Danny wondered what was in the mug. "Yeah, sweet."

"You want to help me plant them?"

Danny pretended to seriously consider it, then shook his head. "I've got some reading to do for my GED."

* * * * *

As soon as Caroline was safely puttering, he went into the office and called Holtz to let him know Joey had agreed to meet. They decided on the following afternoon at 1 PM. He hung up and dialed again.

"Two calls in one decade?" Jerry answered, feigning shock. "Now I *know* something must be wrong."

"In my defense, I had trouble dialing last decade," Danny replied dryly.

"So is everything okay?"

"Maybe."

"Meaning?"

"How well did you know Bill Gardner? I know you weren't friends or anything, but you knew him a little, right?"

"Very little. I talked with him maybe a dozen times. Small talk in line at the hardware store. That sort of thing. Why?"

"Did he strike you as the kind of guy who might have molested his kids?"

"Jesus, Danny, why would you ask that?"

"Because the other night Joey told me he did."

"My God, that's horrible."

"The problem is, now I'm not sure if it really happened."

"Why would he lie about something like that?"

"I don't think he would, and I believed him when he told me, but I just saw him again and now he's saying it never happened and that he never told me that. He said I must have dreamt it, but I know I didn't."

"But why would he tell you something like that, then say he hadn't?" Jerry asked. "Seems strange."

"Maybe he's feeling some kind of perverse guilt for telling me, or maybe he's not really sure that it happened. Either way, it definitely seems like he wants me to forget about it now."

"What would make you think he's not sure?"

"He said that sometimes he can't tell dreams from reality. I have a feeling that even when he's awake he can't always tell what's in his head from what's real. Maybe he's afraid he imagined it, and now he's worried that I'm going to tell the cops."

There was a long pause before Jerry said, "I'm not sure about that, but guilt may not be as perverse as it sounds from what I've read about those kinds of things."

"So do you think it could have happened?" Danny asked. "From what you saw of Bill Gardner? Holtz does."

"Holtz?" Jerry replied. "Holtz the cop? Why would you be talking with him about it? Or at all?"

"I guess I need to tell you a few things," Danny said.

* * * * *

Danny finished talking and lit a cigarette. There was a long silence before Jerry said, "I should have told you about the sexual assault and your relationship with Tim Walczak. Obviously you were going to find out at some point, but we didn't think you were ready."

"Why not?"

"You know what Dr. Price said. You'll remember things as you're able to handle them emotionally. You obviously didn't have any memories of Walczak or that night, so I assumed you weren't ready. I didn't want to risk stirring them up too soon." Jerry sighed. "I guess I thought I was protecting you. I was afraid it might set back the progress you were making. Of course, if I'd known Holtz was planning to recruit you..." he trailed off.

"I guess that makes some sense," Danny said, "though I wish you'd explained that to me. I thought you were just being a dick."

"Kind of hard to explain without getting into specifics. 'Hey, Danny, there's a lot of stuff that happened but I'm not going to tell you about it because it might trigger painful memories.'"

"I just don't think it's a smart idea, Dan. You need to move forward with your life, not go backward."

Danny took a drag on his cigarette. "So that's why you didn't want me to come back here?"

"That was part of it."

"The other part being mom?"

A brief pause. "Yes."

Through the back window, Danny watched her digging in the corner of the yard. She stopped to wipe her forehead with the back of her glove, and took a long drink from her mug. Again Danny wondered what was in it.

"Do you hate her?" he asked.

After a much longer pause, Jerry said, "No. Not hate."

"Then what?"

Jerry laughed uncomfortably. "Wow, getting right into it."

"It's about time, don't you think?" Danny said, then regretted the sharpness.

"Yeah, it is, though I wish we could do it face to face."

"We will at some point," Danny said more gently. "You don't really think we're going to get all the shit out of the way in one call, do you?"

"Probably not. You want me to be completely honest?"

Maybe.

"Please."

"On some level, I'll always love her. She gave me you, and she gave me a chance at the life I thought I wanted, and for both those things I'll always be grateful."

"Even though she's been a total bitch to you ever since?"

"Well, I didn't say it's been easy," Jerry replied with a wry chuckle, "but yeah, I still love her. And I'm also frequently pissed off and frustrated and hurt and guilty and a dozen other things. The emotions aren't as strong anymore, but they're always there."

Danny puffed his cigarette for a few seconds. "Did you know you were gay when you married her?"

"Well, I knew I liked men."

"So, why did you do it?"

"Because I didn't want to like them. I wanted the life I'd grown up watching on TV and in the movies, the life I saw with your grandparents and all our neighbors. A wife, a family, a nice home in the suburbs, two vacations a year, and happily ever after."

"Sounds pretty naive."

"It was a more naive time, or at least less cynical. And I wanted to believe. I thought that if I had all that, I'd be happy, too, and I'd stop wanting that other thing that was shameful and wrong."

Danny sat on the edge of the desk. "You really thought it was shameful and wrong?"

"That's what I was raised to believe. Gay people were sick, perverted. Their lives were tragic and lonely. I didn't want that. I wanted to be happy like everyone else." Jerry let out a rueful bark. "Of course, looking back I realize that not everyone was actually happy. I can see the fractures and tensions that I missed as a kid. I guess hindsight is 20/20."

Not for all of us.

"I know this is going to sound strange," Danny said, "but it never even occurred to me that I might be gay before the fall."

"It didn't?"

"No. I mean, I knew I liked to fool around with guys, but I thought that was something different because it wasn't an emotional thing. It wasn't like you and Karl. I loved Joey as a friend, but I never considered him my boyfriend or anything. I never thought about a future together.

"Do you think he ever did?"

It caught Danny by surprise.

"Because love was meant for beauty queens."

"What's that supposed to mean?"

He felt a sudden stab of guilt. "I think so, but I was too stupid to realize it at the time."

"You were a teenager. You were probably too stupid to realize a lot of things. No offense."

"None taken. That's become abundantly clear," Danny sighed. "I had this whole narrative from my childhood. You were an asshole, mom was the way she was because you were an asshole, Holtz was a different kind of asshole, and we had the most fucked up family I knew. I was wrong about at least three out of four."

"I don't know if this will make you feel any better," Jerry said, "but to some extent, it happens to everyone. First you discover Santa Claus isn't real, then you find out your parents and teachers aren't perfect, and eventually you realize most people are small-minded and vindictive and all governments are corrupt."

"No, that's not making me feel any better."

"My point is that it usually happens over a long period of time. You got hit with twelve or thirteen years of disillusionment all at once. Eventually it won't seem so overwhelming."

"I'm not sure it's really disillusionment," Danny began, then stopped to consider how to explain it. "It's just that, I came back because I felt like I belonged here. It was a part of me and I needed to reconnect with that. But now I know a lot of it wasn't real."

"The important things were real."

"I suppose."

A few seconds of silence ticked by. Danny stubbed out his cigarette. "I should probably let you get back to work."

"Yeah, probably. I have a meeting in a few minutes, but I can call you back afterward."

"That's okay. Just one last thing. What about Bill Gardner?"

"I wish I could tell you, Danny, but I hardly knew him. He seemed okay, but it never would have occurred to me that anyone I knew might do something like that to their kids. For Joey's sake, I hope he didn't. Regardless of whether it really happened, though, Joey's obviously got a lot of emotional issues. Are you sure you're up to dealing with that?"

"I think so. And you're okay with me helping Holtz?"

"Does it matter?"

"Probably not, but tell me anyway?"

"I understand that you need to put the pieces together for yourself, too, but I'm worried about you forcing things. I'm also concerned Holtz isn't being completely honest. It seems like he's got his own agenda for re-investigating the case on his own."

"I have the same feeling," Danny admitted.

There was a brief pause. "Maybe I should talk to him."

Danny fought the urge to say yes. "No, I can do it."

"And will you?"

"Cross my heart."

"Okay, just be careful. If it gets to be too much, don't be afraid to back off."

"I won't."

"By the way, does your mother know any of this?"

"No. You think I should tell her?"

"No. She'll just find a way to make it about herself."

CHAPTER 30

"So what's Caroline up to today?"

Danny knew it was just nervous chatter. "Playing tennis with Beth Wallace, Grace, and Paulina Cahill."

Joey nodded mechanically as he rechecked the stove clock.

"He should be here any minute," Danny said, trying to sound relaxed despite his own nerves. He shook a cigarette out of his pack. "Maybe I should wait for him out front."

"Afraid he's going to miss the house?"

Danny stared back dumbly, then laughed. "Yeah, I guess that was pretty stupid."

"Why are you nervous? He's questioning me, remember?"

Danny shrugged. "It's just kind of weird to know you'll be talking about us but I probably won't remember any of it."

"Sorry, I keep forgetting that part."

"That's okay."

Joey fidgeted in place for a few seconds, then pushed away from the counter. "I better pee again before he gets here."

Danny nodded and held up the cigarette. "I think I'll go outside, anyway."

* * * * *

Holtz pulled in just as he was lighting up. Danny gave the older model brown Caprice Classic sedan a deliberate once-over.

"What, you couldn't find anything that screamed cop a little louder?" he asked as Holtz stepped out.

Holtz showed a ghost of a smile. "The department sells them to us for next to nothing."

"That seems about right," Danny smirked.

Holtz pointedly ignored it. "So how's Joey doing?"

"He seems okay. Definitely nervous, but he's..." He searched for the word. "...present, I guess. Mentally."

Holtz nodded. "Let's hope he stays that way."

"Are you going to ask about Bill molesting him?"

"Probably not directly, but I want to see if I can get a sense of the truth."

The back door opened and Joey stepped onto the porch. His eyes flitted between them warily. "Getting started without me?" he asked in a strained voice.

Holtz smiled reassuringly. "Hey, Joey. How've you been?"

"I'm okay."

Danny interpolated the missing "for someone with a gun to my head," and tried not to smile.

Holtz walked to the porch and shook Joey's hand. "What do you say we go inside and talk?"

* * * * *

"It's up to you," Holtz said. "You can start at the beginning and just tell me what you remember, or I can ask specific questions. Whichever is more comfortable for you."

They were in the living room, Joey and Danny at opposite ends of the couch, Holtz facing them across the coffee table from a ladder-backed dining chair. Joey chewed his lower lip for a moment, then rubbed his right ear. "Questions, I guess."

Holtz nodded, took a small notepad from his shirt pocket, opened it, reviewed the first page for a moment, then looked back at Joey. "Okay, let's start with who was home that night?"

Joey gave him a puzzled look. "Everyone, I think. My parents were in here watching TV with Amy. Bryce's bedroom door was closed but his stereo was playing, so I assume he was there."

"And you and Danny had plans to get together?"

Joey shook his head. "We hadn't talked that day."

"Was that unusual?"

"Yeah, but my parents had shipped us off to our grandparents' for a few days and we'd just gotten back that night. I remember we stopped for Chinese at Chin's Village on the way." Joey's lips curled slightly. "Do you want to know what we ordered?"

"That's okay," Holtz replied. "So you called Danny, or just stopped by?"

"I called," Joey said, then added, "I was horny." He stared at Holtz, the challenge in his eyes obvious, but Holtz's expression remained impassive. Joey's mouth tightened almost imperceptibly.

"About what time?" Holtz asked.

"Nine-thirty."

"And you made plans to get together?"

Joey crossed his arms and sank back again the couch. "Yeah, I asked if I could come over. He said he was worried that Caroline might come home, so we agreed to meet."

"Where?"

"The back yard," Joey said, nodding at the French doors. "I told him I'd meet him at Lovers' Rock, but he didn't want me walking around in the woods by myself because of the killings."

"Lovers' Rock?"

"That boulder that sticks out into the pond on the opposite side from the Campion Center," Danny said.

Holtz jotted something in the notepad, then looked back at Joey. "Did you tell your parents you were going out?"

Joey made a face. "What do you think?"

Holtz didn't show any signs of registering it. "Then what?"

"He showed up ten minutes later and we went to the orchard."

"The one off Concord Road?"

Joey nodded impatiently.

"Then?"

Joey stared at Holtz for a long moment with what looked like teenage petulance, then smiled. Danny's stomach tightened. It was the same malicious smile he remembered from Bryce.

"Then I fucked him," Joey said, drawing each word out. He arched his eyebrows. "Is that the part you wanted to hear?"

Holtz met his gaze without blinking. "Joey, I've seen you and Danny going at it," he said evenly, "except at the time, you were on the receiving end. I didn't care then, I don't care now. So you can save it." He raised his own eyebrows expectantly. After a few seconds, Joey nodded. "Then what?" Holtz asked.

"Then we just lay there and talked for a while."

Suddenly Danny could feel the heat of Joey's naked body, see Joey's tears in the moonlight again. "Because love was meant for beauty queens," he whispered. Holtz and Joey looked at him curiously. "Because love was meant for beauty queens," he repeated more clearly.

"You remember," Joey said.

Danny tried to pull the memory back, but it was gone. "Just that," he said, looking into Joey's eyes. "You said it was from a song, but I didn't know it."

"Janis Ian," Holtz said. "*At Seventeen*."

Joey looked at him with surprise.

"What's it about?" Danny asked.

"Ugly girls and pathetic little gay boys," Joey said.

Danny blinked incomprehension, but Holtz nodded. "I never thought of it that way." He frowned, staring into the middle distance for a moment, then nodded again to himself. He turned back to Joey. "Okay if we go on?"

Joey nodded less reluctantly.

"How long were you there?" Holtz asked.

"Maybe an hour total. Then Danny walked me to the foot of the path that ran up to our house."

"Did you see anyone or hear anything unusual on the way?"

Joey thought about it, shook his head. "I walked to the back yard and waved, then I went inside."

Danny closed his eyes, trying to find the memory. He saw only a flash of a ghostly body moving through the trees

"How did you go into the house?" Holtz asked.

"Through the garage, into the kitchen. Same way I went out."

"And you didn't hear anything outside?"

"Just the usual night noises. Nothing special."

Holtz pointed at the door between the family room and kitchen. "Was that open or closed?"

"Closed," Joey said, wrinkling his forehead. "It was always closed. My mother had this weird thing about food smells getting into the rest of the house. She kept the door from the side hall closed, too. "

"Did you notice the time?"

"Yeah, it was almost eleven."

Holtz wrote it in his notebook. "And did you check to see if your folks were still in here?"

Danny felt a charge pass through the air and turned to Joey. Joey's upper body was perfectly still, but his legs were bouncing so furiously that the couch was vibrating.

"Danny told you about my father, didn't he?" he said, less question than accusation. "That's why you're really here. You think my father killed Bryce and those kids."

Danny's mouth went dry.

Holtz hesitated a moment before responding. "Yes, he told me what you said about your father the other day," he said carefully, "but he also told me what you said yesterday." He shrugged as though both were inconsequential. "I've wanted to talk to you for a long time because you were the only other person we know of who was in the woods that night." He paused, then added, "But if you want to talk about your father, we can."

Joey's body began rocking back and forth and he let out a low pained moan. His head pivoted toward Danny. "You had no right to tell him."

"Joey, I'm sorry, but..."

Joey's eyes locked back on Holtz. "Just because he raped his own children doesn't mean he raped and killed any others."

Danny was sure he heard a note of indignation in it.

"So are you saying he did molest you now?" Holtz asked.

"*But maybe he raped you after we had sex. He raped all those other kids, didn't he?*"

The memory hit with almost tangible force, and Danny sat back. "Wait, how did you know that?" he asked, turning to Joey.

"Know what?" Joey replied angrily.

"That the boys were all raped."

Joey's mouthed worked for a few seconds, but all he managed was, "What?"

"Friday night when you came over, you already knew. How?"

The anger drained from Joey's face and his legs abruptly stilled. "You told me."

Danny closed his eyes for a moment, then shook his head sharply. "No, I didn't. I might not remember shit from thirteen years ago, but I remember the present just fine. I only said *I* was sexually assaulted, but when I told you Holtz didn't think Walczak had done it, you said, 'He raped all those other kids, didn't he?'" He leaned forward. "How did you know they were raped? It wasn't in the papers or on the news."

Joey's eyes moved slowly from Danny to Holtz, then back, as though calculating his best option.

"How did you know, Joey?" Danny pressed.

Joey just hugged himself tightly and looked down at the floor.

Holtz leaned forward, his hands steepled toward Joey. "Look, Joey, you knew something that you shouldn't." His tone was reasonable, concerned. "How?"

"I have to go the bathroom," Joey said.

"Oh, come on, cut the bullshit, Joey," Danny said.

"No, I really have to go," Joey said, looking pleadingly from Danny to Holtz. "I always have to pee when I'm nervous."

Holtz sighed, nodded at Danny. "Go with him."

"Thank you," Joey said, jumping up.

Danny cut a worried look at Holtz, then got up. Joey was already halfway to the kitchen.

"Wait," Holtz said, but Joey didn't slow. "I said, wait," Holtz warned more emphatically, getting to his feet.

Joey stopped in front of the door, but didn't look back. "Sorry," he said coldly, as Danny came up behind him.

"No prob..." Danny swallowed the rest as Joey's left elbow hit him just below the sternum. He staggered back, and Joey pushed through the door. As it swung shut, Danny saw him rushing toward the garage.

Holtz was already beside Danny, catching him by the shoulders. Danny waved him off. "The garage," he managed.

He blocked the door open behind Holtz and stood in the doorway trying to catch his breath as Holtz raced to the garage door. As Holtz yanked it open, the air in the kitchen rushed out, then stopped. For a split second, everything was silent, then the newspapers against the back wall of the garage erupted into flames with a loud "whoomp." Holtz fell back.

For a moment Danny was back in the woods, fighting panic as the fire spread around him and Bryce's laugh echoed. He forced the memory away and lurched across the kitchen. Holtz was still holding tight to the door, staring into the garage as if mesmerized by the flames. Danny shook him and Holtz turned his head.

"Are you okay?" Danny shouted over the rising crackle.

Holtz's eyes slowly focused and he nodded once. Danny looked past him to where Joey lay on the floor a few feet in front of the fire, a can of lighter fluid next to him. He appeared conscious but dazed. Danny made a move forward but Holtz blocked him.

"I'll get him," Holtz rasped. "Call the fire department and find a hose." He stepped through the door.

* * * * *

Danny raised both garage doors and stepped outside. Gray smoke billowed out into the driveway. He moved onto the porch and attempted a deep breath, but immediately began coughing. In the distance he heard sirens.

It had all happened so quickly that it seemed unreal. After the initial fear, he'd stopped thinking and just acted. He'd been calm, focused. It had all felt...

...*hauntingly familiar?*

As the smoke curling up the front of the garage thinned, he opened the side door and poked his head inside. Holtz stood just outside the back door, Joey sitting on the grass behind him, wrapped in a blanket, eyes staring listlessly at the ground.

"How is he?" Danny asked, coughing again.

Holtz shrugged.

Danny surveyed the damage. The back wall and ceiling were scorched but intact. One stack of newspapers still leaned crookedly, while the other two had toppled. They appeared only superficially charred. "Why didn't they burn more?" he asked.

"Fire needs air. They were stacked too densely, though if he'd managed to get enough lighter fluid on them the house still probably would have caught."

"You think that's what he was trying to do?"

"Sure seemed like it."

Danny remembered Joey's comment about the papers being a fire hazard. At the time, his interest in cleaning them out had seemed more manic than calculated.

"They were his dad's," Danny said absently, as he moved closer to the debris. "He told me he was going to take them to the dump." He squatted down and tilted his head slowly from side to side. What had appeared to be a shadow or burn mark on the wall behind where the middle stack had stood, gained dimension. "I think there's something back there," he said, pointing.

Holtz came into the garage and knelt beside him for a moment, then straightened up. He grabbed a pair of gardening gloves from the shelf to the left of the door and put them on.

"I probably shouldn't do this," he said, stepping over soggy mounds of paper, "but what the hell?" He reached down and pulled out a stained and flattened canvas backpack the color of overcooked asparagus. The front flap was singed, but Holtz could still make out a faded Boy Scout insignia. He hefted it appraisingly.

A shadow fell across the floor and they both turned to see Joey standing in the back doorway, clutching the blanket tightly around his shoulders. His eyes were fixed on the bag. Danny thought he looked like a bewildered child.

"What's in it, Joey?" Holtz asked.

Joey blinked twice before shifting his gaze to Holtz. "Their underwear," he said quietly.

CHAPTER 31

"So much for keeping things under wraps," Holtz said under his breath as he and Danny watched a team from the state crime lab join a dozen state troopers and most of the Weston police and fire departments in the driveway. Thirty feet away, Joey sat in the back of a patrol car waiting for a nearby group of men in impressive-looking uniforms to finish sorting out jurisdiction so someone could arrest him.

"This is going to be bad for you, isn't it?" Danny asked.

"I'm definitely not counting on a promotion," Holtz deadpanned, "though if it leads to the actual killer and the department doesn't look too bad, I may be able to keep my job."

"That's not right," Danny replied angrily. "You were doing the right thing." He was surprised by how protective he felt.

"But I was also doing the right thing I was told specifically not to do."

"Shouldn't matter."

"Welcome to the real world."

"No, thanks."

The conference broke up and one of the men walked toward them. He had a few inches, fifty solid pounds, and at least ten years on Holtz. Above his thick graying mustache, his eyes were serene.

"Rick," he nodded.

"Marty," Holtz nodded back. "This is Danny Tyler. Danny, Deputy Chief Marty Thornton."

Thornton gave Danny's hand a surprisingly gentle shake. "Ah, our fair town's most famous coma survivor."

"I wasn't aware there was a lot of competition," Danny replied neutrally, trying to get a read on the man.

Thornton flashed an amused grin at Holtz. "I like him. He's funny."

"So is this good cop doing bad cop's dirty work?" Holtz asked.

"Actually, you're in luck," Thornton replied. "Apparently Field Marshall Smith of our beloved state police is a big believer in both justice and due process."

Danny shot Holtz a questioning look. Holtz nodded discreetly toward a trooper. "Marty thinks their uniforms bear an unfortunate resemblance to Hitler's Brownshirts."

"In any case," Thornton continued, "Smith convinced the chief to put you on paid suspension pending a disciplinary hearing, provided that you make yourself available to his investigation."

"Disciplinary hearing? For what?" Danny asked too sharply, drawing looks.

"Relax," Holtz said. "Marty's one of the good guys. He's just delivering the message."

"If I'm such a good guy, why didn't you tell me about this in the first place?" Thornton asked. "You know I wasn't one of Cronin's cronies."

"Because I didn't want to put you in that position," Holtz replied, realizing how weak it sounded. He frowned. "Suspension for how long?"

"Probably until the chief decides whether he can come out of this looking good. If so, I'm sure he'll waive the hearing and give you just a ceremonial slap on the wrist."

Holtz grunted. "So the staties are catching?"

Thornton shrugged. "It was their ball to begin with."

"And look what an awesome job they did with it last time," Danny scowled.

Thornton cocked his head back and looked down at him. For the first time Danny saw flint behind the amiability. "You might want to learn to curb that," Thornton said evenly. "Petulance is cute at fifteen. Not so cute at thirty."

Thirty? Bitch.

"Yes, sir," Danny replied hastily.

Thornton nodded, looked back at Holtz, then toward the patrol car. "Did the kid say anything useful before the Mongol hordes descended?"

Holtz grimaced. "Yeah, he said he committed the murders and had been planning to take the backpack to the dump because he was worried I was on to him. Said he figured it would be buried under a few tons of garbage within a week."

"And you don't believe him why?"

"The kids' underwear was obviously taken for trophies. The real killer wouldn't just throw them away, even if he thought he was about to go down. He'd do something ceremonial."

Thornton cut a look at the garage. "Like burn them?"

Holtz shook his head. "He said that was spontaneous. He just panicked."

"Maybe that was a lie, too."

"He just confessed to killing his brother and four little boys. Why would he draw the line at admitting to premeditated arson?"

Thornton nodded thoughtfully. "So he's protecting someone. Any guesses?"

"Most likely his father. There was a history of sexual abuse, and just before Joey ran out to the garage, he made a point of saying that just because his father raped his own kids didn't mean he raped and killed any others."

"Pretty clumsy way of averting suspicion, wouldn't you say? Kind of like, 'Pay no attention to that man behind the curtain.' Any other reason to suspect the father?"

"That backpack's almost an antique."

"Not exactly a smoking gun, but okay for now." Thornton turned his attention to Danny. "You know him better than anyone. You think he did it?"

"Maybe if I met him now I'd think so," Danny replied, "but not the way he was back then. I mean, first of all he was never very big. I don't think he physically could have done it. But he was also really gentle."

Unless he was fucking.

Thornton raised his bushy eyebrows skeptically.

"I don't know," Danny started again, then stopped. He took out his cigarettes, caught himself, looked questioningly at Thornton who nodded. Danny lit one. His throat and lungs were still raw, but he managed to keep from coughing. "It's just that when I came by yesterday he didn't seem like someone who was worried. He actually seemed...light. I assumed it was because he'd finally admitted to someone that his father molested him." He shook his head. "It just felt like cleaning out the house was..." He fumbled for the word.

Rhymes with Caroline...

"Symbolic?" Holtz asked.

Caroline...Alcoholic...same thing.

Danny nodded.

"Not to play amateur shrink, but it would make sense if he'd been protecting his father," Holtz said. "Getting rid of the papers and the evidence would be liberating."

The corners of Thornton's mustache pulled down. "So would putting the old man behind bars."

"He's in a nursing home and basically a vegetable," Holtz replied. "He'd never stand trial. Besides, the psychological hold may still be too strong for Joey to turn against him."

Danny shook his head. "I'd want to kill the motherfucker."

Thornton chuckled. "Obviously you have a normal relationship with your parents."

Danny wondered if it was meant to be ironic.

"Unfortunately, it's not unusual," Holtz said. "Some abuse victims seeks vengeance, some follow in the abuser's footsteps, but too a lot become emotionally dependent on their abusers."

"That doesn't make any sense."

"Not to us, but the long and short of it is that the abusive relationship becomes the central one in the victim's life. In essence, it's what forms his identity and he feels he doesn't exist outside that framework. Take away the abuser, and he feels he becomes nothing."

"On a scale of one to ten, how sure are you that's what's happening?" Thornton asked.

"Why?"

"Because Smith seems like a pretty decent guy and I don't imagine the DA's office will be any too anxious to jump on a thirteen-year-old murder case they apparently fucked up the first time around. I can talk to them about recommending a psych evaluation at the arraignment. That'll keep the kid out of jail for thirty days. Not that the state hospital is exactly Club Med."

Nine point five," Holtz replied.

"Good enough. I'll set it in motion. In the meantime, they're going to need statements from both of you, so don't go anywhere."

"Joy," Holtz said as Thornton walked away.

"Is this enough to get Tim out?" Danny asked.

"Not nearly," Holtz replied. "Even if forensics links the underwear to the murders, that's not proof that someone other than Tim was responsible. If they find Bill Gardner's DNA all over everything, though, it should be enough to file an appeal." He looked at his watch and sighed. "I need to call my wife and let her know I won't be home for dinner."

Danny felt a tremor of anxiety in his stomach. "I guess I better call Caroline, too."

CHAPTER 32

Danny got out of Holtz's car, waved goodbye. Caroline's reaction when he'd called had been surprisingly calm and appropriate. He wondered how many minutes that had lasted. The excitement of the fire and subsequent tedium had drained him, and he wasn't in the mood for manufactured drama. He squared his shoulders and walked up to the porch.

Through the window he could see her sitting at the kitchen table. Her eyes were on the mug cradled in her hands. A spent tea bag lay nearby, but from her slack expression and unfocused gaze, he suspected she'd been sipping more than just tea.

For a moment he wondered whether he could get in the truck and slip away unnoticed, but her eyes suddenly lifted and found him. He took a deep breath and opened the door.

"Are you all right?" Caroline asked in an oddly formal tone.

Danny crossed to the refrigerator and took out a Coke. "Yeah, I'm fine, but I'm worried about Joey. They're putting him under psychiatric evaluation." He turned, popped the tab, and took a sip. Caroline just stared at him, her lips pursed disapprovingly "What?" he asked.

"Is this why you came back, Danny? So you could dig all this up again?"

Danny moved to the counter separating them. "No," he said evenly, "I'm here because you asked me to help you out until you get your license back. Remember?"

Caroline suddenly lowered her head in mock genuflection. "And thank you so much for that. You're *such* a wonderful son." She looked up, a smirk twisting her lips. "And you've been so helpful to me while you've been out playing detective and doing God-knows-what with that half-wit cop."

Danny just shook his head and took another sip, though his anxiety level was climbing. It was the side of Caroline he'd been fearing. The side that paced the house in the middle of the night, or woke him to revisit all of the injuries and indignities she'd suffered, primarily at the hands of Jerry. It was also the side that could be unbelievably cold and cruel.

"What's the matter?" she asked, her voice rising sharply. "Eleven and a half years in a coma wasn't enough? You need to dredge it all back up so you can remind everyone who you are?" Her face became flushed and she waved her arms in the air. "'Oh look, there's the boy who was in the coma. Poor thing. Look at his arm.'"

She banged her hands down on the table and sat back, breathing hard, then seemed to remember her mug and took a sip. Her expression turned solemn. "Your father was right." The formality and restraint were back in her voice. "You should never have come back." She shook her head with pity. "When is it going to be enough, Danny? When are you going to stop rehashing the past? It's time to stop being a victim."

Danny stared at her in disbelief for a few seconds, then burst into laughter. "You first."

Caroline came up out of the chair so quickly that his laugh became a startled choke. She lunged across the counter and grabbed for him, her perfectly manicured nails just grazing his chest as he pulled back. She glared furiously for a moment, her right arm still outstretched, then collapsed back into the chair and buried her face in her hands. She began to sob.

All the colors of the psychotic rainbow tonight.

For the first time he could remember, Danny felt no sympathy for her tears. He walked to the doorway, but stopped and turned back. "By the way, if you don't want me to know you're drinking, don't hide the bottles in the barrel."

* * * * *

As he reached the top of the stairs, he heard the screen door slam, and went to the corner window in the guest room to make sure Caroline wasn't going for her car. He saw her standing just below him on the porch steps. In the fading light, he could make out an unlit cigarette clamped between her lips and a pint bottle in her left hand. She didn't move for almost a minute, then dropped clumsily onto the edge of the porch and lit the cigarette. In the flickering glow of the flame, her expression was blank.

Danny turned away and walked down the hall to his room. He closed the door and dialed the phone.

"Hello?" Karl answered on the second ring, his soft Dutch accent managing to give it a few extra syllables.

"Hey, Karl, it's me. Is my dad around?"

"He's watching TV with his eyes closed," Karl replied chattily.

"Can you wake him?"

"Is everything all right?"

Danny imagined Karl pushing his glasses up from where they'd settled while he read the latest Strachey or Brandstetter mystery, his eyes suddenly alert with concern. It made him feel surprisingly more relaxed. "Yeah, I just need to talk with him."

There was a pause, then, "All right, hold on."

Danny thought he heard hurt. "Wait, Karl?" he said quickly. "Yes?"

"How are things with you?"

There was another pause, then what sounded like a murmur of surprise. "I'm fine," Karl said, "though I miss having you around. Despite your questionable dishwasher skills."

They both laughed.

"I miss you, too," Danny said, realizing he actually meant it.

Karl's voice dropped to a theatrical whisper. "Though he's a fine man in many ways, when it comes to music, your father's taste is rubbish. He still thinks the *Saturday Night Fever* soundtrack represents the artistic and cultural highpoint of dance music."

"Philistine!" Danny gasped. "So, anything good I should know about?"

Karl drew an excited breath. "The second...or is it third?... coming of Miss Donna Summer."

"Wait, I thought you told me we were boycotting her since she went all born again and denounced us."

Karl tutted. "Yes, but all is forgiven now that she's pledged her faith to the new holy trinity."

"What new 'holy trinity?'" Danny laughed.

"Stock, Aiken, and Waterman," Karl intoned reverentially. "The first single is fabulous."

* * * * *

"Does Joey have a lawyer?" Jerry asked.

It was a typically practical response that left Danny feeling typically dissatisfied. He lit a cigarette. "I'm not sure."

"See if you can find out. I'd hate for him to be stuck with some inexperienced public defender. One of my clients is a big criminal defense attorney up there. I'm sure I could get him to at least take a look at it."

"Okay," Danny said, dissatisfaction turning to disappointment. *And you were hoping for?*

There was a long silence, then Jerry exhaled loudly. "I was still trying to get my head around the idea that Gardner could have molested his own kids, but this? It's...overwhelming." He grunted disbelief. "Are you okay?"

That.

"I guess. It doesn't feel entirely real yet. It's just so hard to believe that Mr. Gardner might have tried to kill me." He shuddered. "And it's weird to think that I spent all that time at their house and had no idea what was going on."

"I hope you're not blaming yourself," Jerry said, equal parts compassion and scolding. "There's no way you could have known."

"I know that. Logically." Danny took a drag on his cigarette. "No wonder Joey turned into such a freak. Can you imagine keeping a secret like that?"

"Are you angry at him for it?"

Danny considered it a moment. "No. I don't understand it, but I'm not angry. I just wonder how long he knew."

They lapsed into silence again, this time more comfortable.

"So how's your mother dealing with all this?" Jerry asked after a while.

Danny let out a brittle laugh. "She basically accused me of getting involved because I can't let go of the past. She said I have to stop being a victim. Kind of ironic, don't you think?"

"I'd go with straight up hypocritical. Do you think you should get out of there, at least temporarily?" It came out more suggestion than question.

"No, I'm okay. It's a big enough house for both of us, and I can always escape outside if I have to. She's been gardening, but I'm pretty sure she wouldn't venture beyond the edge of the lawn."

"Not without a safari outfit, anyway," Jerry replied, then his tone became serious. "Just be careful."

"Of what?"

"I worry that you're still a little naive about her."

Danny laughed. "I forgot a few months of my life, not the whole thing. I know what she's like."

"But you think her manipulation is always obvious. You underestimate how subtle she can be. It's when she's not beating you down with guilt that you have to watch out. She's got a gift for finding weakness and exploiting it to keep you emotionally dependent on her."

"*So does it make you self-conscious?*"

"*What?*"

"*Your arm.*"

"Trust me," Jerry said. "That was my life for too many years."

"I promise, if she takes out a pocket watch and starts swinging it in front of my face, I won't look," Danny said, trying to make light of it despite his sudden disquiet.

"I just don't want you turning into Little Edie Beale, okay?" Jerry said.

So much for that new head scarf.

"Okay," Danny said. "I promise I'll be careful."

CHAPTER 33

Danny put his toothbrush back in the holder, swished water through his teeth a few more times, and spit into the sink. He wet the fingers of his right hand and ran them through his sleep-matted hair, squinting appraisingly at the results in mirror. From somewhere below he heard the muffled sound of breaking glass, followed by Caroline yelling, "Shit!"

Now what? he wondered. He opened the bathroom door and stepped into the hallway, cocking his head. From the hallway between the foyer and kitchen he heard hurried footsteps, then a door sliding and more footsteps. He went downstairs.

"Be careful, honey," Caroline said as he reached the kitchen doorway. "You've got bare feet."

She was kneeling in front of the sink with a dustpan and broom, sweeping up the remains of a Wild Turkey bottle. Seven other bottles were lined up on the counter. Danny recognized them from the bar in the basement.

"Grace coming for brunch?" he asked.

"I'm dumping them out," Caroline said evenly. "Fortunately I'd already emptied this one before I dropped it."

"That's a nice empty gesture considering you don't drink brown liquor," Danny snorted contemptuously.

Caroline paused and shook her head sadly. "I remember when you used to be sweet in the morning."

Danny shook his head back at her and said, "Don't even try it. I know all your tricks." Jerry's warning from the night before was still fresh in his mind.

Caroline didn't respond. She finished sweeping, stood, and laid the dustpan on the counter. She unscrewed the top from the Southern Comfort and began pouring it down the drain.

Danny noticed that she'd brewed coffee, crossed gingerly to the counter, and poured a cup. He took a tentative sip and was pleasantly surprised that it wasn't too strong.

"So what's this all about?" he asked as he walked around to the table. "Don't tell me you had a moment of clarity in the middle of the night." He sat and lit a cigarette, waiting for a response.

Caroline finished emptying the bottle, put it in the drainer, and turned to face him. Her eyes were clear, direct. "Haven't you ever wondered why you were out there in the woods all night?"

Danny immediately felt uneasy. He'd been expecting her usual arsenal of excuses, apologies, and tears. Again he thought of Jerry. "No, it hadn't occurred to me," he said.

Caroline took a slow, deep breath, then said, "It was my fault. When I got home that night, I passed out in my car. I didn't even know you were missing until the police showed up the next morning. I'd just woken up and was standing right here making coffee when they knocked on the door."

Danny gripped the mug tighter as if it might anchor him. "Why are you telling me this now?"

"Is it all right if I sit down?"

Danny nodded warily. Caroline came around the counter and sat in the chair to his left. He had to fight the impulse to slide back to keep some distance. He watched as she lit a cigarette, exhaled, and smiled weakly.

"I know I was never a nurturing mother," she began. "It just never came naturally for me. I wanted a child, and I loved you... still love you...but I was never quite sure what to do with you. That's why your father and I were a good match. At least until he decided he liked men. He instinctively knew what you needed. He may not have been the most affectionate or warm father ever, but he was solid and stable. I was impulsive. I wanted to be able to pick up at a moment's notice, go have fun, and the truth is that I resented you a little bit." She gave a "what can I say?" smile. "In the vernacular of the times, you cramped my style."

Danny started to smile back but caught himself. "So?"

"So, I let your father do all the hard work and just showed up for the fun parts." She looked at Danny as though he might contradict her, but he just nodded for her to continue. "After the attack I was wracked with guilt," she said. "I kept thinking that if I'd noticed you were gone and you'd been found sooner, things would have been different. You might not have gone into a coma. The doctors said that wasn't the case, that there was nothing that could have been done, but I couldn't help feeling it was my fault. It was actually a relief when your father moved you to Shady Meadows because every time I saw you I was reminded of how I'd failed you."

Danny realized Jerry had been right about the last part. He also realized how shamelessly Caroline had exploited the situation for her own gain despite her supposed guilt. "Be sure to tell me when we get to the part where I should feel sorry for you," he said.

"I'm not looking for sympathy," Caroline replied calmly, though Danny noticed the tiny flash of anger in her eyes that preceded it. "I know I don't deserve it. I'm just explaining what happened so you can understand what I'm doing now."

Danny regarded her coldly as he took another drag on his cigarette, then nodded. "I'm listening."

Caroline nodded back gratefully. "After you were gone, I began drinking heavily. Not with the girls. Just on my own. Usually at home, but sometimes I'd go to the Red Coach for lunch and stay through dinner. It went on for almost a year until Beth and Grace did an intervention of sorts. It wasn't anything official, but they sat me down and convinced me that I was killing myself and had to slow down."

Danny thought it had the ring of truth. If she'd told him Grace had tried to get her to stop entirely he would have known it was a lie, but it was believable that she might have advocated for moderation. Grace had managed to spend her own adult life in a state of only mild intoxication.

"After a few failed attempts, I got things under control," Caroline continued. "Until you recovered." Her eyes dropped

159

to the long ash on her cigarette and she stared at it for a few seconds before tapping it into the ashtray. She looked back up at Danny. "You have to believe me about this," she said, on the edge of pleading. "When I talked to you about coming back to the area while you went through rehabilitation, I really wanted it." The certainty in her eyes faltered. "Or maybe I just wanted to want it because I thought it was a way to make up for what I'd done." She shook her head. "I'm really not sure. Self-awareness has never been one of my strengths."

Danny frowned at the clumsy attempt at humility. "So what happened? Change your mind?"

"Not consciously, no," Caroline replied, "but the old feelings came back. The guilt and wondering how I was going to face you. I started drinking alone again, then I'd go for drives. The counselor who ran our AA meetings in prison suggested I might have been sabotaging myself, hoping to get caught, or maybe even to die. Thank God I didn't hurt anyone else. When I think about it…" She looked at Danny for a reaction before continuing, but didn't get one. "When I went to jail, I made a promise to myself that I was going to get sober. That I was going to stop fucking up my life and yours. So I went to meetings, and I prayed to God for strength, and all the things I was supposed to do." She paused and her lips twitched. "Except one."

She reached toward Danny's face but he drew back. She lowered her hand. "The goal of Alcoholics Anonymous isn't simply to stop drinking. It's also spiritual recovery. The ninth step is to make amends to the people we've hurt. The book says, 'If we are painstaking about this phase of our development, we will be amazed before we are halfway through. We are going to know a new freedom and a new happiness. We will not regret the past nor wish to shut the door on it. We will comprehend the word serenity and we will know peace.'"

So it's still all about you?

Danny was impressed that she'd at least done some research to make it sound plausible.

160

"I never did that," Caroline went on. "I was hoping maybe I could skate past it, but I've realize I can't. I can't just show up for the fun parts, anymore. The guilt is always there, and when I drink to escape it, it just comes back stronger. I can't do it anymore." Her voice was thick with conviction rather than self-pity. "I can't keep avoiding you and what I've done. I'm sorry, Danny, and I hope that eventually you can forgive me."

Danny didn't respond as he finished his cigarette. Finally he said, "For what it's worth, I don't think it would have made any difference if you'd been standing right there when I fell, unless I landed on you. The doctors said the damage was immediate and there wasn't much blood loss." He pursed his lips and studied her appraisingly for a few seconds, then nodded as if responding to a silent question. "But we both know I'd be an idiot to get too excited. We've played this apology scene before. In fact, we just played it five days ago."

Caroline nodded. "But making amends doesn't mean just apologizing. It means trying to restore justice, and to do that I have to permanently change the way I live and the way I behave toward you." She looked at the bottles. "I understand why this seems like an empty gesture to you, but for me it's about accepting the fact that I'm powerless over my disease. I can't be around liquor right now. I'm not strong enough."

"So are you planning to dump Grace, too?" Danny asked archly, then regretted it.

"I know you don't think much of her," Caroline said, "but Grace really is a good friend, and though she enjoys her cocktails, she doesn't need them the way I do. She helped me before and she's going to help me now. When I called her last night she offered to start taking me to meetings. There's an open meeting every Tuesday at noon at the Friends' Meeting House in Wellesley and a Sober Sisters meeting on Saturdays at 10:30 AM at St. Andrew's Episcopal Church next to Wellesley College."

Danny eyed her suspiciously. "How do you know about those?"

"The counselor gave me a list of local meetings before I was released," Caroline replied without hesitation. "I was supposed to attend at least two a week."

"And there aren't any in Weston?" Danny asked, surprised.

Caroline dropped her eyes. "I'm not quite ready for that yet."

So it's okay to admit you're a drunk in front of criminals and strangers, but not the other drunks in your own town?

"Look, if you really mean it, that's great," Danny said, "and I'll be happy to drive you to meetings, too, but don't expect me to just forget last night or last week or all the other shit that's happened over the years."

"You shouldn't forget," Caroline said. "The goal is to accept the past, make peace with it, and move forward."

For whose benefit? Danny wondered.

* * * * *

As he padded barefoot down the driveway, Danny imagined a tiny angel on his right shoulder and tiny devil on the left, both whispering into his ears.

To err is human, to forgive, divine.
To fall for the same crap again and again, pathetic.
Everyone deserves a second chance.
John Hinckley, Jr., will be thrilled to hear that.
Do unto others...
...before they do unto you.
Honor thy mother.
Fuck the bitch!

He wished he could muster more enthusiasm for Caroline's latest commitment to self-improvement, but even if it was something she genuinely wanted, experience had taught him that her own enthusiasm would fade after a few days or a week. Still, at least one genuine positive had come from the morning. He hadn't backed down or allowed her to emotionally manipulate him. He felt proud of himself.

He stooped to pick up the paper and caught movement out of the corner of his eye. Tom Parker was slowly making his way home down Cherry Brook.

"Wow, eight-fifteen already," Danny thought.

CHAPTER 34

Holtz set the cardboard tray on the picnic table in the back corner of the empty Dairy Joy patio and dropped onto a bench.

"Thanks," Danny said as he began unloading their lunches. "So how are you enjoying your vacation so far?"

"I've learned that the key to a happy marriage is time apart," Holtz replied with mock sageness. "Lots and lots of time apart." He snatched up a few fries. "I'm trying to stay busy and keep out of the way, but sometimes I catch my wife staring at me like she's measuring me for a coffin." He stuffed the fries in his mouth, took a sip of Coke.

Danny chuckled. "And that's unusual?"

"Even the kids seem on edge about having me around so much. First few days it was, 'Yay, dad's home. Wanna play catch?' Now it's more like, 'Don't you have someplace to go, old man?' And it's only been nine days." He bit the corner off a packet of mustard and squirted it on a hot dog.

"I visited Joey yesterday," Danny said.

Holtz raised his eyebrows as he took a big bite.

"He's doing okay," Danny said. "Considering. They put him on some new meds that are supposed to even out his mood. It seems to be working if dazed is the mood they're going for." He dumped tartar sauce from a small paper cup onto his clam roll and spread it with a plastic fork. "He still says he's the killer."

Holtz washed his mouthful down with more soda. "I know. I talked with Marty Thornton this morning. He said the State Police have actually been very courteous about keeping the Weston PD in the loop."

"So what's going on?" Danny picked up his clam roll, took a bite. For a moment he was twelve again, giddy with excitement and anxiety on his first double date with Bryce, Diane Costello, and Nancy Gorman. Holtz's voice brought him back.

"The underwear has been positively identified. Michael Frazier and Davey Talbot were both headed to camp that summer and their mothers had already sewn name tags on theirs. Mrs. Levitt and the ex-Mrs. Parker confirmed their boys wore brands and styles matching the other two pairs. Not conclusive enough to stand up in court, but good enough for now."

"Can the lab do tests to confirm it?"

"That's the plan."

Holtz pushed the rest of the hot dog into his mouth and chewed it slowly as he dribbled mustard onto the second. Danny took another bite of clam roll. The memory wasn't as intense.

"They found traces of semen," Holtz said after a minute. "Blood type O-positive. Same as Joey and his father, same as Tim."

"Same as forty-five percent of the population."

Holtz gave a wry smile. "Yeah, but presumably they'll start by matching it just against those three."

"Did they find the knife?"

"About a dozen of them, not to mention assorted guns and bows and arrows. Was Bill Gardner some kind of survivalist nut?"

"Go ahead, you pussy," Bryce taunted.

He felt a flutter of trepidation but drew his bow back, sighted down the target-tipped arrow, and released it. There was a quick "pffft" as the arrow split the air and near-simultaneous "twack" as it struck the ground six feet away, exactly halfway between Bryce's bare feet. He let out his breath.

"Nice shot," Bryce said, sliding his left foot to the arrow. He pulled it out of the ground and notched it into his own bow, then smiled. "My turn."

"You okay?" Holtz asked.

Danny looked up and saw concern on his face. "Yeah, sorry. Just spaced out for a second." He sipped his Coke and tried a reassuring smile. "I think he was just really into camping and hunting when he was a kid. His family had a cabin somewhere up in Maine and he spent summers there." He blinked away the ghost of memory. "Bryce was really into that stuff, too. He was always taking his dad's old stuff out of the attic."

"What about Joey?"

Danny remembered Joey in the backyard shooting cans with Bryce's BB pistol. "Not really," he hedged. "I mean, we all had BB guns and bows, but Joey never seemed that into it. Maybe because Bryce was so competitive." He watched Holtz seemingly inhale a third of his second hot dog, then cocked his head curiously. "You don't really think he might have done it, do you?"

Holtz shook his head as he wiped mustard from his lips. "Not a chance. I was just curious. Trying to get more of a sense of him."

Danny nodded. "You know what's weird?"

"Only one choice?"

Danny looked down at his left arm and shifted it an inch. "He hasn't apologized."

Holtz gave him a bemused look. "For your arm? Why would he? He didn't have anything to do with it."

"I know, but..." Danny closed his eyes, waiting for the idea to fully form. "...but he's trying to make us believe he did," he said finally. "You'd think he'd try to show some false remorse."

"Not if he's pretending to be a stone-cold sociopath."

"But he's not. He's just being the same Joey, and Joey would apologize if he really thought he'd hurt me."

Holtz frowned, trying to follow the logic. "Okay, maybe, but what's the significance?"

"Maybe subconsciously he really doesn't want me to believe he did it."

"Because he's afraid of losing your friendship?"

"Or because he wants me to help him."

Holtz chewed some fries contemplatively for a moment, then nodded. "Interesting."

"That's it?" Danny blinked. "'Interesting?'"

"By George, Magoo, you've done it again!" Holtz said, pumping his right fist once in the air. "Better?"

"No wonder your wife and kids don't want you around."

Holtz smirked. "It is interesting. I'm just not sure what to do with it." He took another bite of hot dog, chewed it slowly, swallowed. "By the way, Captain Smith and his boys are trying to track down Amy Gardner. Joey claims he doesn't know where she is. He didn't mention anything to you, did he?"

"Just that she's a mess, so they must keep in touch. Why are they looking for her? Wasn't she questioned in 1975?"

"Yeah. She didn't see or hear anything. Said she fell asleep watching TV with her folks. Her dad carried her up to bed around 10 PM. She said the last thing she remembered that night was watching *The Bob Newhart Show*. Hopefully that was the case."

Danny caught the implication, nodded somberly. "So then why do they want to talk with her?"

"For one, they want to confirm that she and her brothers were actually molested, but they also want to see if she remembers anything that might connect her father to the other victims. Whether she ever saw him with any of them, that sort of thing. "

Danny nodded again as he gnawed on a fry. "I've been thinking about what you said," he said, "that Bryce and I might have been attacked by someone else. If Bill Gardner was the killer, do you think it makes it more or less likely he attacked us, too?"

Holtz looked mildly impressed. "I've been thinking about that, too. I'd say much more likely."

"Why?"

"It could explain why neither of you fit the profile and why the ritual wasn't followed. The other killings were definitely about satisfying urges, but Gardner may have had another motive for killing the two of you."

"Such as?"

"Necessity, maybe. Suppose Bryce was threatening to go the cops about being molested and Gardner got scared about having us poking around in his business. Or maybe Bryce even knew what was going on and threatened to turn him in. That would be a pretty good motive."

"But what about me?"

"Hate to say it, but you may just have been incidental damage. Wrong place at the wrong time. Or maybe Gardner was afraid that Bryce told you what was going on. It's even possible that he did tell you."

Danny felt a chill pass through him and sat up straighter. It hadn't occurred to him that there might have been a motive beyond craziness for what happened to him. The possibility made the memories still locked in his head feel more dangerous. "That's comforting," he said dryly. "Seems like a lot of speculation, though."

"It's a theory," Holtz shrugged before stuffing the last of his hot dog in his mouth.

They finished eating, then Danny lit a cigarette. "Any word on Tim?"

"He's out of intensive care. They'll be transferring him back to Cedar Junction in a day or two. Looks like he dodged a bullet." Holtz smiled teasingly. "By the way, Angel was asking about you. I think he might be interested."

"That's great," Danny replied with mock excitement. "When does he get out? I'll pencil him into my calendar."

Holtz chuckled. "How are things with your mother?"

"For what it's worth, she's apparently been sober for a week and she's gone to two AA meetings with Grace O'Neill."

"So I heard."

Danny cocked an eyebrow. "What happened to anonymous?" He waited a moment for an explanation but saw none was coming. "I'm not sure which is worse," he said, shaking his head. "Self-centered Caroline or self-consciously humble Caroline."

"Sounds like either way she gets to keep the attention on herself," Holtz said.

CHAPTER 35

Danny finished loading the dinner dishes and surveyed his work. He knew Karl would have put the taller glasses toward the back of the top rack, but everything seemed secure. He filled the dispenser with Cascade powder, flipped it shut, closed and locked the door, hit START. The dishwasher rumbled to life.

Caroline was already on the couch, her feet tucked up under her, thumbing through TV Guide. A cup of chamomile tea steamed on the table to her left. Danny crossed to his now-usual chair and sat down. He'd been making a conscious effort to spend more time with her at night, even staying up to watch the late movie the previous Saturday, though he'd managed to make it through only the first half-hour of *Mrs. Miniver*.

"*MacGyver*, some new sitcom called *Live-In*, *Alf*, or a movie?" Caroline asked, her inflection making her own preference clear.

Danny frowned indecisively.

"*Sabrina*," Caroline coaxed, as though it should have meaning to him.

Danny returned a blank look.

"With Audrey Hepburn. You always liked Audrey Hepburn."

"I think you're confusing me with your other son."

Caroline gave him a saccharine smile. "I didn't have another son because the first one turned out so perfectly."

Danny rolled his eyes and laughed. "Okay, fine, *Sabrina*. But I'm not staying up for the second feature."

* * * * *

Danny was just drifting off when Caroline's voice cut through the fog. "Look at that dress. It's gorgeous."

169

Danny opened his eyes and blinked at the screen. Audrey Hepburn was floating through a crowd in a white strapless ball gown embroidered with delicate black flowers. The bodice was fitted, the skirt full, with a bustle in the back.

"Edith Head," he said without thinking.

Caroline looked at him. "What?"

"Edith Head," Danny repeated. "She designed it and won an Oscar for best black-and-white costume design."

Caroline pursed her lips skeptically. "And how would you know that?"

Danny thought about it a moment, then laughed. "I have no idea. Maybe it's a gay thing."

Or just a Karl or Jerry thing.

He saw Caroline's lips tighten slightly, then she looked back at the TV and her expression turned wistful.

"I wore one like that for my sweet sixteen party, except it was the most gorgeous pale pink and didn't have any embroidery. Your grandmother and I made a special trip into Manhattan to Macy's because everyone knew they had the best collection of junior gowns every spring."

Danny's brow furrowed with surprise. "You really had a sweet sixteen party?"

"All of the girls in my circle did."

"You had a circle?"

"Well, it wasn't *my* circle," Caroline said, though her tone made it clear she was at least part of its center, "but, yes, I had a group of girls I chummed around with all through school." She sipped tea. "I was very popular. I've always found it easy to make friends for some reason. Even with the girls in prison." It came off as reflective rather than boastful.

"So did you go to your prom?"

"Of course I went to my prom," Caroline sniffed. "I was prom queen my senior year."

Danny frowned thoughtfully. "What was it like?"

Caroline stared back with a mix of incomprehension and

annoyance, then her face softened. "Oh, Danny, I keep forgetting how much you missed out on," she said. "I'm so sorry, honey."

"It's okay," Danny said. "It's not like you pushed me."

Right?

"I've actually been meaning to thank you."

"For what?"

"Keeping my senior yearbook for me."

Caroline looked confused again, then her eyes cleared and she sighed. "I'd forgotten about that. Joey put it there."

"Joey?"

Caroline nodded. "I remember he stopped by just before Christmas that year and asked if he could have a picture of you. He wouldn't say why, just that it was a surprise. I gave him that one because it was always one of my favorites. The day you would have graduated he brought the yearbook over and showed me the dedication. It was one of the sweetest gestures I'd ever seen." Her eyes began to shimmer and she took a shaky breath. "He said we should put it in the drawer so it would be there when you came back." She wiped her eyes. "Not if. When."

Danny swallowed, unsure what to say.

"Were the two of you in love?" Caroline asked suddenly.

Danny felt his body grow warmer and had to fight not to fidget. "I think he was," he said, "but I don't think I was capable of it back then." He knew it wasn't that simple, but didn't feel up to explaining the intricacies of hormonal teenage boy emotions or his own particular separation of love and sex at the time.

"And what about now?" Caroline asked.

"I don't know."

"So you've never been in love?"

Danny shook his head.

"I want that for you," Caroline said. "For you to know what it feels like to be in love." She took a deep breath and managed a semblance of a reassuring smile. "So what do you want to know about the prom?"

"Everything."

"The real everything or the romanticized version?"

Danny considered it a moment. "Tell me your favorite memories. I don't care if they really happened."

CHAPTER 36

"It's Rick Holtz," Caroline said, holding her hand over the mouthpiece of the phone.

Danny jumped up from the kitchen table, grabbed his coffee and cigarettes. It had been over a week since he'd heard from Holtz. "I'll take it in the office," he said, already halfway down the hallway.

He picked up the extension and yelled, "I have it," then held the receiver close to his ear, listening for the click. He suddenly felt silly, like a secretive teenager. "Hey, where have you been?" he asked. "I tried calling a few times."

"My wife figured that since I'm home I may as well put in that vegetable garden she's been wanting for the past five years," Holtz replied dourly. "Lots and lots of vegetable garden. Besides, I didn't have any news until now."

"Good news?"

"Unfortunately, no. The DNA tests were inconclusive."

"What does that mean?"

"It means that it could have belonged to Bill or Joey Gardner or both, but they couldn't pinpoint it any more than that."

"I thought DNA was unique."

"It is if you drill down deep enough, but within families a lot of it is common because kids get half from their mother and half from their father. The part that gets passed along the Y chromosome is almost identical from generation to generation."

"But what about the mother's half?"

"Some of the semen is old, probably dating back to the original killings. The DNA was probably already degraded. But the main problem is that the water cross-contaminated everything."

"Shit," Danny sighed.

"Better wet than incinerated. At least the DNA is still there. But different tests would be needed."

"Would?"

There was a long pause before Holtz said, "That level of testing would have to be done at a lab in Britain. It would take a few months and cost a lot of money. The DA doesn't feel it's justified given the circumstances."

"The circumstances?" Danny replied more sharply than he'd intended. "What the fuck does that mean?"

"Look at it logically. They've got possession of items belonging to the victims, they've got an attempt to destroy evidence, they've got a plausible DNA match, and they've got a confession. It doesn't get much more solid than that."

"Yeah, but..." Danny stopped himself, knowing that arguing wouldn't change the situation. He lit a cigarette.

"For what's it worth," Holtz said, "I don't think the DA's office is just going for the easy resolution. To order those kinds of tests, they'd need a compelling reason to believe Joey is covering for his father. Unfortunately, our opinions aren't enough. They have to follow the evidence."

"Yeah, I know," Danny said. "But there's still a chance the psychiatric evaluation could say he's not mentally competent to stand trial, right?"

"Sure, and then he'll spend the rest of his life in the state hospital. Personally, I don't think being locked up with a bunch of violent mental patients is a step up from prison."

Danny took a long drag and held the smoke, letting the nicotine do its magic. His body relaxed, his thoughts focused. "Okay, let's assume he goes to trial. His attorney..."

"If he pleads guilty it's going to be a very short trial," Holtz cut him off. "I think it's time to find out if you were right, that he subconsciously or secretly or whatever wants you to help him. You need to try to convince him to retract his confession. I'm sure the DA would still charge him based on the evidence, but at least there'd be a real trial."

Danny felt uneasiness settling over him. "Any suggestions on how I do that?"

"Seems to me he needs a way out. Something he can live with emotionally."

"Such as?"

Holtz didn't respond for a moment. When he did, his tone was deliberate, pensive. "Well, I think it's safe to assume he isn't afraid of his father physically anymore, so it's about breaking the emotional control." He paused. "If you were in his situation, what would free you to tell the truth?"

Danny laughed uncomfortably. "I'd let the bitch fry."

"I'm being serious."

"Our relationship isn't parallel," Danny snapped. "Caroline is just emotionally manipulative. It's not the same."

Why so defensive, cupcake?

There was an awkward pause. Danny felt heat creeping up into his cheeks.

"Who said it was?" Holtz asked. "I was just talking about Joey and his father. I wasn't trying to insinuate anything else. I'm asking you because you have a connection with Joey that I don't. Nothing more." He let a few beats pass. "But we can talk about your mother if you'd like."

Danny caught the teasing undertone and smiled. "No, that's okay. I've humiliated myself enough for now."

"So what do you think?"

"It can't hurt to try. Let me give it some thought."

"One more thing," Holtz said.

"Am I going to like this one?"

"The tests didn't find any DNA matching Tim's. With that and Joey's confession, his lawyer plans to file an appeal."

"But what if I convince Joey to take back his confession?"

Holtz grunted. "Another bridge for another day."

* * * * *

175

Caroline was standing at the sink when he walked back into the kitchen. She turned to face him, clutching a mug to her chest with both hands. "Is everything okay?" she asked.

"The results of the DNA tests came back. It could have come from either Joey or his father or both."

"So what does that mean?"

"It means that Joey's probably going to be charged and have to stand trial."

"Even if he admits he didn't do it?"

Danny nodded. "Holtz thinks the DA would still charge him at this point."

Caroline shook her head sadly. "I'm sorry, Danny. I know you couldn't have foreseen what would happen."

Danny was sure he heard a note of judgment. "What are you talking about?"

"Well, if you and Holtz hadn't gone digging around, I'm sure none of this would be happening right now." Caroline sipped from her mug and shrugged. "Sometimes it's just better to leave the past alone."

It hit Danny like a gut punch as Jerry's words echoed back.

"She's got a gift for finding weakness and exploiting it to keep you emotionally dependent on her."

"Of course, it's really not your fault, but Holtz should have known better." Caroline paused a beat. "Then again, if his judgment were better, those girls might not be dead."

Danny's pulse quickened. "What girls?"

Caroline squinted in concentration for a few seconds. "Delia Lee, I think the older one's name was. He never mentioned it?"

"Mentioned what?"

"I don't really remember the details," Caroline replied cryptically. "It was a few years ago." She waved her hand as though giving up on trying to remember. "But you should ask him why he spends all day sitting behind a desk."

CHAPTER 37

Bridgewater State Hospital had gained national notoriety in 1967 as the subject of *Titicut Follies*, a documentary detailing the abuse of inmates. During a subsequent investigation, it was discovered that dozens of prisoners had been committed there in error over the years and become lost in the system, some remaining for decades after their sentences should have ended.

Who knew there were so many shades of institutional blue? Danny thought, looking around the waiting room. He checked his visitor pass again, then reflexively patted the right front pocket of his jeans. The No Smoking signs posted every ten feet seemed to mock him.

A phone rang and the blowzy middle-aged blond behind the glassed-in desk picked it up without speaking. After a moment she hung up and barked, "Thirty-seven," though Danny was the only one in the room.

He jumped up and held up his pass. The woman seemed to smirk contemptuously before nodding toward the barred doorway to her left. Danny walked to it and waited as a lanky older guard came down the hall to usher him in. As soon as the door clanged shut behind them, his palms began to sweat.

All right, Mr. DeMille, I'm ready for my cavity search.

* * * * *

Joey was at a corner table, a styrofoam cup in front of him. Like the previous time, he was dressed in pale green pajamas and a thin white robe, but now his beard was heavy and his hair wild.

"Hey," Danny said.

"Hey," Joey replied dully, his lips barely moving.

Danny eyed the vintage vending machine with COFFEE in peeling silver letters across the front, thought better of it, and took the chair across from Joey. A guard discreetly stood watch in the opposite corner.

"So how are you doing?" Danny asked. He noticed that Joey's eyes were bloodshot, the pupils dilated.

"Okay, I guess," Joey shrugged. It seemed to require a lot of effort.

"Have you been sleeping?"

"That's about all I do."

"What have they got you on?"

Another labored shrug. "I don't ask. How are you?"

Danny frowned. "I've been better. Have you talked to your lawyer since yesterday?"

"He called but I was busy. I haven't called back yet."

"You should. The results of the DNA tests came back. They were inconclusive. Basically the semen could have come from you or your father."

Joey looked down at his hands but didn't respond. His features remained slack.

"That means the DA is probably going to formally charge you," Danny said. He watched carefully for a reaction, thought he saw a small flicker of apprehension. He decided to follow his gut. "Do you think your father loved you?"

Joey looked up, his eyes registering mild surprise. "Of course."

"You're sure about that?" Danny gave it an edge of skepticism.

"Yes," Joey replied more forcefully.

Danny nodded. "I think so, too." He hoped he hadn't oversold it. He leaned closer, cutting a quick look at the guard to make sure it was okay. "Which is why I think what you're doing is wrong."

"I'm not doing anything. I'm just telling the truth."

Danny kept his voice low. "But if your dad loves you, do you really think he'd want this for you?"

As opposed to raping you?

Uncertainty flickered in Joey's eyes for just a split second.

"I told you, I'm just telling the truth," he said stridently enough to draw a throat clearing from the guard.

Danny decided to change tack. "I didn't say you weren't, and honestly, it doesn't matter. I still don't think your dad would want you to go through this."

Joey looked momentarily confused. "But I have to pay for what happened."

Danny cocked his head at the phrasing. "For what happened," not, "for what I've done." A thought began to take shape. He tried to relax and let it come.

Not cause and effect...different...less direct...overall...bringing back balance...

...*restoring justice...*

...amends.

Suddenly it made sense. Joey wasn't just trying to protect his father. He wanted to make amends for what his father had done by sacrificing himself.

"Joey, it's not going to matter to him," Danny said. "You said it yourself, he's not really even living anymore." Joey stared back dumbly for a few seconds, then Danny saw comprehension come into his eyes. "It doesn't matter if you did it or not," he continued in a near-whisper. "Just say it was him. It's not like they can arrest him or put him in jail at this point. He can't stand trial. He won't even know it's happening." He gave an offhand shrug. "Why throw away your own life?"

Lukewarm coffee splashed his face and chest as the styrofoam cup sailed past his left shoulder.

Joey was on his feet. "You fucking piece of shit!" he screamed, his face red and twisted. "How could you say that?"

Danny slid his chair back though Joey made no move toward him. The guard moved in quickly, slipping his left arm around Joey's neck and twisting Joey's right arm up behind his back.

"He loved me!" Joey cried.

Footsteps thundered down the hall and two burly orderlies rushed into the room. The guard released his hold and each grabbed one of Joey's arms. He didn't resist. His anger seemed already spent. He began to wail. Danny looked helplessly at the guard who just shrugged.

"He loved me, he loved me," Joey kept repeating between sobs as he was guided from the room.

Holtz's words suddenly came back to Danny: "He needs a way out. Something he can live with emotionally."

* * * * *

"I fucked up," Danny said. He trapped the phone between his ear and shoulder and lit a cigarette. "I didn't even get inside my own head. I got stuck trying to imagine how a normal person would react in that situation."

"There's your mistake," Holtz said flatly. "No such thing."

"Sorry."

"At least you tried."

It wasn't the reaction Danny had expected, and for some reason it made him angry. He blew smoke in frustration. "I'm starting to feel like one of those kids on the short bus, like I get a gold star just for showing up."

"How about a gold star for self-pity?" Holtz said.

"What?"

"Isn't that what I'm hearing? Self-pity?"

Danny felt another rush of anger, but didn't reply.

"Look, if you want someone to rub your nose in it every time you make a mistake, get married," Holtz said.

"Ouch," Danny said. He wondered if Caroline was starting to get to him. "You're right. Sorry." He took a drag on his cigarette. "So now what?"

"Now we let the wheels of justice continue their slow turn and hope he has a change of heart before the trial. Maybe his lawyer can do something with the idea that he wants to make amends."

Danny almost said, "It would be nice if my visit wasn't a total loss," but realized it would come off as more self-pity. He looked at the stove clock, then out the front window. Tom Parker was just passing the end of the driveway on his late afternoon walk. Danny wondered for a moment why Caroline wasn't home yet.

"I hope so," he said.

"Me, too," Holtz replied. "Anything else?"

Danny wanted to ask about Delia Lee, but decided against it. He had the feeling it was something they should talk about face to face. "No, that's it," he said.

He hung the phone back in the cradle, stubbed out his cigarette, and lifted the lid of the trash to dump the ashes. The stink of old chicken bones make him grimace.

Disgusting, he thought, as he wriggled the bag free. He tied the drawstring, then carried the bag out to the porch. As he opened the garage door, he froze. Caroline's car was gone.

CHAPTER 38

Buy me some peanuts and Crackerjack. I don't care if I never get back...

Danny sat up, not sure what had woken him. He could hear the soft patter of rain against the windows. The faint echo of the song lingered, and he realized how often it had been in the back of his mind lately. Before he could ponder why, the doorbell rang three times, followed by muffled banging. He looked at the glowing display on the clock: 12:14 AM. The doorbell rang again and he jumped up and opened his bedroom door. Light from the kitchen still filtered into the foyer downstairs. He flipped on the hall light. Caroline's bedroom door was open. His heart began racing as he had a vision of a grim-faced policeman standing on the back porch waiting to deliver bad news.

His senses were fully alert, his brain buzzing, but his body seemed to be moving too slowly as he crossed to the stairs and started down. The air felt thick. As he reached the bottom step and turned toward the back door, the banging abruptly stopped. At the end of the hall he could see a backlit shadow through the sheer curtains. It swayed slightly from side to side.

"Danny, let me in!" Caroline's hoarse voice shouted.

Danny felt a rush of relief and hurried to the door. He turned the key in the deadbolt and yanked it open. Caroline stood on the porch, her hair plastered to her head, clothes dripping, arms crossed tightly across her chest. Steam rose from her skin and her whole body was shaking.

"Holy shit," Danny said. He pushed the screen door open and she stepped stiffly inside. He slipped his right arm around her and pulled her against his chest. A shiver ran through him as his body began absorbing her chill through his now-soaked t-shirt.

"Come on," he said after a minute, guiding her into the kitchen. He propped her against the counter and grabbed the quilt from the back of the family room sofa. As he turned back, he noticed the pale pink stain down the front of her white t-shirt and the faint trickle of blood along the left side of her nose.

"What the fuck happened?" he exclaimed. "Are you all right?" He wrapped the quilt around her shoulders, then gently lifted her bangs. An inch-long gash ran just above her left eyebrow. He grabbed a napkin from the table and dabbed at it, but it immediately began weeping blood again. "I think I should take you to the emergency room," he said.

Caroline tried to shake her head but stopped, gasping in pain. "No," she protested. "I'm fine. I just hit my head."

"On what? Where have you been?"

"On the windshield...or the steering wheel...I'm not sure." Her eyes rolled up for a moment then came back to Danny, though she didn't seem to be looking at him. Danny snapped his fingers, watching carefully for a reaction. Her eyes slowly cleared.

"You had an accident?" he asked. "Where?"

"Off Concord Road. Down by the old tracks."

Danny knew the spot, a short dead-end forking down to abandoned railroad tracks about a quarter-mile from the center of town. He and Bryce had spray-painted obscenities and enormous cocks on the walls under the bridge one night. "How did you get down there?" he asked.

Caroline frowned as though struggling to remember, then her breathing grew heavier and ragged. "I couldn't see where I was going. The rain was so heavy and it was foggy. I kept thinking I should pull over, but I was afraid someone might hit me from behind so I kept going. I saw the rock at the last minute and tried to stop, but the pavement was wet." Her voice hitched and her lower lip began to tremble. "I'll never forget that sound."

Danny could see she was heading for hysterical tears and touched her left cheek to keep her focused on him. "Was anyone else hurt?"

"No, I don't think so. I didn't see anyone."

"What do you mean, you don't think so?" Danny asked sharply. "The police didn't tell you?" Caroline's eyes dropped and Danny's concern turned to foreboding. "Oh fuck!" he cried, running his fingers through his hair. "You left the scene?" He turned and paced a few steps away, then turned back. "You've got to be shitting me. You just drove home?"

The dam burst and tears streamed down Caroline's cheeks. "I just...panicked," she managed haltingly around wracking sobs. "The car stalled...and I couldn't start it...then lights went on in the house nearby...and I thought they might call the police...so I ran."

Danny looked down. Below the quilt, her once-pink Espadrilles were caked with mud.

Caroline took several deep breaths, but they didn't seem to calm her at all. "And I dropped the keys when I got out...but I couldn't find them in the dark...so I couldn't get into the house."

Let me guess, then your dog ran away?

Danny shook his head with a mixture of sympathy and disbelief. "Please tell me you weren't drinking."

"I swear I wasn't," Caroline replied adamantly.

Danny handed her a clean napkin and she wiped her eyes and blew her nose. The first wave of tears seemed to be receding.

"You need to take a warm shower and put on dry clothes," Danny said. "Then do something about that cut."

"But what about the car?" Caroline asked.

"I'll take care of it. Assuming I can get it started."

"But what if the police are there?"

Danny considered it a moment. "If the neighbor had called or the police found it, I'm sure we'd have heard by now."

"But what if they are?" Caroline pushed, her eyes beginning to shimmer again. "What are you going to tell them?"

Danny gave an unconcerned shrug. "I'll just tell them Grace borrowed it."

CHAPTER 39

The angel and devil were back, having a new debate.

It's not the same.

How is it different?

She didn't kill anyone.

This time.

Fuck off. It's not the same.

Danny cleared the grove of crab apple, willow, and bittersweet, and switched off his flashlight. The rain had passed and the clouds cleared. The field shimmered silver in the moonlight.

Initially he'd had a few moments of anxious deliberation about which route to take, but the real dangers of walking narrow twisting roads dotted with few streetlights and fewer sidewalks had finally won out over his fear of woodland phantoms and whatever memories might be stirred. Now, as he breathed deeply the cool sweet air, he felt a sense of calm settle over him.

He walked to the bottom of the hill and stopped. The path toward town lay to the right, not far from Lovers' Rock. He heard a soft noise to his left and turned, half expecting to see Tom Parker sleepwalking up the road. For a moment he saw nothing, then a doe stepped out of the heavy brush along the edge of the trees twenty feet away. She seemed to look at him, then lowered her head and began nibbling at the grass.

He'd seen deer in the fields and woods at dusk and dawn, but never at night. "Are you my spirit animal?" he asked, not entirely sure he was joking.

The doe's head popped up, ears alert, eyes wide. This time it was clear she saw him. Danny slowly raised his right hand and waved. The doe turned and bounded off toward the far treeline.

"Guess not," he said.

But maybe it was a sign.

He watched her top the gentle rise and cut right, disappearing into the cave-like opening in the trees. Sweat popped out on his back despite the chill.

Yeah, maybe, he thought.

* * * * *

Danny suddenly felt vulnerable, imagining eyes more accustomed to the dark watching and ears more attuned to normal night sounds listening to his uncertain footsteps. His heart fluttered and he took a deep breath. It didn't bring calm. The air was redolent of decay and permanent damp. It suggested death and slithery creatures under the leaves and beneath the still water. He had a sudden vision of Bryce's body, his blood slowly seeping into the pine needles as the creatures watched, lying in wait for their chance to claim him.

"Stop it!" he commanded himself, shaking his shoulders to release the tension. He took a slower breath and raised the flashlight, slowly scanning the woods. No glowing eyes caught the light. He trained the beam back on the trail and continued for another two dozen yards.

Though no lights were on inside, he could just make out the Gardners' house through the early summer foliage. He studied the ground along the left edge of the trail, searching in vain for a hint of where the path had been, then turned back toward the head of the trail. If he'd walked Joey back to the house and they parted there, presumably he'd met up with Bryce somewhere along the way back to his own house. He began retracing his steps.

Fifteen feet from the edge of the woods he stopped.

Nothing.

It all felt familiar, but no more. No emotions, no sense memories he could be certain were specific to that night. He turned off the flashlight and put it in his back pocket, fixed a cigarette between his lips, and flicked his lighter.

"What? Did you think I was going to stab you? Lighten up."

The cigarette and lighter dropped to the ground as Danny jumped back, adrenaline banging his heart and turning his spit metallic. He froze for a moment, then spun around, convinced Bryce's voice had had to have been real. He'd never had a memory so intense.

He yanked the flashlight from his pocket, fumbled it on, and turned in a slow circle. There was no one else there physically, but he sensed he wasn't quite alone either. The memory seemed to still be hovering nearby, as though he could just close his eyes and find it again.

But am I really ready for that? he wondered. He chewed his lower lip anxiously for a few seconds, then braced himself and closed his eyes. For a moment there was nothing, then he heard a low sinister chuckle.

Danny, it's me, Bryce. I've come to suck your blood! Muah ah ah!

Danny opened his eyes and muttered, "You're such as ass sometimes."

You're the one talking to yourself in the woods in the middle of the night.

He let out a sigh and scanned the ground with the light until he spotted the cigarette and lighter. He bent to reach for them. Suddenly Bryce was sprawled in front of him, just beyond the edge of the beam. Someone moved in the shadows beyond.

Danny screamed, scrambling back on his heels, and jerked the light up. Bryce was gone, the shadows empty. He straightened slowly, waiting anxiously to see if there would be more, then snatched up the cigarette and lighter.

Fuck this, he thought. I'm so done with Memory Lane for tonight.

* * * * *

Danny pulled into the garage, hit the remote control on the visor to close the door, and turned off the car. The radio clock read

1:38 AM. It hadn't been quite an hour and half since Caroline had woken him, though it felt like he'd been awake for days. He hoped she'd gone to bed because he was too tired to talk.

He noticed that the door latch was within easy reach of his left hand, hooked it with his index finger, and pulled. The door popped open and he climbed out.

Small victories.

He closed the door and walked around to the front of the car. The damage was substantial but appeared to be just cosmetic, centered above and below the inside right headlight, which had escaped without being cracked. The car had started without any problem and driven smoothly. He wondered why it had stalled in the first place. He suspected Caroline actually turned it off in her confusion, then flooded the engine when she tried to restart.

He began to turn away but stopped. Something didn't feel right. He looked back at the car, then squatted down and studied it for a minute.

"Any thoughts?" he whispered.

Silence.

"Sure, now you keep your mouth shut."

CHAPTER 40

Danny hung up just as Caroline walked into the kitchen. She paused a moment, her bloodshot eyes fixed on the receiver, then continued to the coffeemaker and poured herself a mug.

"How are you feeling?" Danny asked. Nothing about her physical state the previous night—unfocused eyes, slow reactions, confusion—seemed surprising given the circumstances, but he still couldn't help wondering if she'd been drinking.

Caroline took a long sip before turning around. Her expression was both tired and wary. "I have a horrible headache and I can barely move my shoulders and neck."

"I really think you should go to the doctor," Danny said. "You might have a concussion or cracked bones. You don't want to risk making things worse."

Caroline took another sip, then went to the refrigerator and added cream. "Who was that?" she asked, pointedly ignoring his suggestion. She crossed back to the counter and added sugar.

Danny frowned. "No one. I was trying Holtz, but no answer."

Caroline stopped stirring. "So you can tell him about last night?" It came across as an accusation.

"Yes, but not about you or the car. When I was cutting through the college last night, I remembered something. At least I think it was a memory. It might just have been my imagination, but it seemed too real."

"Did you get the car?" Caroline asked, as though she hadn't heard him. She laid the spoon on the counter.

Danny blinked at her. "Yeah, it's fine. Just needs some body work. I didn't have any trouble starting it."

Caroline studied him for a few seconds. Her expression lost its challenge. "So this memory you had, what was it?"

Danny sat at the table and lit a cigarette. "First I heard Bryce's voice. It freaked me out. Usually when I remember things I can tell they're not real, but it really sounded like he was right there."

Caroline lowered herself stiffly into the chair to his left and took a cigarette from his pack. "What did he say?"

"'Did you think I was going to stab you? Lighten up.'"

"Stab you? He had a knife that night?"

"I don't think so. It definitely triggered a sense of anxiety, but I didn't really feel...threatened."

No?

Caroline lit the cigarette and smoked it pensively for a moment. "So then what do you think it meant?"

"I don't know," Danny shrugged.

"And that was it?"

"I wish. I saw his body and someone standing behind him."

Caroline's body tensed and she sat up straighter, grimacing at the effort. "Tim Walczak?"

Danny shook his head. "It was just a shape in the shadows. It makes me wonder if I actually saw who did it." He took a drag on his cigarette. "At least now I'm sure I was really there."

"What that ever a question?"

"Yeah, kind of. At least for me. I mean, I knew I was in the woods and my blanket was found by Bryce's body, but it still didn't feel possible that I was there when he was killed. That seemed like something I'd *have* to remember." He shrugged, gave a hollow laugh.

Caroline reached over and gave his left arm a gentle squeeze. It took him by surprise because he'd sensed that she found it unsavory.

Maybe she's just reminding you it's there.

"Remember what the doctors told you," she said. "You'll remember things when you're ready."

"It's still frustrating," Danny sighed. He took another drag on his cigarette, then fixed Caroline with a sober look. "So can we talk about your night?"

Caroline's lips tightened, but she nodded.

"What were you thinking, driving with a suspended license? Especially in that kind of weather?"

"I only drove to and from Grace's house, and when I left to come home it was barely drizzling."

"But you're not supposed to be driving at all."

"I couldn't help it," Caroline replied. "We decided to try a new Wednesday meeting in Waltham because the people at the Tuesday meeting in Wellesley are so tedious. Grace was supposed to pick me up, but she had a flat tire." She shrugged. "I couldn't very well ask her to walk over here."

"What time was the meeting?"

"One."

"So where'd you go after that?"

Caroline rolled her eyes. "The Natick Mall. Then we had dinner at Ken's Steakhouse, then we went to see *Big*," she recited like a put-upon teenager. "Is that okay with you? I called to let you know, but there was no answer."

Danny knew it was possible. "I was just asking," he said.

"Because you wanted to make sure I wasn't in a bar all night?"

"No."

Yes.

Caroline pursed her lips sourly. "I've been going to meetings. I've been working my program. I've been home almost every night. I don't know what more I can do." She jabbed her half-smoked cigarette out in the ashtray. "I get it. I made a mistake. Trust me, it won't happen again."

Danny knew she was trying to put him on the defensive, but refused to play along. "Good," he said.

He could see the wheels working in Caroline's eyes. Finally she just nodded penitently. "By the way, did the paper come yet?"

"I can go look," Danny offered.

Caroline waved him off and pushed slowly to her feet. "The exercise might help loosen up the kinks a little." She rolled her shoulders and moaned. "Besides, I want to take a look at the car."

"You should call your insurance company."

"In a few days. When I'm feeling better."

* * * * *

Danny finished dressing and opened his bedroom door. Caroline's door was closed. He considered checking to make sure she was all right, but decided to let her rest and headed down to the kitchen. The sports and entertainment sections of the *Globe* were lying on the kitchen table. He perused the front page of each, then grabbed his cigarettes and went to the office. He tried Holtz again, then dialed Jerry's office and closed the door.

"Hey, Danny, what's up?" Jerry came on after a short wait.

By his tone, Danny could tell he was busy. "Caroline took her car out yesterday and had an accident."

"Is she all right?"

"She banged her head and cut it. She seemed pretty out of it when she got home, but this morning she's okay, other than a headache and some pain."

"Was she drinking?"

"I don't know. I don't think so. She said she wasn't, and I didn't smell it on her, but like I said, she was kind of out of it. But that could also have been from smacking her head."

"Did she say where she'd been?"

"She and Grace went to an AA meeting, then shopping, then dinner and a movie."

"Why wasn't Grace driving?"

"Because she supposedly had a flat. Caroline said she just drove to Grace's house and back. Grace did the rest of the driving."

"Maybe you should ask Grace."

Danny hesitated. "You want me to check up on her?"

"Wouldn't it be better to know for sure?"

"I suppose, but I think Grace might be a little suspicious if I called her out of the blue. And I'm pretty sure she'd mention it to Caroline."

"That might not necessarily be a bad thing," Jerry replied. "Put your mother on notice that things have changed. You're not just taking her word for things anymore."

Did I ever?

"Easy for you to say," Danny said, glossing over the sting. "You don't have to live with her."

"Neither do you," Jerry replied brusquely.

Danny realized Jerry was slipping into default mode. Surprisingly, it didn't bother him the way it had in the past. He decided his recovered memories could wait. "I'll think about it," he said, then pointedly added, "I'll let you go since you've obviously got your mind on other things."

How's that for notice?

There was a long silence, then Jerry chuckled. "You caught me. Sorry."

"It's okay. Just don't be afraid to tell me when you're busy. I'd rather know than think you're just being an asshole."

"Point taken. I'm pretty sure Karl might have mentioned the same thing a few times. How about we talk tonight?"

"Sounds good."

CHAPTER 41

"I'll clean up," Danny said. "You relax. No offense, but you don't look so good."

It was true, though it wasn't just Caroline's physical appearance. Since she'd come out of her room late that afternoon, she'd seemed distracted and anxious.

"Thank you," she replied with enough ambiguity that Danny wasn't sure if it was sarcasm or gratitude.

"Are you sure you don't want to go see a doctor?" he asked.

"Yes, I'm sure," she replied, "but thank you for your concern. I think I'm just going to go back upstairs and read for a while."

"*My Fair Lady* is coming on in half an hour."

Caroline gave a wan smile as she headed for the door. "Maybe I'll watch in my room."

The phone rang and she stopped. Danny picked it up.

"Tyler residence."

"It's me," Holtz said.

"Hey," Danny replied brightly, then mouthed, "Dad" at Caroline. "How's Karl?"

"What?" Holtz squawked. "What are you talking about?"

Caroline said, "Say hello," without feeling, and shuffled out of the room.

Danny waited until he heard her climbing the stairs. "Sorry about that. Caroline was standing right here."

"So?"

So I don't know.

"I tried calling you a few times today."

"I'm back at work," Holtz replied.

"Your suspension is over?"

"At least temporarily."

"What does that mean?"

"I take it you haven't seen the news today?"

"No, why? Somebody not separate their recycling?"

"A hit-and-run, last night around ten-thirty. A guy got hit while he was putting out his trash..."

Most of the rest became lost in the sound of Danny's own breathing and the pounding in his ears.

"...route 20..."

Danny had a sudden vision of Caroline's car. What about the damage wasn't right?

"...so I'm manning the desk and answering calls for now."

There was a few seconds' silence.

"You still there?" Holtz asked.

"Huh?"

"I asked if you're still there," Holtz repeated. "You okay?"

"Yeah, fine. Where did it happen?" Danny realized how anxious he'd sounded and took a slow breath.

"I told you, Boston Post Road."

"I know, but I mean where?" Danny hoped it sounded like just casual interest.

"Eastbound, next to the Gifford School."

Danny pictured the stretch of road. It was on the east edge of town near the Route 128 interchange. It was nowhere near Grace's house.

Assuming that's where she really was.

The tightness in his chest eased a bit. "So it must have been someone coming off the highway."

"Most likely."

"Is the guy alive?"

"For now, but he's in critical condition. Severe head injury. He hasn't regained consciousness yet."

"Poor guy," Danny replied automatically.

"It also looks like the driver may have tried to hide him. Blood indicates he was hit at the end of the driveway, but he was found in the yard about thirty yards away."

The tightness in Danny's chest returned. "Maybe he crawled."

"Not with those injuries, and marks in the grass indicate he was dragged."

By someone prison yard strong?

"He was lucky he didn't bleed to death. The wife had taken a pill and gone to bed around nine, so he was out there all night. The housekeeper found him when she arrived this morning."

"I can't believe someone would do that," Danny said because it seemed like the natural response. "That's really cold."

"And ballsy. That stretch is pretty heavily traveled even at night. We're hoping someone noticed the car parked by the side of the road."

"So you don't know anything about it yet?"

"No, but if they find any paint the lab should be able to trace the make, maybe even the model. It's usually pretty distinctive."

I'm going with BMW silver.

Danny looked down and realized he'd unconsciously taken out a cigarette. He lit it and took a drag.

"So why were you trying to reach me?" Holtz asked.

Danny tried to think of a plausible reason for being in the woods the previous night, but couldn't. "I just wanted to say thanks for not giving me shit about the way I fucked up with Joey," he said. "I appreciated it."

"Um, yeah," Holtz replied stiffly. "We can exchange gimp friendship bracelets the next time we have lunch. Anyway, I just wanted to let you know I'll be at the station during the day for the foreseeable future, but you can always reach me here at night."

"Okay," Danny said. "And congratulations, I guess, even if it's only temporary."

"Thanks. Should add weeks to my marriage."

Danny hung up and worried his cigarette for a minute.

"I'd let the bitch fry."

Sure you would, cupcake.

It had to have been a coincidence, he thought. He'd retrieved Caroline's car himself. He'd seen where the accident happened.

And yet something about the damage...

The phone rang and he snatched it back up. "Forget something?"

"Excuse me?" came Grace O'Neill's voice.

"Sorry, Mrs. O'Neill," Danny replied. "I was just talking to... my dad. I thought he was calling back."

"Oh." Danny could hear the ice. "Be sure to say hello the next time you talk with him. So is your mother around, handsome?"

"She's resting, actually."

A long pause. Danny imagined Grace squinting at her Cartier watch while balancing a martini in the other hand. "It's not even seven yet. Is she feeling okay?"

"She had an accident while she was driving home last night." Danny wondered if Grace would play dumb.

"Oh dear, is she all right?"

"She hit her head, cut her forehead."

"Does she have a concussion?"

"I don't think so, but she won't go to the doctor."

"I don't blame her," Grace said. "Sick people go to doctors. There are germs on everything. Every time I go, I end up with someone else's disease."

I didn't realize so many sick people visited the plastic surgeon.

"Well, give her my love and tell her to give me a call later if she's up to it. I'm sure I'll be up." She sighed ostentatiously. "It seems there just aren't enough hours to get everything done."

Doing nothing can be so time-consuming.

"I will," Danny replied, his mind racing for a way to subtly check Caroline's story. "By the way," he asked quickly, "how was the movie?"

"Oh, it was delicious," Grace replied without hesitation, drawing out the last word. "That Tom Hanks is so cute, and who knew he was so talented? And did you know it was directed by Laverne from that TV show?"

"Yeah, I read that in *People*," Danny said, relief settling in. "Glad you liked it. Have a good night."

Told you so, he thought.
Silence.

CHAPTER 42

Danny opened his bedroom door. The hallway smelled of coffee. He inhaled deeply, smiled, and went into the bathroom to empty his bladder. He considered a quick shower, decided the coffee was more important, and headed down to the kitchen. Caroline was sitting at the kitchen table, reading the paper. She looked up and smiled.

"Good morning, honey. How did you sleep?"

"Fine. How about you?"

"Much better. The headache is gone and my shoulders and neck aren't nearly so sore."

"That's good. Guess you didn't need to go to the doctor, after all." Danny crossed to the coffeemaker, poured a mug, and blew on it as he walked to the table. "Anything interesting in the paper?"

"Did you hear about that hit-and-run accident on route 20 on Wednesday night?" Caroline asked without missing a beat. "Just awful."

"Yeah. That was the same night you had your accident," Danny said casually, watching for a reaction.

Caroline just nodded. "I'm not surprised. That rain and fog were terrible. I'm sure there were a lot of accidents. But can you imagine leaving that poor man lying there like that?"

Can you?

"The police think the driver actually dragged him into his yard so he wouldn't be found right away," Danny replied.

Caroline frowned. "It doesn't mention that in the paper."

"Holtz told me."

"When did you talk to him?"

"Last night, after I talked with Jerry. By the way, Grace called. She said to give you her love. She wants you to call her."

Caroline's eyes dropped to her tea. "How sweet. Did you have a nice chat?"

"No, I just asked how she liked the movie. She said it was 'delicious.'"

Caroline offered a convincingly relaxed smile. "I don't know that I'd go quite that far, but it was very entertaining." She looked back at the paper, turned the page, and shook her head. "Imagine that, trying to hide the body. How awful. What's this world coming to?"

To Danny it sounded more obligatory than heartfelt, but not deceitful. It was just the sort of automatic response people made when they didn't really care but knew that something wasn't right. "So are you up for a trip to the grocery store?" he asked. "I'd rather go today. Saturday it's all soccer moms and their brats."

"Since when don't you like children?" Caroline asked.

Danny took his cigarettes from his robe pocket and lit one. "I'm not sure," he said, blowing smoke toward the family room. "Did I ever like them?"

Caroline stopped skimming the paper and gave him a puzzled look. "I thought so. At least I assumed you did because you were always good with the younger kids in the neighborhood."

"I was? When?"

"Whenever the neighbors got together. The other parents loved having you around because they could forget about their kids for a few hours. You'd organize games, make sure they ate. You had a natural gift for it. I though maybe you'd be a teacher some day." She smiled wistfully. "And remember, you babysat Andy Parker? Of course, that was a few years later."

Danny shook his head in bewilderment. "There were neighborhood get-togethers? Why don't I remember that?"

Caroline shrugged. "I'm sure I don't know. It went on for a few years. Cookouts, cocktail parties. At least once a month during the summer from the time you were four or five."

"Are you sure you're talking about my life?"

"Yes, I'm sure. Ask you father if you don't believe me."

Danny frowned. "But he told me he didn't really know Bill Gardner, that he'd only talked with him a few times."

"Because the Gardners weren't invited."

"Why not?"

Caroline hesitated, her eyes roving to Danny's cigarettes. He slid the pack to her and she lit one. "Because of Bryce," she said through a veil of smoke.

"Bryce? Why?"

"Because he was a bit wild, and the Gardners didn't do anything to control him. I always adored him, of course, but a lot of the other parents thought he was a bad influence. It seemed like there was always trouble when he was around. And to be honest, he could be cruel at times, even to you, though I never thought it was malicious. He just got overly excited and didn't know when to stop."

Danny knew that was true, though he hadn't recognized it while they were still best friends. "So the whole family got excluded because some people didn't like Bryce?"

"Would it have been better if they'd asked Bill and Bobbi to leave him at home? And it's not like the parties were held in the middle of the street where they could see them. It was all very discreet. No one wanted to hurt Bobbi or the other kids."

"What about Bill?"

"I don't think he would have cared. I always had the sense he wasn't particularly interested in getting to know the neighbors."

Or having the neighbors get to know him.

Danny nodded and took a long drag on his cigarette. "So why did the parties stop?"

Caroline shrugged a bit too casually. "The Woods and the Howards moved, and I guess the rest of us just got busy with other things. You know how it is. But that was one of the reasons I wanted to finish the basement. I was hoping we could start getting together again. Then your father left." She stared into the middle distance for a few seconds before smiling self-consciously. "Life moves on."

It hadn't sounded like an attack or a plea for sympathy, so Danny decided not to comment. "So what do you think about the grocery store?" he asked.

"If you don't mind, I think I'll just stay here. I still have some planting left, and I don't want to overdo it."

"Sure," Danny said. "I already started a list."

* * * * *

Danny gave the cantaloupe a squeeze and sniffed the stem cavity the way Karl had shown him. The rind was still firm, the aroma sweetly fruity. He put the melon into his cart and pushed on down the aisle.

"Danny?" a voice called behind him. He turned and saw Grace O'Neill striding toward him in seersucker ankle pants, a pale pink sweater tied casually over the shoulders of her crisp white t-shirt. She kissed him on both cheeks, then stepped back and looked him up and down, conspicuously ignoring his left arm. "So how's your mother today? I haven't had a chance to call her yet." She patted the bottom of her freshly colored and styled bob.

"Better. Less pain and her mood seemed better."

"Oh good." Grace picked up an avocado, squeezed it, put it back. "I have to admit my first thought when you told me she was resting was that she was sick from that awful food. I know she likes it, but it's not for me, and the restaurant just doesn't seem very sanitary."

"Ken's Steakhouse?" Danny asked.

Grace tested another avocado and dropped it into her basket. "No, that Star of Calcutta or New Delhi or whatever it's called." She gave a little shiver of distaste.

"In Waltham?"

Grace nodded though her attention had drifted to a rack of rotisserie chickens in the back corner.

Danny's pulse quickened. "What were you doing in Waltham? I thought the movie was in Framingham."

Grace looked back, though she seemed momentarily surprised to see him there. "No, we went to the matinée in Chestnut Hill, right after..." She looked around dramatically, then raised her eyebrows "...the meeting. Then your mother insisted we go to that place for dinner." She stopped, frowned. "Why would you think we went to Framingham?"

"I just assumed it, I guess," Danny replied quickly. "I forgot about Chestnut Hill. It had just opened when..." He nodded at his arm and got the "let's move on" look he'd wanted.

"Lord knows I'm not a racist," Grace sighed, "but that food was just too spicy, and like I said, the place just seemed dirty." She pouted disapprovingly. "I also wasn't a big fan of that Loretta."

"Loretta who?"

"One of 'the girls,'" Grace air-quoted, "from your mother's 'time away.'" Another air quote. Her eyes widened suddenly. "I probably wasn't supposed to tell you any of this, was I?"

It struck Danny as contrived, a play to ensure Loretta didn't stay part of Caroline's life for long. He decided to ignore it. "So what time did you leave the restaurant?" he asked, trying not to sound overly interested.

"I left before eight. Like I said, I really wasn't enjoying Loretta's company, and when your mother suggested going for dessert and coffee, I bowed out and had the restaurant call me a cab."

"So Caroline didn't drop you off?" Danny asked numbly.

Grace looked toward the ceiling and unleashed a put-upon sigh. "That's what I just said, isn't it?"

Danny stared back without seeing her for a moment, then felt a flash of anger. "You know, you don't have to be such a cunt all the time," he snapped.

CHAPTER 43

Danny pulled into the driveway and stopped. Caroline's garage door was open, her car gone. The asphalt was wet and the hose lay in a tangle at the end of the walk.

Fuck, she really did it, he thought.

He'd sat in the parking lot for a half hour after he stormed out of the store, trying to come up with another plausible scenario that fit the facts. He hadn't found one. Still, he couldn't believe...didn't want to believe...that Caroline was capable of doing something so monstrous. He was sure there had to be a missing piece of the puzzle, something that would explain it all away, and he'd nursed that hope all the way home. Now it was gone.

She hadn't just hit someone and tried to hide the body, she'd faked another accident to cover up the damage. That was why it hadn't been right. The rock was barely the height of the bumper, but the hood had been creased, too. He wondered if she'd faked not being able to start the engine, too, knowing he'd retrieve the car for her? Had she been setting him up to verify her story?

He parked in the turnaround and got out, hoping she was gone. He needed time to think. He suddenly wished that Joey were there. Not that Joey would know what to do, but at least Joey would understand what he was feeling.

As he stepped over the hose, the screen door banged open and Caroline stepped onto the back porch. Her eyes were red-rimmed and puffy, her hair disheveled. She stared at him for a moment, then her whole body sagged and she burst into tears.

Danny fought an unwanted welling of sympathy. "Let's go inside," he said.

* * * * *

A half-empty bottle of Stolichnaya stood on the kitchen table. Caroline dropped into her regular chair and filled the tumbler of ice in front of her, but didn't drink.

Hmmm, the good stuff. She must have been saving it for a special confession.

"I know everything," Danny said. "I ran into Grace at the store. She told me you were in Waltham on Wednesday and about Loretta. I know you didn't drive her home." He paused to make sure she was listening. She wiped her eyes and nodded. "Did you and Loretta go drinking after Grace left?" he asked.

Caroline nodded again without hesitating.

"Then you hit that man on the way home."

Caroline's eyes widened. "No, I swear, honey. I didn't have anything to do with that. I hit a dog. A golden retriever on Deer Path Lane."

Danny cocked his head challengingly. "Why would you be on Deer Path? That's the opposite side of town from Waltham."

"Because I was afraid to come home. I knew you'd be mad at me, so I was going to ask Grace to let me spend the night, but then..." She took a hitching breath "...I hit the dog and got scared. I thought I heard someone shouting."

It sounded like she believed what she was saying, but Danny knew she'd had almost two days to practice. "Then why were you so desperate to read the paper yesterday? You were looking for information on the hit-and-run."

"No, no. I didn't know about that until I saw the news last night. I thought there might be something about the dog."

"In the *Globe*?" Danny replied skeptically.

Caroline dropped her eyes to the glass, then closed them. "I wasn't thinking straight. I just..."

"Bullshit," Danny cut her off. "Then why fake the other accident? To hide the fact that you hit a dog?"

Caroline's eyes jumped to the glass again for a half second. She licked her lips, took a slow breath. "Because I thought I could get you to take the blame for it."

"What?" Danny asked incredulously.

Caroline took a moment, then said, "Danny, I'm on probation. If they found out I was driving, never mind that I'd been drinking and hit a dog, I'd automatically be sentenced to another six months." Her tone was steady, reasonable.

"So you wanted me to take the fall?"

"Just for hitting the rock, not the dog. There's nothing illegal about having an accident on a rainy, foggy night. The insurance company would have settled the claim without a second thought."

Danny studied her. She returned his gaze evenly.

"Why didn't you just tell me the truth?" he asked.

"Because I didn't trust you. I thought you might say something to your friend Holtz."

Danny knew he would at least have considered it. "Where's the car now?"

"Loretta's brother owns a garage in Waltham. I had it towed there." Her eyes began to fill with tears again and she wiped snot away on the back of her hand. "I called Loretta last night after I saw the news about the hit-and-run and told her what had happened. She said her brother could take care of it and he'd do it all in cash so the insurance company wouldn't have to get involved."

"Wasn't that big of her? And I'll bet there's an extra charge for discretion, right?"

Caroline sniffed. "I just wanted it to be taken care of."

"While I just happened to be at the grocery store. You didn't think I'd notice it was missing? And why did you wash it?"

"Because there was blood under the lip of the hood." She looked at him pleadingly. "I swear I didn't hit that man. I was nowhere near there."

Danny took out two cigarettes, gave her one, stuck the other between his lips, and lit them both. Separately, nothing she'd said seemed impossible, but together it all seemed too improbable.

Then why do I believe her? he thought.

Because you're a momma's boy?

No.

Because she's not stupid?

That was true. The fact that the whole story was a series of short-sighted improvisations that made her look guiltier actually worked in her favor. If she'd hit a person—or even known someone had been hit that first night—she would have planned more carefully. Instead she'd winged it, just trying to create a plausible explanation for the damage to the car. Unless he'd happened on a notice about the dog in the *Town Crier*, he would have taken her word for what happened and covered with the insurance company. It would have all turned out fine.

"What's done is done, I guess," he said, then saw the tears returning. "What now?"

"I think the tow truck driver was suspicious." She began sobbing again. "He kept...asking me questions...and...looking at the damage."

Danny blew out a hard breath. "Fuck. The police probably alerted all the tow companies and body shops in the area because of the hit-and-run." Caroline let out a guttural moan. "We need to call and tell them what happened," Danny said. "Holtz is back at work. I can call him. He'll believe me."

I think.

Caroline whimpered pitifully. "I can't go back to jail."

"They'll test your car and rule you out," Danny reassured her.

"But I'll still go back. I violated probation."

"Maybe you should." For a moment Danny wondered if it had just been in his head, then he saw the flash in Caroline's eyes. "I mean, maybe you just need some more time to get your life back together," he backtracked, angry at how weak it sounded.

The set of Caroline's jaw suddenly shifted, her expression became determined. "You hit the dog," she said matter-of-factly.

"What?"

She nodded with certainty. "That should work. You'll have to say you hit the dog."

And if she really was responsible for the hit-and-run?

"You've got to be fucking kidding," Danny cried. "You don't think they're going to wonder about that gash on your head?"

Caroline picked up the glass and downed a third of it, nodded to herself again. "I was in the passenger seat and hit my head when you slammed on the brakes. It makes sense. You'll get a slap on the wrist. Probably less given your circumstances." She tilted the glass at his withered arm. "I'll pay the fine, then in a few months when I can drive again, I'll get you a condo."

Danny blinked in disbelief. "With what? Jerry's money?"

"I don't need your father's money," Caroline scoffed. "I have my own."

"Since when?"

"Since your grandfather died. More than Jerry *ever* had."

Danny gaped at her. His grandfather had died a few months after Jerry moved out. "Does he know that?"

"Of course not. It was hidden in a trust."

"And you've been sponging off him for all these years?"

Caroline's upper lip curled with contempt. "He owed it to me, and you owe me this."

"I owe you? How do you figure?" Danny shook his head at her and let out a small humorless laugh. "You know what? That coma may have been the best thing that ever happened to me. At least I still have my life ahead of me. If I'd stuck around here, I probably would have thrown it away trying to save you."

"Don't be insipid," Caroline replied coldly.

A phantom slap stung Danny's right cheek.

And yet in the bathroom, she hit you...

He had a sudden vision of Caroline's arm flailing up toward him and flinched.

"...on the other side," he whispered.

"What?" Caroline said, her hard stare turning uncertain.

Danny closed his eyes and went through again. In the kitchen, too, he thought. When she'd lunged across the counter, it had been with...her right hand.

"You fucking bitch," he said, opening his eyes. "You're left handed. It wasn't an accident. You knew exactly what you were doing. I couldn't protect myself from that side."

He saw the fear in her eyes, then the twitch of her right arm. As it cleared the table, he just managed to catch hold with his left hand. Pain shot up his arm and for a moment he saw pinpoints of light exploding in front of his eyes, but he didn't let go.

"Not this time," he said. "Never again."

CHAPTER 44

"You can't survive without me! You're too weak! You've always been too weak!"

There's irony. A memory I'll probably never be able to forget, Danny thought. He wondered if any of the neighbors had seen Caroline chasing the truck down the driveway or heard her ranting as he pulled away down Cherry Brook.

He slid open the glass door and stepped out onto the balcony. His room overlooked a wide bend in the Charles River. To the left, a few kayakers paddled near a stone and timber boathouse that looked like it would have been more at home on the Danube. Directly across, geese floated in front of a boat rental parking lot, no doubt waiting for someone to come along and feed them. To the right lay Norumbega Road, the Metrowest's infamous hub of open, gross, lewd, and lascivious behavior.

He lit a cigarette and sat down. He'd probably gone past the Newton Marriott a thousand times, but it was the first time he'd been inside. His room was clean and relatively spacious, if a bit rundown, and the balcony and view were nice bonuses. It was also relatively cheap, though he'd still have to make sure it was okay to charge it on the credit card Jerry had given him.

But that could wait, he decided. He wasn't ready to relive the events of the day or figure out his next move just yet, and Jerry would want to do both. For the moment, he just wanted to relax and try to clear his mind.

A red convertible cruised slowly into the boat rental lot and pulled to the front edge by the water. The geese immediately moved toward it like an armada. The driver got out but ignored them, and after a few moments they moved away. Danny sat forward, intrigued.

He couldn't make out the driver's face from that distance, but from the way the man moved, he appeared to be younger. His hair was blond and longer in the back, and he was wearing acid-washed jeans, white high-tops, and a red tank top.

A tank top? Danny thought. It's not that warm.

The man lit a cigarette and leaned against the driver's side door, facing the entrance to the lot. He pulled the front of the tank top down and the crotch of his jeans up, then folded his arms across his chest, leaving his right hand free to work the cigarette. The pose seemed practiced, calculated. Danny was surprised to feel his penis thickening.

That could be relaxing, he thought.

Or terrifying.

* * * * *

"Randy" had been sweet and nervous. As soon as Danny pulled into the parking lot, the seductive posturing had turned to shifting feet and shy glances. At one point he'd even gotten back into his car, but hadn't left. Danny had finally climbed out of the truck, walked over, and introduced himself.

"Randy" said he was a student at nearby Brandeis University, though Danny assumed that meant grad student since he appeared to be in his mid-to-late twenties. They'd gone back to the hotel, and Randy had had two Heinekens to relax while they talked.

When it had come time to take the next step, Danny had faltered. He told himself it was moral qualms because "Randy" had revealed he had a fiancée, but the truth was that he simply wasn't ready. He still had too much anxiety around sex. So instead they'd just stripped and watched one another jerk off.

For Danny it had been exhilarating. For the first time since the coma, he'd felt sexual, desirable. "Randy" had been curious about his arm, but not repulsed, and had gone into graphic detail about which of Danny's body parts he found exciting and what he wanted to do with each of them.

They'd cum simultaneously, then "Randy" had quickly dressed and left amid a flurry of mumbled excuses and suggestions they get together again sometime. Danny didn't mind. He went out on the balcony and had another cigarette, then climbed into bed, though it was just past 7:30 PM.

Baby steps, he thought, as he drifted off to sleep.

* * * * *

"Come on, let's go!" he whined.

"In a minute, honey," Caroline replied with an overly sweet smile at odds with the irritation in her voice.

Familiar faces watched from around the table, though they all looked younger than he remembered. They exchanged furtive, anxious glances with one another, brittle smiles plastered on their faces.

"Danny, why don't you go play with the other kids for a little while?" Charlie Gerstner's father suggested with a subtly pleading look. "Let your mom finish her lunch."

He looked at Caroline's plate. It was empty, but her plastic cup was still nearly filled with what looked like orange juice.

"No!" he shouted, knowing that if they didn't leave soon she'd fall asleep when they got home and he'd be alone with nothing to eat until morning. He reached out and grabbed Caroline's left arm just as she picked up her cup. The orange liquid slopped over the sides and onto her lap. "Come on," he cried again, tugging on her wrist.

He didn't see the warning in her eyes until it was too late.

* * * * *

Danny sat up, reaching for his left arm. The blissful calm he'd been feeling as he fell asleep was gone.

Awesome, my first semi-sexual experience in thirteen years and it triggers memories about my mother, he thought. How perverse is that?

CHAPTER 45

"She broke my arm, didn't she?"

He'd called Jerry just after 6 AM, hoping to catch him before he and Karl left for the Hamptons. They'd been talking for almost a half-hour. Danny imagined Karl pacing the room, knowing that each passing minute could translate into another five minutes in traffic through Queens and Nassau, and felt a small pang of guilt.

"A hairline fracture, yes," Jerry replied.

"When?"

"You were seven."

"I don't remember ever having a cast."

"You didn't. I was in London at the time. She was afraid she'd get in trouble if she took you to the doctor, so she just set it herself and wrapped it in an ace bandage."

"And you didn't take me when you got back?"

There was a long silence, then, "I'm sorry, Danny. I just... I guess I was afraid of what she might do."

After what he'd just experienced with her, Danny decided he couldn't blame Jerry. "Is that why the parties stopped?" he asked.

"I don't think they stopped. We just stopped being invited."

"That's sad."

"No more endless conversations about lawn care and the Red Sox? Not as far as I was concerned."

"I meant for her," Danny said, immediately feeling pathetic for it.

"To be blunt, she earned it," Jerry said. "I ran into Carol Gerstner a few weeks later. She was circumspect, but made it clear that more than a few people thought your mother hurt you intentionally. They were afraid to have her around their kids anymore, especially when she was drinking."

There was another long pause. Danny carried the phone out to the balcony and sat down. The cord just reached. He lit a cigarette. On the far side of the river, rush hour traffic was beginning to back up on Route 128.

"Do you remember asking me why I moved you to Shady Meadows? Jerry asked finally.

"Technically I asked why you *bothered*, but yeah, I remember."

"I never really answered."

Danny thought about it. "No, I guess you didn't. Why not?"

"Because at that point it seemed like things with your mother could go either way, and I was hoping for the best. I didn't want to say anything negative that might color your view of her."

"I guess that makes sense. So why did you move me?" Danny took a drag on his cigarette.

"To get you away from her."

Danny laughed and coughed out smoke. "Okay, that was a little more direct than I was expecting,"

"Let's face it, your mother is a professional victim," Jerry said. "She uses it to manipulate people and to be the center of attention. I was afraid that you were going to become her crowning glory."

Danny wasn't sure what to say.

"But the thing I worried about most," Jerry continued, his voice suddenly breaking, "was that every day for the rest of your life, you'd have to listen to her spew self-pity and venom about what a burden you were and the sacrifices she had to make for you. I didn't want that for you."

Jerry took a wet breath, and Danny wiped his eyes.

"Thanks, dad," he said.

CHAPTER 46

Danny turned onto Cherry Brook. There'd been a light drizzle all morning, but now the darkening sky threatened something harder. He hoped it would be brief. Driving in heavy rain made him nervous, and he didn't want to spend any more time at the house than necessary. The plan was to just grab more clothes and head right back to the Marriott, preferably without drama.

He glanced at the dashboard. 7:40 AM. There was a good chance Caroline wouldn't be awake yet if she'd continued drinking into the night. If she was awake, he prayed she'd be in her usual morning-after contrition mode. Regardless, he wouldn't tell her about his plan to temporarily go back to Manhattan until he came back to pack up the truck.

As he rounded the curve in front of Tom Parker's house, he saw a flash of red fifty yards ahead, and slowed. Through the trees he could see someone in a hooded slicker moving quickly down Joey's driveway toward the house. He tapped the gas, then coasted to a stop by the Gardner's mailbox. There was no one in sight.

As he stared at the house, the rain began falling harder. Was it just a neighbor checking on the house, or someone wanting to get a closer look at the home of the alleged child murderer? No, he hadn't gotten enough of a glimpse to get a sense of build or gender, but he'd definitely gotten the sense that he or she was in a hurry and hadn't wanted to be seen.

Common sense told him to continue home and call Holtz, but he was sure that whoever it was would be long gone before the police arrived. He drummed his fingers on the steering wheel for a few seconds, then pulled into the driveway and parked in front of the left garage door. He jumped out and sprinted to the cover of the back porch as the skies released a thunderous downpour.

Even pressing himself against the screen door, the wind-whipped rain soaked through his sneakers and the legs of his jeans within seconds. He peered through the glass into the back hallway. The red rain slicker that had been hanging there the first time he visited Joey was gone, and the door to the kitchen wide open. He opened the screen and tried the door knob. It was locked.

He closed the screen and turned back to the truck. The walkway was already under a half-inch of water and the rain showed no signs of letting up. He thought about the pristine leather seats of Karl's truck and muttered, "Fuck." He needed to get someplace dry and wait it out.

As he turned toward the side door to the garage, he froze. It was open a crack, and a light blue eye was watching him through the gap. For just a moment he thought it was Joey.

"Danny?" a cautious voice asked.

The door opened wider and a woman in the red slicker took a step onto the porch. She eyed him anxiously for a few seconds, then pushed back the hood. She wasn't wearing any makeup, and her dark hair was pulled back into a loose ponytail.

"Amy?" Danny exclaimed. "Holy shit!"

Amy Gardner gave a forced smile, then her expression turned worried. "Where's my brother?"

*****

Danny finished talking and sipped his coffee. It had gotten tepid. Amy faced him from the other end of the couch, her knees drawn up into her chest in a pose eerily reminiscent of Joey. Unlike Joey, though, her energy was calm.

Her eyes were closed for nearly a minute as though she were meditating on what he'd said, then she exhaled deeply and looked at him. He was struck again by the brightness of her eyes. Had he forgotten that, or just never noticed because he'd always been so focused on her brothers?

"I knew something had to be wrong," she said quietly.

"I'm surprised he didn't call you when he was arrested."

"He couldn't. There's no phone at the ranch where I live." She saw the skepticism in Danny's eyes and added, "By choice. It's a spiritual retreat for women. Phones, TVs, radios, they all get in the way of that. Joey and I had a standing date. I'd call him at midnight on the second Saturday of every month."

"Midnight?"

"There's a little lesbian bar in the town. Technically everyone who lives at the ranch is supposed to be sober, but two of the other girls and I go into town and have a few drinks most Saturday nights before the next batch of Earth Mama-wannabes arrive."

Danny thought he heard judgment on the last part, but decided to ignore it. "So you're gay, too?"

Amy shook her head. "No, but women tend to understand that 'not interested' means not interested. At least where I live."

Danny took her meaning. "So he didn't have any way of reaching you?"

"Not directly, but he could leave a message at the cafe in town." She picked up her tea, sipped it. "I wasn't too concerned at first because I figured maybe he'd finally gone on a date or something, but I'd asked Darlene, the girl who owns the cafe, to keep trying him. When she still hadn't gotten an answer by midweek, I began to worry. Unfortunately I couldn't leave until yesterday. I arrived late last night."

"Why didn't you call the police? They would have told you what happened. In fact, they've been trying to reach you."

"No doubt," Amy replied, "but I prefer to keep my life...and location...private. Joey respects that."

Danny was sure there was an implied "Will you?" He wondered if she was just paranoid or hiding from someone.

"I would have called you," she said, "but I didn't know you were back."

"I just came back a month ago."

Amy nodded. "Joey had told me you were out of the coma. So what was that like?"

Danny almost laughed at the childlike directness. It had come across like, "I heard you went to Disneyland. What was that like?" He wondered if the artlessness was genuine.

"Kind of a long story," he said.

Amy shrugged. "I'm not in a hurry to go anywhere, and I get the feeling you're not either. Am I right?"

Psychic, or that obvious?

"You don't want to visit Joey?" Danny asked.

"Not yet. I have to figure out a few things first."

Danny arched his eyebrows. Amy responded with a placid but resolute smile.

"Sorry, I didn't mean to pry," he said.

"It's okay. I just wasn't expecting all this. It's a lot to take in. I need to think about it for a bit."

"I understand, but can I ask you one question?"

Amy studied him a moment, nodded.

"Do you think he's covering for your father?"

A flicker of something he couldn't read crossed Amy's face before she said, "Of course. And please don't call him my father. He lost that right a long time ago."

Danny waited for more, realized it wasn't coming. "Sorry. How about just 'Bill'?"

"How about Child-Fucking Scumbag?" Amy replied with sudden ferocity, then seemed to catch herself. She breathed in deeply, exhaled slowly, smiled sheepishly. "Sorry, you didn't deserve that. When I was younger, I used to call him Sidewalk." It was an obvious peace offering.

"Sidewalk?"

"What's lower than dog shit? The sidewalk. Get it? Ha ha," she recited mechanically, then gave a small bitter laugh. "I thought it would make me feel better, but it didn't."

"And now?"

Amy stared at her tea. "Now I don't call him anything because I don't think about him. At least not very often."

Danny was sure it was a lie.

"'Bill' is fine, I guess," she said, looking up and forcing a smile. "So are you living with your mother?"

Danny decided to just go with it. "I was. Until yesterday."

"You got a place of your own?"

"Yeah, my very own room at the Marriott. I'm going to go back to New York and stay with my dad and his boyfriend for a while. Figure out my next step."

"I guess that means things didn't work out here?"

Danny took a moment to consider it. "Things with my mother didn't work out," he said. "Everything else was actually okay."

"So why not stay?"

"I can't stay in a hotel forever."

"Stay here," Amy shrugged. "At least until you figure out what you want to do next."

"I don't know, I just think that..."

"You're making excuses," Amy cut him off, and Danny sensed she meant it on a deeper level. "At least stay until I go back. Too many ghosts in this house. I don't like being here by myself."

Danny suspected the last part might be a lie for his benefit, but he was intrigued by the idea of spending more time with Amy. Still, he decided not to give up his hotel room yet.

"Okay," he said, "but I've got to go to the house to pick up some more stuff."

"You want me to go with you for moral support?"

"No, that's okay. I need to face Caroline on my own."

CHAPTER 47

Danny let himself in and walked into the kitchen. The house was quiet. He flipped on the light. The glass and now-empty Stolichnaya bottle were still on the kitchen table. Caroline's everyday purse lay on the counter, the contents dumped beside it.

Nip bottles? Danny wondered absently, then felt a jolt of panic as he noticed the two pill containers under the table. A vision of Caroline dead in a pool of vomit on her bathroom floor popped into his mind and he raced down the hall and up the stairs.

As he reached the top, he heard a sound coming from Caroline's bedroom and froze. It took him a moment to realize what it was, then his face flushed with anger.

"You're a sick bitch!" he called sharply.

Caroline's laughter grew louder.

CHAPTER 48

Amy sipped a glass of white wine while Danny smoked. The plates from the dinner they'd thrown together had been pushed to the side.

"So how long have you been living at the ranch?" he asked.

"Just for two years, though I've known most of the girls since my freshman year of college. We met in an incest survivors support group. One of them, Kara, went to a retreat during our junior year and fell in love with the area. After graduation we all drove out together and never left."

"Do you mind if I ask where it is?"

"Do you mind if I tell you it's none of your business?" Amy replied, then showed a teasing smile. "New Mexico, about twenty miles outside Sante Fe."

Danny smiled back. "You said it's a spiritual retreat. Does that mean religious?"

"Quasi. There are elements from a lot of eastern and western religions. Buddhism, Taoism, Hinduism, Judaism. Even Christianity. But also elements from philosophical movements like Esotericism, Gnosticism, Hermeticism..." She paused when she saw the blank look on Danny's face, then added, "Plus a whole crock of self-help bullshit."

Danny laughed. "So you don't actually believe it?"

"Oh no, I do. At least the core concepts. But a lot of what we offer is definitely tailored to appeal to Type-A's trying to fill a hole in their lives. You know, the type of women who hang dream catchers from the rearview mirrors of their Mercedes to show enlightenment?"

"Isn't that kind of cynical?"

"It's practical. I don't think spirituality and capitalism have to be mutually exclusive. There's nothing noble about being a burden on your community. Poverty doesn't make you spiritually purer."

A Zen Republican?

She emptied her glass. "The thing is, there are some women who come genuinely seeking a path to understanding and inner peace. If hot stone massages, yoga, mud baths, and New Age mumbo jumbo are the necessary evils to stay in business for those women, so be it." She suddenly looked self-conscious and nodded at the wine bottle. "I probably shouldn't have any more of that."

"So what do you actually believe personally?" Danny asked.

"Idle curiosity, or are you really interested?"

"No, I'm really interested." He frowned thoughtfully. "At the risk of sounding like New Age mumbo jumbo, ever since I came out of the coma, I've been trying to figure out what I'm supposed to be doing with my life. I never had a path from who I was before to who I am now. I was just suddenly here, and I feel like I've been waiting for my life to begin again. I thought that if I came back and remembered the missing parts of my past, I'd be able to move forward, but now I'm starting to feel like the missing memories aren't what's holding me back. I just don't know how to move forward, if that makes sense."

Amy seemed to carefully consider what he'd said, then flashed a sly grin. "You want a job?"

"Very funny."

"First of all," Amy said, "I don't think there's a 'supposed to be doing' in life. We all have lots of choices, lots of possible paths. I'm not big on destiny because it gives people an excuse not to take responsibility for their actions. Secondly, whether you make any decisions about where you're going or what you're doing or not, your life is already moving forward." She raised her eyebrows. "It sounds to me like you just haven't gotten used to the idea that this *is* your life now."

"So, how do I do that?"

"Fake it until you make it."

It was the same thing Holtz had said. "That's it?"

222

"Usually works for most people. No need to make it more complicated than it has to be."

Danny laughed. "And you actually get paid to tell people that?"

Amy shrugged. "Sometimes the most important step is just getting out of your own way."

"I suppose that's true," Danny replied, thinking of all the times Caroline had sabotaged herself. He bit his lower lip. "You know, it's funny, but Joey told me you were 'kind of a mess.' I don't see that."

Amy chuckled. "I wouldn't consider smoking pot in a bathrobe all day as having one's shit together either." Her expression lost its lightness. "Let's just say I'm a high-functioning mess."

Danny suddenly wondered if she played at serenity and enlightenment, hoping they'd become real some day. He decided not to ask. "So, how long has he been like that?"

"A few years. He had sort of a nervous breakdown."

"What happened?"

"He made the mistake of trying to follow in Bill's footsteps."

Danny stared dumbly back, realizing he had only a vague sense of what Bill Gardner had done for a living.

"Investment banking," Amy clarified. "Joey was smart enough. Graduated near the top of his class from Wharton, got a job with Goldman Sachs. But he didn't have the temperament for it. I guess he's not enough of an amoral asshole. He barely made it a year."

Danny noticed she didn't sound sympathetic. He wondered if she thought she'd have been more suited to the job. "How did Bill deal with that?" he asked.

"According to Joey, he was supportive, but I assume that was bullshit. I don't really know. I was already gone by then." Amy's eyes darted to her empty glass, then back. "Shortly after that, Bill's mind began to go, so it worked out for both of them."

"Joey mentioned that you'd only come back once since you left for college," Danny said.

Amy just gave him her placid but resolute smile and he knew the subject was over.

They sat in awkward silence for almost a minute, then Amy's forehead puckered with concern. "So do you want to talk about what happened with your mother?"

* * * * *

"I guess on some level I always knew she was manipulative, but my dad was right, I underestimated her. I always figured that underneath it all she really loved me. That when push came to shove, she'd put me first." He shook his head. "Obviously I got that completely wrong. She's a fucking sociopath." It felt like he'd been blathering nonstop for hours. He took a deep breath. "Sorry, I didn't mean to just unload like that."

Amy waved it away. "Sometimes it's hardest to see the truth about the people who are closest to us."

"But I can see it clearly now. She isn't just careless or self-centered. She's evil."

A small smile curled Amy's lips. "Evil is relative."

"Yeah, I guess it is," Danny replied. "Sorry."

"So what are you going to do about it?" Amy asked.

"Well, I'm not going back until I need to get my stuff."

"I mean about the accident. Are you going to call the police?"

Danny felt a prickle of anxiety. "But I really don't think she hit that guy," he said quickly.

"But she at least hit a dog. And she was driving drunk and left the scene of an accident."

A dozen justifications passed through Danny's mind, but he knew the truth was simpler. He shook his head. "I can't."

"Because you still love her."

Danny nodded. "How pathetic is that?"

Amy reached across the table and squeezed his left hand. "We're supposed to be hardwired to love our parents no matter what shitty things they do to us, and they're supposed to be hardwired to love us the same way. Your mother and Bill aren't normal, but that doesn't mean we don't still love them on some level." She flashed a wry grin. "And hate them at the same time."

Danny lit a fresh cigarette, took a few drags. "You know what's funny?" he asked. "Even before I realized it about Caroline, I was starting to see how fucked up my perceptions were about my friendship with Bryce."

Amy looked suddenly uneasy, but nodded for him to go on.

"I mean, I'm not even sure why I was friends with him the last few years. No offense, but he was an asshole to me a lot of the time." He smoked, shook his head. "Yet I kept coming back for more, just like with Caroline. And I held onto the idea that we were best friends long after it stopped being true, like I couldn't recognize or admit that part of my life was gone."

Amy's gaze was distant, and for a moment she didn't seem to notice that he'd stopped. Then her eyes cleared and she tried to cover with a thoughtful nod. "Why do you suppose that is?"

"I don't know," Danny said, wondering if she'd even heard him, "because since I've started remembering specific events, I've realized that I was on edge a lot of the time I was with him."

Amy nodded knowingly. "Acknowledging what happened in the past is important, but deciding what you're going to change in the future is even more important."

Danny knew it was a nonresponse. It was the sort of generic aphorism she probably tossed whenever she zoned out while an "Earth Mama-wannabe" prattled on about the emptiness in her life. She'd clearly disconnected from the conversation.

"Yeah, you're probably right," he said, forcing a yawn. "I think I'm going to get some sleep."

"Okay," Amy replied. "I'm sleeping in the living room, so take whatever room you want." She seemed to lose her focus again for a second, then added, "We need to go grocery shopping in the morning, but not the one in town. Do you mind driving? I don't want to take my rental out of the garage."

* * * * *

Danny put his bag down on the landing, closed his eyes, and inhaled deeply. The hallway outside Bryce's and Joey's rooms was no longer ripe with the essence of teenage boys. He wondered if he'd still find the scent as intoxicating as he had before, or if he'd just find it rank now.

He crossed to Bryce's room, opened the door, and flipped on the ceiling light. The room was empty, the walls bare and painted cream. All traces of Bryce were gone. It was a stark contrast to the way his own room had been preserved, though he was sure that had been more the result of Caroline's laziness than a desire to hold onto his past.

Had it just been too painful for Bobbi Gardner to be reminded of Bryce, he wondered, or had the changes come after she was gone? He shivered as he pictured her lying in a fetal position on Bryce's bed, slowly slipping toward unconsciousness and death.

Quick, let's try the next room, Goldilocks!

He turned off the light, closed the door, and moved down the hall to Joey's room. The door was open. He flipped on the light. Other than the bed being neatly made and a lack of clothing on the floor, it was exactly as he remembered it. The white walls, sleek blond furniture, Marimekko Unikko bedspread, and brown shag rug were a reflection of Bobbi Gardner's early 70s experiment with Scandinavian design. The posters and magazine pages taped to every wall and clutter on every available surface were pure Joey. Fortunately for Bobbi, her fascination with minimalism had passed almost as soon as she'd finished decorating.

Danny stepped into the middle of the room and turned in a slow circle, taking in the details. Was it really possible that Joey hadn't wanted to change anything during all those years?

Maybe he was sleeping somewhere else.

Was that why Amy was sleeping in the living room? Had Joey taken over her room? Or was it because her room held too many bad memories?

Danny decided he didn't want to know. If Joey hadn't moved to Amy's room, there was only one other possibility, and the idea that he might have chosen to sleep in his father's bed was too disturbing to contemplate.

Especially if he started right after Bobbi offed herself.

He went out in the hall and picked up his bag. Joey's room would do.

* * * * *

"What's wrong?" Bryce asked.

They were walking along the road by the pond. The sun was just beginning to dip behind the tree tops.

"Nothing," he pouted.

Bryce studied him for a moment, then gave a coaxing smile. "Come on, lighten up. Today was awesome. The Sox kicked the Yankees' asses and your dad got us Yaz's autograph."

"But now he's going away," he said quietly.

Bryce shrugged. "So? Just for a few days."

His pulse quickened and his throat constricted. He took a deep breath to hold back tears. "But what if something happens and he never comes back?" he swallowed hard. "I'll be alone."

Bryce stopped, frowning confusion. "No, you won't. You'll still have your mom."

I know, he thought.

CHAPTER 49

Amy had been subdued all morning. Danny wondered if being back in the house was taking a toll on her.

"If you really want to move forward with your life," she said suddenly, "you have to put your big boy pants on first."

Danny looked up from the paper. "Excuse me?"

"You've got to stop relying on your father and take care of yourself." Her expression was impassive, her eyes unreadable. "I know he loves you and thinks he's doing what's best for you, but if he keeps supporting you and lets you come running back every time you face a little adversity, you're never going to learn to stand on your own."

Danny sensed that whatever she was feeling wasn't really about him, but the words still stung.

Because they're true?

"No offense," he said, "but you weren't there."

Where have we heard that before?

He tried to keep the hurt from his voice, but couldn't mask his anger. "You have no idea what I've gone through to get this far. When I came out of the coma, I couldn't even sit up. The doctors told me I'd need at least a year of in-patient therapy and might never be able to walk normally, live on my own, or drive. I left Shady Meadows after nine months, I'm fine on my own, and I'll be driving your ass to the store. Yeah, Jerry's been great, and he and Karl have helped me in a lot of ways, but I did the work on my own. I think I've proven that I can deal with adversity."

Amy's expression didn't change, but she settled back in her chair. "All I'm saying is that you don't need a GED and two arms to work a cash register or tell fat women they look great in leg warmers. If you really want to stay, you can find a way."

Or I could just run away to New Mexico.

Amy cracked a faint smile as if she'd heard the thought. "Expressing your anger is good," she said. "It's healthy. You don't always have to be nice. That's part of being an adult. Sometimes you get to be a bitch. Like me." She drained her mug and smiled more brightly. "You ready to go to the store?"

Danny smiled back though he was still bothered. "I'm going to take a shower first," he said.

* * * * *

"She sounds like an interesting character," Jerry said.

"At least one," Danny replied dryly. "Her moods swings are kind of dramatic. Guess it runs in the family." He lit a cigarette. "She said I need to put on my big boy pants and stop relying on you to take care of me."

Jerry chuckled softly. "That's not exactly how I'd characterize our relationship. So far as I can remember, you haven't asked me for anything since you were ten. You were the kid who started mowing lawns in the neighborhood just so you wouldn't have to ask for money and I wouldn't have a say in what you bought."

"Yeah, but you bought the lawnmower."

"A seventy-dollar investment you paid back a few times over by mowing the lawn for the next five years. You did the rest on your own. I just helped create the opportunity. There's a difference between that and propping you up. I never did anything because I thought you couldn't succeed on your own."

"But I still knew I had you as a fall back, and since I recovered, you've been supporting me entirely."

"That's what parents are supposed to do. Sure, you've had to rely on me more than usual since then, but I know it's temporary. And to be honest, it's been kind of nice for me. I've gotten to indulge my fantasy that you might actually need me a little." A one beat pause. "Despite your apparent indifference while you were living here."

Danny felt a flush moving up his neck. "I'm sorry about that. I had to stop being angry at you first."

A longer pause before Jerry asked, "And have you?"

"Yeah, I have," Danny replied, then quickly added, "though that doesn't mean you don't still annoy me sometimes."

Jerry released a pent-up breath. "I think I can live with that."

"I've also figured out why I was mad at you in the first place."

"Leaving you and being gay weren't enough?"

"That was what I always thought, too, probably because that's what Caroline drummed into my head, but the truth is that I never really cared that much about you being gay. That was pretty much just an excuse to rip on you with Bryce and Joey."

"Nice to know I could provide some amusement."

Danny took a drag on his cigarette. "And I was mad at you long before you left. I just didn't realize it until now."

"You were?"

"Yeah, I had a dream last night about when you took Bryce and me to the Sox-Yankees game for my eleventh birthday. It should have been one of the happiest days of my life, but afterward I was pissed at you because you were going on a trip."

"I never realized it bothered you when I traveled."

"I don't think it did for a long time, but once I started to understand what Caroline was like..." Danny trailed off. "I was afraid something was going to happen to you and I'd be stuck with her. Kind of ironic given that I came running back to her as soon as I could, huh?"

"Danny, I'm so sorry," Jerry sighed. "You were worried I might abandon you with her, and that's exactly what I did."

"I don't blame you for leaving," Danny said. "I get it. I think on some level I always knew you would, knew you had to, but I couldn't admit that without also admitting that she was selfish, irresponsible, and manipulative." He took a contemplative drag on his cigarette. "I realize now that she was like that long before you left, but at the time it was easier to blame it on you."

"I understood that," Jerry replied.

"It was your own fault," Danny teased. "I held you to a higher standard because you were always the responsible one. Caroline was just being herself, and for some reason, I always found it much easier to forgive that. I guess I still do."

"That's one of your mother's gifts," Jerry replied. "She's got a certain something that makes people want to be around her and makes it easy to forgive her shortcomings."

Danny laughed. "Sucker punching your gimpy son isn't just a shortcoming."

"No, I suppose not, but it's still hard to stay mad at her. Bryce had that quality, too."

"Yeah, he did," Danny agreed. "I've realized they were alike in a lot of ways, though all Caroline's victims lived."

"Except the dog."

"Danny?" Amy's impatient voice called from the downstairs hallway. "Are you almost ready?"

"I better get going," he said, though he didn't really want the call to end. "I have to take Amy grocery shopping."

"Okay," Jerry replied. "I'll call tomorrow."

Danny swallowed a sudden lump in his throat. "Okay. Say hi to Karl for me, okay?"

* * * * *

Danny finished loading the groceries into the back of the truck, sat on the tailgate, and lit a cigarette. To his surprise, Amy was just hanging up the pay phone outside the entrance of the Star Market.

"I thought you were going to CVS," he said as she approached.

"I lied. I was calling the Weston police. I didn't want to call from the house because I assume they can trace calls and I didn't want them to know I was back in town. At least that was the original plan."

The hair on the back of Danny's neck stood up. "The police? Why?"

"To report your mother's accident."

"Not funny."

"I'm not kidding. You said yourself that you couldn't turn her in, so..."

Danny laughed uncomfortably, still not sure it wasn't a joke.

"Look, I just did what you tried to do for Joey," Amy said, her tone removing any doubt. "I gave you a way out. Now you don't have to feel guilty. You didn't turn her in. You just confided in a friend."

Danny's eyes widened. "But what if..."

"Don't worry," Amy cut him off. "She didn't hit that guy. It was on the news this morning. His wife did it because he was leaving her for a younger model. The cops found the car she used under a tarp in the carriage house."

She gave a reassuring smile, and the anxiety Danny had been carrying for days suddenly lifted. He laughed unexpectedly. Amy nodded and he could see that whatever had been bothering her earlier was gone, too. She radiated calm, gentle authority. She sat beside him and took his hand.

"I've realized over the years that there are always consequences to hiding the truth. If Bryce had told the truth about what happened to him, it probably wouldn't have happened to Joey, and if Joey had told, it wouldn't have happened to me. Your mother only hit a dog this time, but what if she got away with it? What about next time? A kid? A school bus? Would you be able to live with yourself if that happened?"

Danny shook his head.

"And keeping secrets is like a cancer," Amy said. "Look at poor Joey." She frowned, nodded to herself. "And that's my fault."

Danny cocked his head curiously.

Amy gave his hand a gentle squeeze and stood up. "We need to get going. Your friend Holtz is going to meet us at the house in a half-hour."

Danny blinked confusion. "I thought you said you didn't want the cops to know you're in town."

"I said that was the original plan, but on the way here I realized it was time for me to put on my own big boy pants and tell the truth about something. Joey only thinks he's covering for Bill. The truth is that he's covering for Bryce."

CHAPTER 50

"About two months after Bryce was killed, Bill took us to our grandparents for the weekend. He said mom needed time alone to go through Bryce's things and say her goodbyes. Up until that point, she'd been acting pretty much like you'd expect from someone whose child had been murdered, but when we got back, all traces of Bryce were gone. All of the stuff in his room, every picture in the house. I asked her why, but she wouldn't talk about it. In fact, she wouldn't talk about Bryce at all after that. I figured it was how she was dealing with her grief."

"And she never explained it?" Holtz asked.

Amy shook her head. "She was nearly catatonic most of the time by then, but a few weeks before she killed herself, she suddenly started going on about something Bryce had done. She wouldn't tell me what, but said it was something no one could ever know about."

"The killings."

"Yeah, though I didn't figure that until last year."

"What happened then?" Holtz asked.

"One day Joey called the cafe in town and told Darlene, the owner, that he really needed to talk to me. He sounded upset enough that she drove right out to the ranch to get me. By the time I called back an hour later, he could barely string a sentence together. He just kept crying and begging me to come home. I assumed the stress of putting Bill into the nursing home was getting to him." Amy frowned at the memory. "I'd vowed to never step foot in this house again until Bill was dead, but I was worried that Joey was headed for another breakdown, so I agreed to fly back. When I got here he showed me the backpack, and I started putting the pieces together."

"How?" Holtz asked.

"I recognized it. It belonged to Bill's grandfather. I was with Bryce when he found it in the attic. I never saw him use it, but I knew he'd taken it. The way I figured it, my mother must have found it while she was going through his room and that was what drove her off the deep end. Erasing him was her way of dealing with what he'd done, though obviously the guilt was still too much for her."

"But if she didn't want anyone to ever know, why not throw it away?" Danny asked.

"I've thought about that a lot. Maybe subconsciously she wanted to be sure the truth would come out someday, even if she couldn't bring herself to tell it. I think that's also why she told me Bryce had done something."

Holtz nodded thoughtfully, then furrowed his brow. "But why does Joey think your father was the killer?"

"Because he found the backpack in the back of the closet in the master bedroom." A slight hesitation. "And because I encouraged that assumption."

"Why?" Danny asked.

"Partly because I was hoping he might finally be able to hate the fucker, too, but mostly because I wanted payback." She shrugged her lack of remorse. "Bryce was already dead. It wasn't like he could be punished again."

"You were going to frame Bill?"

"I knew he'd never go to jail, but I wanted to make sure no one would ever say what a great guy he was again."

"How were you planning to do that?" Holtz asked.

"I was going to turn the backpack over. But before I did, I made sure the underwear would definitely be tied back to him."

"How?"

Amy lifted her chin defiantly. "I jerked the senile prick off, just the way he taught me when I was nine."

Holtz's and Danny's faces made it clear she didn't need to fill in the blanks.

"So why didn't you go through with it?" Holtz asked.

"I couldn't. For Joey's sake. I told him to take the backpack into the woods and bury it. I assumed he had until now."

They lapsed into silence for a minute, then Holtz looked at Amy. "It all sounds logical, but unfortunately it's not evidence. Just because Bryce had the backpack at some point and your mother said he did something, doesn't prove he was killer. And I'm afraid the DA isn't just going to take your word for everything. We're going to need to find some hard evidence before he'll kick Joey or Tim Walczak free."

"It's in my room," Amy said. "Under a floor board in the closet. At least I assume it's still there."

"What is?"

"The evidence. There were photos in the front pocket. Polaroids. Joey never knew about them. He wouldn't touch the backpack after he saw the underwear. I found them that night after he went to bed and hid them."

"Why?" Danny asked.

Amy's face reddened and she looked down. "Because they didn't fit with my whole framing-Bill plan."

"What kind of photos?" Holtz asked.

Amy hesitated a long moment and her eyes began to shine. "Some are just kids playing baseball," she began.

Take me out to the ball game...

* * * * *

Danny lit a cigarette and leaned against the truck. "He umpired Little League games. I know Andy was on a team."

"Michael Frazier, too," Holtz replied. "He was wearing his uniform in the picture with his obituary. I'm not sure about Talbot and Levitt, but I'm guessing yes."

"Our speculation was right. Bryce was able to hide in plain sight because he was supposed to be there."

Holtz nodded.

"You were also right about two separate killers."

"Yeah," Holtz replied without enthusiasm. "Now they just have to find the other one."

"Will Amy and I be able to stay here tonight?" Danny asked.

"It's not my call, but I can't imagine why not. The house has already been searched once, though obviously they neglected to check under the floors." Holtz cracked a wry smile. "I'm sure Smith's boys will just want to get Amy's statement and take the photos into evidence."

Danny nodded, chewed his lower lip thoughtfully

"What?" Holtz asked.

"I just don't understand how she could live with that for a year, seeing the kind of photos she described and not telling anyone the truth. That's not normal."

"Probably by not thinking about it. That's how some people cope. Out of sight, out of mind. If they don't see something, they don't have to think about it. That was obviously Bobbi Gardner's philosophy. If she wasn't reminded of Bryce, she wouldn't have to think about what he'd done."

"Yeah, but that obviously didn't work. You'd think Amy would have realized that."

"You're assuming she recognizes she's following her mother's pattern." Holtz paused a beat, then smiled slyly. "It's amazing how blind some people can be to that sort of thing."

Danny gave a curdled smile. "Don't you have a family not waiting for you at home?"

CHAPTER 51

Amy was lying on the living room sofa, a nearly empty wine glass cradled in her left hand, a book propped against her thighs. She licked her right index finger and flipped the page. Danny knocked on the doorway.

"I just wanted to say goodnight."

Amy grunted as she pushed up on her elbows and sat back against the pillows. She pulled her knees up and nodded at the empty space. Danny sat down facing her.

"So, how come you're sleeping in here instead of your old room?" he asked. "It doesn't look very comfortable."

"With all that pink? I'd have nightmares for a month." The smile slowly faded. "There are no ghosts in here. No real memories. In eighteen years, I think I was in here twice. It's emotionally neutral territory." She raised her eyebrows. "But you didn't come in here to ask me about that or to say goodnight. What's up?"

Danny licked his lips anxiously. "Did you ever think about Tim Walczak when Joey found the backpack?"

Amy studied her glass for a long moment, then sighed. "This place is poison for me. When I'm here, I become a different person. The hate comes back and I just want to hurt Bill for what he did to us. Even last night I kept wondering if there was a way I could save Joey but still get revenge." She looked back up at Danny. "So no, I didn't think about Tim Walczak then, and by the time I got back to New Mexico and could think straight, it was too late. I was afraid that if I told Joey what I'd tried to do, I'd lose him. He's the only family I have.""

"No offense," Danny said, "but you talk to him once a month, and you've only seen him once since you graduated high school. I'm not saying you don't love him, but what exactly would you be losing? Tim lost everything. You could have given him back at least one year of his life."

He braced for the fallout, but Amy just nodded ruefully.

"You're right. About that and my relationship with Joey. I wish we could spend more time together, but he's afraid to leave and I'm afraid to come back, so we make do."

"But that doesn't really seem to be working out for either of you. He's a hermit, and you can't be here without going over to the dark side. Wouldn't it be better to just deal with the shit instead of avoiding it? I mean, isn't that what you help other people do?"

Amy laughed. "Clearly you've never heard the saying, 'Those who can, do. Those who can't, teach.' Back in New Mexico, when I'm surrounded by people who make me feel safe, I can almost be the person I want to be, the better version of myself who feels at peace and counts my blessings and appreciates the smaller gifts of life. At least most of the time. I don't know that I'll ever get to a point where I can be that person here."

"But shouldn't you at least try?"

"Not yet. Not while he's still alive." Amy looked past Danny, and her face lost all its softness. "Maybe once he's gone. In the meantime, I'm better off as I am."

A high-functioning mess?

Danny nodded, started to get up.

"Does it bother you, knowing the truth about Bryce now?" Amy asked suddenly.

It took Danny by surprise and he sat back down. "I'm not sure yet." It was the truth. "I already felt like I didn't really know him during the last few years. Now I wonder if I ever did."

"You did," Amy replied with surprising certainty. "I think there were two Bryces, and both were equally real."

"A good one and a psycho one?"

Amy gave a little laugh. "Good might be pushing it, but there was definitely good in him."

Danny nodded. "But it's hard reconciling the Bryce I remember—even when he was being a dick—with the pyscho."

Amy nodded back knowingly. "You know, he tried to protect me from Bill."

"He told you that?"

"No. I heard them arguing a few weeks before Bill started coming to my room. It didn't make any sense at the time because I didn't know what was going on, but later I realized he was offering himself in my place. I'm betting he did the same for Joey."

"Kind of strange given that he ended up molesting kids himself, don't you think?"

Amy shrugged. "Like I said, I think there were two sides to him, and up until the point, Bryce was a really good brother. Once Bill started in on me, it was like I didn't exist anymore."

"That doesn't make sense. Why would he shut you out then? It should have been the opposite. He should have been sympathetic because he'd been through it himself."

"Guilt. I think that was actually why he ran away, too."

Danny frowned. "Sorry, I don't follow."

"He left a few days after Bill touched me the first time. I think it was because he blamed himself for not being able to stop it. When he came back, he was reminded of that every time he saw me, and it made him angry. Of course, if he'd been normal he would have turned his anger on Bill, but he couldn't allow himself to do that. Instead, it became my fault I was being molested." She stopped and studied Danny's face for a moment. "Is this all sounding like New Age mumbo jumbo?"

Danny shook his head. "No, I get it, I think. At least the shifting blame part. I did the same thing to Jerry."

"Sounds about right."

They lapsed into thoughtful silence for a few minutes, then Danny nodded to himself.

"Although it makes me sick to think about what Bryce did and all the things that happened to you guys when you were younger, I guess I'd still rather know the truth. I mean, that's why I came back, right?"

CHAPTER 52

They stopped at the foot of the narrow side path.

"I'll be okay from here," Joey said.

He looked at the lighted windows less than a hundred yards through the woods and decided not to argue. "Okay. I'll call you in the morning, assuming Caroline doesn't kill me tonight."

They kissed awkwardly, then he watched Joey work his way toward the house, white t-shirt floating like a ghost through the trees. He waited until Joey waved from the backyard, then turned and started back toward the field.

As he rounded the bend, he moved carefully, keeping to the right so he could feel his way along the edge of the path with his foot. Despite the heat and humidity, he hugged the blanket tighter against his chest.

The path dropped toward a narrow stream, then rose again and curved left. The field came into view and he felt a surge of relief. He exhaled and began moving more quickly.

Suddenly something moved to his left, and he let out a sharp cry. A shadowed figure stepped into the middle of the path.

"Hey, homo," a familiar voice said.

He took a few tentative steps until he could make out the contours of Bryce's face. "Jesus fuck, you scared the shit out of me," he said shakily, letting out a slow breath.

"So how long have you and my brother been fucking?" Bryce asked, taking a step forward.

"What are you talking about?" he tried, hearing how unconvincing it sounded.

"I saw you," Bryce said. "He fucked you. And you kissed."

He wasn't sure how to respond. Bryce's voice wasn't accusatory or angry, but something in it made him uneasy.

Bryce took another step forward. "Why not me?"

"What?" he replied.

"Why not me?" Bryce's voice broke plaintively. "He's just my brother. I'm supposed to be your best friend."

He began stammering. "I just...I didn't think..."

"Well, you were wrong," Bryce cut him off with sudden coldness, jerking his hands from his pockets.

He flinched away in response, adrenaline spiking his heart.

Bryce brayed derisively. "What? Did you think I was going to stab you? Lighten up."

He felt Bryce's eyes burning into his own as Bryce lifted a small silvery pipe, flicked the Zippo lighter in his right hand, and inhaled deeply. "Here," Bryce said without exhaling, extending the pipe with his left hand as he snapped the lighter shut and slipped it into his right pocket.

"I can't," he said. "I have to get home. Caroline's probably freaking out."

Bryce tilted his head back and blew smoke at the sky. "Right. You can fuck around with my brother for a half hour but you can't hang out with me for a few minutes. You're an awesome friend."

He closed his eyes and chewed his lower lips for a second, then nodded. "Sure."

He reached for the pipe, but as his fingers touched the warm brass, Bryce's hand spasmed open and it dropped to the ground, scattering glowing embers.

"What the fuck?" he cried angrily, stamping them out. "That was such a douche move."

He snatched up the pipe and looked expectantly at Bryce, but Bryce didn't reply, just stared down at his own chest for a moment, then gasped wetly and dropped to his knees.

"Stop fucking arou..." he started, but his vocal chords constricted as he saw someone standing behind Bryce.

Bryce toppled sideways, his body barely making a sound as it hit the soft ground.

He dropped the blanket and ran.

* * * * *

He crouched behind the trunk of a fallen pine. His lungs burned and a stitch throbbed in his left side. His eyes and the tiny cuts crisscrossing his face, hands, and arms stung. He could smell his own piss and breathed through his mouth.

He didn't know where he was or how long he'd been running. He'd missed the path to the Gardners' house and tried another a hundred yards farther along, hoping it would lead him out to the road, but it had taken him deeper into the woods. He'd been too afraid to backtrack, so he'd left the trail, circling to the left.

He looked around. The ground had a gentle slope and was rockier than the woods he knew. The trees were all less dense, almost entirely pine. He closed his eyes, straining to listen for cars over the throbbing chirp of heat bugs. Instead he heard a faint crack from the direction he'd come.

His eyes snapped open as panic tightened his chest again. He couldn't see anything moving. He took quick breaths to fight back a wave of nausea. He realized he needed to make a stand soon. If he kept running he wouldn't have enough energy to fight back if it came down to that.

He crouched lower and scanned the ground nearby. A few feet behind him lay a tangle of broken branches. He crab-walked to it and quietly pulled out a thick three-foot section. It was heavy and felt solid against the palm of his left hand.

Farther to his right, a wide, jagged slab of granite rose almost vertically. Higher ground, he thought. It was something he'd read or seen in a movie. Always take the higher ground. Though it was only a bare sketch of a plan, it made him feel slightly better.

The rock was no more than forty feet away, but he'd be in the open the whole time. It was a risk he had to take. He clutched the branch tightly in his right hand and rose to a crouch, carefully watching the trees for a long moment.

On the count of three, he thought, taking slow, deep breaths as he unconsciously rubbed the cross around his neck.

One...two...three. He began to sprint.

He heard footfalls behind him immediately, but fought the urge to look back. He cut left instead around a wide hummock, then back right, and ran harder. Over the pounding in his head, he was sure the footfalls were gaining.

He adjusted his gait and readied to jump, but the ground suddenly dipped. He stumbled, tried to recover, knew he couldn't make it. He dodged right around the side of the rock.

The ground dropped sharply away. He tried to stop, but his Chuck Taylor's just skidded in the pine needles. He made a desperate grab with his left hand and felt soft moss pull away in his fingers.

* * * * *

He was falling, his heart banging. He could see his arms flailing and his hands clawing at the air, but beyond them was just blackness. He closed his eyes, waiting for the impact.

Suddenly he stopped falling. There was no pain. Just stillness, the sound of his own breathing, and the rich smell of damp earth.

"Here, Lily, I've got a bone for you. Actually two-hundred-and-six, though a few are busted."

It was his own voice, but he knew he hadn't spoken. In the distance he heard a branch crack.

"Come on, girl! Come on, Lily!"

Another crack, much closer.

He tried to open his eyes, but couldn't.

Excited barking. A hand caressed his right cheek.

"Hang on, sweetie, she's almost here. You're almost safe."

The voice became a whisper.

"Then it'll be time for me to go."

CHAPTER 53

Danny finished dragging the branches away from the break in the wall. Though the ground beyond had been overgrown, he could still make out the gentle curve where the path had cut through the trees. He wiped his right hand on his jeans and checked his watch. 6:28 AM. Still too early.

He turned back to the house. The lights were still off. He wasn't sure if he wanted Amy to wake up before he left or not. He suspected she'd try to talk him out of it. He picked up his mug, sipped cold coffee, and decided he didn't need any more. He was already wired enough, though it wasn't just the caffeine.

In the four hours since he'd woken up, everything had come back to him. Little by little, the seconds, minutes, hours, days, weeks, and months leading up to his fall had returned. His memory of his life before that moment was whole again.

"Then it'll be time for me to go."

Logically he knew it was just a dream, but he hadn't felt that other part of him since. Oddly, it didn't make him sad. He actually felt at peace, contented. He lit a cigarette, kicked off his sneakers, and wiggled his toes in the wet grass, savoring the sensation.

Another fifteen minutes, he thought.

CHAPTER 54

From across the field he could see Tom Parker. Parker was moving slowly, his steps seemingly less steady than usual. Danny took a last drag on his cigarette, carefully crushed it out on the damp ground, and pocketed the butt. He took a step back into the shadows, his heart pounding with anticipation as Parker approached the bottom of the hill.

Just a few more steps. Five, four, three... Parker disappeared behind the rise. Danny took steady breaths, trying to relax as he waited. Seconds passed, becoming a minute.

Fuck, he thought. I was wrong.

Suddenly a backlit halo of thin red hair broke over the crest in the dirt road fifty yards away. Parker's head bobbed into view. Danny moved farther back.

As he stepped under the canopy, Parker paused to let his eyes adjust. When he saw Danny standing in the middle of the trail, he cocked his head curiously as though it might be an illusion, then took a few tentative steps.

"Hey, Mr. Parker," Danny said. "I was hoping I'd find you."

Parker looked at him uncertainly. "Well, you did," he rasped. "I guess I'm a creature of habit."

Danny nodded. "Does it ever freak you out, passing by here?"

Parker cocked his head, his scant eyebrows knitting together.

"This is where Bryce was killed, isn't it?" Danny asked.

Parker looked around slowly, then shrugged. "Somewhere around here. I'm not sure where exactly."

"The police know he killed Andy and the others," Danny said. "Amy Gardner told them yesterday." He wished he could see Parker's eyes more clearly, but the light was behind him.

"I saw all the cars," Parker said flatly.

Danny moved a few steps closer. "You should turn yourself in. It's time."

Parker didn't reply, but looked down. No emotion registered on his face.

"You and Lily walked this route at least twice a day," Danny said. "You would have come across Bryce's body first. I don't know why I didn't see that sooner."

Parker looked up and studied Danny with a calm shrewdness Danny hadn't seen before. Danny found it unsettling.

"You found me because you were looking for me, weren't you?" he asked, watching for a reaction.

Parker just gave a slight nod.

"To make sure the fall killed me?"

Parker's eyes widened. "I didn't know about the fall until Lily found you," he said with surprising passion. "I swear."

"You didn't chase me?"

Parker shook his head. "I was in shock. I couldn't move. I just sat here and cried. I couldn't believe what I'd done."

Danny felt a chill as he realized the implication. He'd lost twelve years of his life out of panic.

"Once I calmed down, I went to your house to make sure you were okay," Parker went on. "I rang the doorbell at least a dozen times, but there was no answer, so I waited. Just before the sun came up, I went home to get Lily and we came back to look for you. I had her sniff the blanket you'd dropped, hoping she'd get your scent."

Danny frowned as he tried to put the pieces together. "You went to my house looking for me?"

Parker nodded.

"But if I'd been there, I would have called the police."

Parker nodded again. "I was willing to accept the consequences for what I'd done at that point."

Danny noted the emphasis on the last three words, decided it could wait. "How did you know Bryce killed Andy?" he asked.

"I didn't. Not until later."

Danny blinked surprise. "Then why did you kill him? "

"I was just reacting in the moment."

"To what?"

"He had a knife in his back pocket. I saw him pull it out. I realized he was going to kill you."

Danny suddenly felt dizzy. He closed his eyes and took shallow breaths. The memories of the final moments replayed in his head. Bryce lighting the pipe, slipping the lighter back into his right pocket, holding the pipe out with his left hand. Where was Bryce's right hand? Had Bryce just been trying to get him to step closer?

His eyes snapped open. "So you were just trying to save me?" he asked. The coincidence of Parker just happening on the scene at that moment seemed too unlikely.

Parker nodded, seemed to read his skepticism. "I was just out walking. Trying to avoid being at home." He paused, tilted his head as though hearing distant voices. "I remember I'd left Lily at home because of the skunks." He nodded to himself. "I didn't even know you were here until I heard voices. I stopped to listen for a moment, then started to leave because it was obvious you were having a private conversation." He pressed his eyes shut. "But something made me stop. Something in his voice that made me nervous, so I moved closer." He opened his eyes, and Danny saw the glint of tears. "That's when I saw him grab the knife. I don't think I even meant to stab him. I think it just happened when I grabbed his wrist." He shook his head sadly.

"But if you were just trying to save me, why didn't you tell the police?" Danny asked. "Especially if it was an accident."

"Because while I was searching for you I had a chance to run through it all again in my head, and I realized it wasn't a sudden thing. It wasn't an argument that got out of control. It was planned. I heard it in his voice, and saw it in the way he went for the knife. He knew exactly what he was doing. He was calm. That's when I realized he'd done it before." Parker's voice broke. "To Andy and the others."

He paused and took a few unsteady breaths, then his eyes turned hard. "And I decided I wasn't going to take a chance on throwing my life away for killing that worthless piece of shit."

Danny knew there was no appropriate response, and decided to give Parker a moment. He took out his cigarettes, lit one, watched Parker's breathing return to normal.

"I'm really sorry about Andy," he said finally, "and maybe Bryce even deserved what you did to him, but what about Tim Walczak? He was innocent and you knew it, but you let him go to jail."

"Innocent?" Parker replied coldly. "He might not have killed anyone, but he was still a pervert. Who knows what he would have done if he hadn't been locked away?"

The sympathy Danny had been feeling died. "He wasn't a pervert," he replied. "He was just a lonely kid. He didn't deserve what happened to him." He gave a Parker a meaningful look. "Like I said, you should turn yourself in."

"Haven't I lost enough?" Parker called after him as he started back toward the path to the Gardners' house.

CHAPTER 55

"I have something for you," Holtz said, pushing an unlabeled BASF cassette tape across the table.

Danny eyed it curiously. "You made me a mix tape? Does this mean we're going steady?"

"Smart ass," Holtz replied. "Consider it part of your re-education."

Danny smiled and slipped it into his shirt pocket. "Thanks. So what's happening with Parker?" It had been a week since he'd confronted Parker in the woods, six days since Parker had confessed to killing Bryce. He knew Parker was back home, though he hadn't seen him out walking at all.

"The DA is still weighing his options," Holtz replied. He squirted ketchup on his burger and fries, signaled the waitress for more coffee.

"Whether to charge him or not?"

"Whether to charge him with manslaughter or murder."

"Murder?"

"They interviewed his ex-wife. She wouldn't go so far as to say she thought it was premeditated, but she said Parker was fixated on Bryce after Andy was killed. He always knew when Bryce was home from Fessenden, where he'd been, who he'd been with."

"You think he suspected all along that Bryce killed Andy?"

Holtz shrugged noncommittally. "That's the big question."

Danny waited while the waitress refilled Holtz's cup.

"Did Mrs. Parker know he killed Bryce?" he asked finally.

Holtz picked up some fries. "She said no. Said they were pretty much living separate lives by then, sleeping in separate bedrooms. But she also said she frequently heard him walking around in the middle of the night, going into Andy's room, leaving the house and coming back hours later, so she was probably aware he wasn't home that night. My guess is that she had suspicions but didn't want to confirm them." He stuffed the fries into his mouth.

Danny nodded, then frowned as a thought began to take shape. He stared into space for a moment, trying to remember exactly what Parker had said.

"What?" Holtz prompted.

Danny looked back at him. "This may be nothing, but he told me that initially he was ready to take the fall for what he'd done. It wasn't until the next morning, after he realized Bryce had killed Andy and the others, that he changed his mind."

"So?"

"So that's when he would have tried to cover it up by making it look like the other killings, right?"

Holtz nodded. "Presumably."

"You said Bryce's throat was cut after he was dead. How long after?"

Holtz's hand stopped, his cup halfway to his mouth. "That's a really good question. If it was right after, that throws the rest of his story into question." He nodded slowly as he sipped his coffee. "You sure you don't want to be a cop?"

Danny took a bite of his BLT and chewed it slowly. "You know," he said finally, "the more I think about it, the more I question a lot of his story."

"Like what?"

"Like whether Bryce was even going to kill me. He may have been pulling a knife out of his pocket, but..." He stopped and shook his head uncertainly.

"What does your gut tell you?"

"My gut tells me that maybe I don't want to know for sure. Especially if he was."

"Mmmm. Sometimes it's easier not knowing the whole truth."

Danny made a wry face. "Yeah, and the not-so-subtle irony of that isn't lost on me." He sipped his raspberry lime rickey and let happier memories intrude. "So are you BMOC now?"

251

Holtz made a face. "For making the original investigators and the DA's office look like incompetent bigots?" He shrugged. "Actually, most of the guys have pulled me aside privately to congratulate me, and Marty Thornton said he's going to see about transferring me to the detective division once the dust settles. Assuming the bug ever crawls out of the Chief's ass."

"Wait, Weston has a whole detective *division*?"

Holtz ignored it. "It would be a nice promotion. Good money..." he trailed off.

"But?"

Holtz hesitated a moment. "I'm not sure I'm ready for it."

"Why not?"

"You asked why this case was so important to me. I gave you a few reasons that were all true, but I never told you the main one."

"Delia Lee?" Danny asked.

Holtz's eyebrows popped up.

"Caroline told me to ask you about her," Danny said.

"Your mother is a piece of work."

"Yeah, I think that's been pretty clearly established. So who was she?"

Holtz looked around uncomfortably before settling his gaze back on Danny. "Delia was a twelve-year-old girl who called 911 and reported that her mother had beaten her and was threatening to kill her. I was dispatched along with a second-year guy.

"When we got to the house, there was no answer, so we did a sweep around the outside. We found the mother and daughter on the patio having a quiet dinner. They both seemed convincingly startled to see us, and equally surprised to hear about the call.

"The mother said her husband had recently moved out, and that someone had been leaving notes in Delia's locker saying the split was her fault. Mrs. Lee suggested the same person had probably placed the call as a prank. I asked Delia about the notes, and she confirmed them. She also said she hadn't called us.

"It came down to a judgment call. My instinct was to take her into custody, get her examined and have a social worker talk with her, and as senior officer on the scene it was my call. I decided not to do anything."

"Why?"

"She was wearing shorts and a halter top and there were no visible marks, and though she was subdued, she didn't seem scared. It was also clear that Mrs. Lee was going to lawyer-up the moment we left, and I'd already developed a reputation for overreacting." He paused and rubbed his hand over his face. "Basically, I was afraid of making a fool of myself."

"But it sounds like you made a reasonable decision based on the situation," Danny said.

"That's what the review panel said," Holtz sighed, "but obviously I missed something. That night, Mrs. Lee beat Delia so severely that she never regained consciousness."

A somber silence stretched out for nearly a minute before Danny said, "I'm sorry. We don't have to talk about it anymore if it's too painful."

Holtz shrugged it away. "In any case, even though the panel ruled that my decision hadn't been improper, they recommended I be taken off the streets. It was pretty clear I'd lost the confidence of my peers by then, so I didn't fight it. To be honest, I'd begun to wonder whether I was cut out for the job, myself." He grunted at the memory. "After a few months of riding the desk, it was apparent I had a lot of free time with no one watching me, so I started reviewing old cases. That was when I remembered the questions I'd had about the Walczak investigation and dug it out again. My gut still told me the pieces didn't fit together, so I started investigating it."

"So basically you were just trying to prove you weren't a total fuck up?" Danny joked, hoping to lighten the mood.

Holtz opened his mouth, seemed to change his mind, and cracked a grudging smile. "Yeah, basically. Plus the other stuff I told you before."

"Well, it seems like you succeeded, so why the reluctance to become Detective Rick?"

Holtz stared at his plate for a moment. "I proved I was right, but I didn't solve the case. You pieced most of it together, and there was more than a little luck involved."

Danny sighed theatrically. "As much fun as it is to watch you wallow in self-doubt, yeah, you lucked out that Amy showed up and that my memory came back, but you recognized the problems with the original investigation and figured out the two-killer part. Plus you cooked up the half-assed scheme to sucker me into helping you. That's got to count for something, right?"

"It wasn't *that* half-assed," Holtz replied. "It worked, right?"

"Exactly, so what's the problem? It seems that despite all early indications, you grew up to be a decent cop."

"And you just grew up," Holtz deadpanned. He sipped his coffee, then gave Danny a stern look. "By the way, ambushing killers by yourself in the middle of the woods? Don't do that again." He picked up his burger and took a bite.

"Oh, come on," Danny laughed. "The guy is like ninety."

"And you've only got one arm to defend yourself," Holtz replied around his mouthful.

"For now."

Holtz quirked an eyebrow. "You're going to have surgery?"

Danny shook his head. "That would just give me an excuse to put my life on hold for another six months, but check this out." He squinted in concentration and slowly lifted his left hand two inches from the table, then lowered it. He smiled triumphantly. "I've been working on it for an hour a day."

"Congratulations."

"Baby steps. My goal is to be able to type with it by the end of the summer. They say everything's going to be done on computers soon, so..." He waggled his fingers. "I'm taking the GED exam in a few weeks, then I'm going to apply to some schools."

"Good for you."

"Thanks. It feels good to finally have some kind of plan."

They lapsed into comfortable silence until they finished eating. Holtz signaled for more coffee and the check.

"Amy left yesterday," Danny said.

"So I heard."

"From who?"

Holtz smiled cryptically.

Danny rolled his eyes. "You and your mysterious sources."

"I also heard you're taking your mother back to the big house tomorrow."

"Wow, you're good."

"That was an easy one. I saw Beth Wallace. So does that mean you've patched things up?"

The waitress topped off both of their cups and laid the check on the table.

"No, it just means Caroline needs a ride. Beth is busy, and Caroline and Grace are on the outs."

"What caused that?"

"My guess is that Grace is pissed that Caroline used her as an alibi without telling her first. Either that or she blames Caroline for my calling her a cunt." He shrugged casually. "I suppose it doesn't matter. They'll have another six months to get over it."

Holtz nodded. "So, seriously, what's happening with you and your mother?"

"Nothing really. I'm actually glad she's going away because it means I don't have to really deal with her for a while. Tough to get into a serious discussion with Matron Mama Morton looking over your shoulder."

"What about after she gets out? What do you want ideally?"

Danny thought it over. "I don't want to cut her out of my life completely. I guess it'll be more baby steps. I'll spend some time with her and see what happens." He nodded to himself. "I guess I'd say I'm cautiously optimistic. The fact that she copped to being guilty could mean she's ready to change. Or not."

"Cautious optimism is good, I guess," Holtz said. "Have you talked about what happened?"

"No. Honestly, I'm not interested in her reasons or excuses. I've heard them all before."

"Kind of harsh, don't you think?"

"Maybe, but I figure the only way to move forward is to stop repeating the same shit again and again. We've already done the apologize-forgive-get-fucked-over-again dance enough. We'll deal with what happened down the road.

"So are you moving back into the house while she's gone?"

Danny widened his eyes in exaggerated disbelief. "Gee, you don't already know?" He cracked a wry grin. "Yeah, until I hopefully start school, though I'm going to spend the last two weeks of July in the Hamptons with my dad and Karl."

"I'm not even going to comment on how pretentious that sounded," Holtz replied.

"Yeah, I guess it did. Sorry."

"So how's Joey doing?" Holtz asked.

"Who?"

"What's that supposed to mean?"

"It means he's been like a ghost since he got home. I knew he and Amy had a lot to discuss, so I gave them space, but since she left, he's been avoiding me."

"He probably just needs to catch up on his rest. I'm sure he didn't get much with all the loonies howling at the moon."

"No, I've heard him pacing around, but he won't come into a room if he knows I'm there, and if he comes in and sees me, he mumbles a bunch of excuses and almost runs out."

"Give him some time. He's been through a lot."

"I know, and it's not like I was expecting him to suddenly turn into Mr. Rogers, but I think he's actually gotten worse. He seems more haunted, more withdrawn. At least around me."

Holtz sipped his coffee for a moment. "I hate to say it, but he might still be pissed at you for trying to convince him to throw his father under the bus."

Danny gave him a questioning look.

"The reality of everything else may have changed, but that moment hasn't," Holtz replied. "Not for him, anyway. He felt you betrayed him."

CHAPTER 56

Joey was sitting on the folding chair on the patio, staring toward the gap in the wall.

"I blocked it up right after my mother killed herself," he said without looking up as Danny approached. "I was having nightmares that there was something evil back there that kept creeping into our house." He smiled self-consciously. "I thought I could keep any more bad stuff from happening."

"I cleared it so I wouldn't have to pass my house. I couldn't deal with both Parker and running into my mother in the same morning. I can cover it back over if you want."

"It's okay," Joey said. "Now I just see woods."

"Good." Danny settled down onto the flagstones a few feet away and watched two squirrels chasing one another along the top the wall until the silence began to feel comfortable. "I'm really sorry for what I said the last time I visited you," he said. "I thought I was doing a good thing."

"I know," Joey replied softly. "Amy explained it. You were trying to save me from myself by giving me a way out."

Danny cut a look at him. "So you're not pissed at me?"

"Not anymore."

"Then why does it seem like you've been avoiding me?"

Joey continued staring into the trees for a moment longer before meeting Danny's gaze. "Probably because I have been a little, but only because I wasn't ready to talk yet."

"Are you ready now?"

Joey just shrugged. Danny decided to take it as a yes.

"So are you okay?"

"Yes, no, getting there."

"That pretty much covers all the bases."

Joey smiled tiredly. "I just feel so stupid and pathetic. Why didn't I realize how fucked up I was about my dad?" He stopped and frowned at what he'd said. "That's not true. I did realize. I just couldn't admit it to myself." He grimaced. "Which is even more pathetic."

"You don't have to explain," Danny said sympathetically. "Believe me, I get it. We both have a parent who abused us and we both kept forgiving them. The only difference is that I blocked out the worst parts because I couldn't let myself get mad at her. In the end, though, we both did the same thing. As soon as they needed us, we came back."

"But you needed to come back for you, too."

"Maybe, but let's face it, I was still being her little bitch. I was willing to shit all over Jerry, but I kept giving her a free pass, hoping that maybe she'd magically change."

"How did that work out for you?" Joey asked.

Danny gave a wry chuckle.

Joey looked back toward the trees and his brow furrowed. "Do you know why I was so willing to go to prison?"

"Because you love your dad?" Danny ventured.

Joey sighed deeply and shook his head. "Because my life had already become a prison."

Danny fought the urge to giggle. He pretended to hear a noise to his right and turned his head away.

"Yeah, that was what I thought, too," Joey said after a few seconds. "A tad melodramatic, huh?"

Danny looked back at him. "Where did that come from?"

"My shrink at the hospital. I had to see him every day."

"And that's what he told you?"

"He also thinks I may have daddy issues," Joey deadpanned before cracking a sly grin.

Danny laughed. It wasn't the old Joey, but he'd regained some of his playful charm.

"Actually it was pretty helpful," Joey said, his expression turning reflective, "and I had a lot of time to think about things."

"Any major epiphanies?"

"My father doesn't know I exist anymore."

Danny gave him an uncomprehending shrug. "You've known that for a long time, haven't you?"

"You can know something logically without accepting it emotionally," Joey replied. "Yeah, I knew he was a vegetable, but I still kept trying to prove myself to him. I was willing to let Tim Walczak die in jail to do that. I was willing to go myself." His eyes clouded over. "I also realized my entire identity pretty much revolves around my father and Bryce's death."

"Not much sunshine," Danny said.

"No," Joey agreed. "That was the night I became the brother of the dead kid, the night my mother started her final slide, and the night I lost you."

"I'm sorry," Danny replied reflexively.

"I've felt guilty about it all for so long."

"Why?"

"Because I thought that I should have heard or seen something and been able to save you, or that maybe it was supposed to be me instead of Bryce." Joey's voice dropped to a near-whisper. "And because I thought I should have been more sorry he was dead."

Danny just nodded.

"But now that I know the truth," Joey said, "I think I can finally let it go."

"That's good," Danny said encouragingly. He leaned back and wrestled the pack of cigarettes from his front right pocket, pulled one out, and lit it. He took a long drag and blew smoke at the clear late-afternoon sky, watching it drift back toward the house.

"Last week I thought I was going to be spending the rest of my life in prison," Joey said after a moment. "I got a second chance. I don't want to waste it."

"Any ideas on what you want to do?"

"Long-term, no, and honestly it's a little too scary to contemplate. The last time I tried to make it in the big world, I ended up crawling back to daddy-who-diddled me. I also know that I'm not going to miraculously stop being fucked up just because I think I've put a few things behind me."

"What about short-term?"

"Oddly, the best thing my father ever did for me was to get sick because it gave me a sense of purpose and something to focus on. Without that, I probably would have just curled up in the corner until they carted me off to a padded cell."

"So you're going to become a candy striper?"

Joey rolled his eyes tolerantly. "Tim's being released on Friday. His parents won't even talk to him, so he's being placed in a state-run hospice."

"How do you know?"

"I went to visit him. Angel says hi, by the way. I think he has a crush on you."

"So I've heard."

"He's cute." Joey arched his eyebrows teasingly. "And it looks like he's got a big package."

"Anyway," Danny sing-songed.

"Anyway, I was thinking Tim could come stay here."

"You serious?"

"Yeah," Joey replied in a way that suggested he was still trying to convince himself. "He's doing better now, and when...if...he gets sick again, he can move into the study. It's still set up from when I was taking care of my dad."

"But are you sure you really want to do that?"

"He deserves a break. He's gotten screwed over for almost half his life."

"But that wasn't your fault. It wasn't even Bryce's fault."

"No, but he went to jail for what Bryce did, and I kept him in there for an extra year. I just feel like maybe I can restore the balance a little."

Danny nodded slowly. "I think it's admirable that you want to help," he said carefully, "but won't you be allowing that night to still define your life? I mean, your only connection to Tim goes through that point."

Joey nodded thoughtfully. "Yeah, but up until now, everything about it has been negative. By helping him, I can make something positive out of it. Kind of take control, in a way. It also gives me something to focus on while I figure out what I want to do when I grow up." He smiled self-consciously, then looked down at the flagstones. "And to be honest, I'm not sure I can handle being alone again yet."

Danny felt a stab of guilt and knew he couldn't ignore the implied question. "Yeah, I'm moving back into Caroline's after I take her back tomorrow," he said.

"You don't have to," Joey replied. "You could move in here. Just as friends, I mean. You could help with Tim." His eyes searched Danny's face with a mixture of hope and anxiousness.

"I can't," Danny said, "I want to get to know Tim, and I'll definitely help out if you need me, but I need...I want...to be on my own. I'm sorry."

"It's okay," Joey said quickly. "I get it." He forced a smile, though Danny could read the hurt in his eyes.

Danny shifted to face Joey. "Joey, you're not an 'ugly duckling girl.' You never were." He pictured Joey lying naked beside him in the moonlight. "You were beautiful."

Joey's eyes widened. "'Ugly duckling girl?'"

"Holtz gave me a tape of the song," Danny said. "I finally get what you were trying to tell me that night."

"You remember it?"

Danny nodded. "I remember everything now, and I'm sorry I was so dense. I realized that we were something more than friends, but it never occurred to me that we might be boyfriends." He smiled shyly. "That you might actually love me."

"How could you have missed that?" Joey asked.

"Maybe because I didn't even realize we were gay."

Joey blinked in disbelief.

"I'm serious," Danny said. "It wasn't until I was recovering and Abby noticed that I was way more interested in the hot guys in *People* that I thought, 'Oh, I must be gay.'"

"But you were twelve when your dad moved in with Karl. You knew all about gay."

"I know, but I thought they were different because they loved one another. I wasn't even thinking about the possibility of love." He saw Joey's lips tighten, and added, "Not just with you. At all. After watching Jerry and Caroline disintegrate, it wasn't something I thought I'd ever want."

"Like Bill and Bobbi were better?"

"I know, but I guess I lacked imagination. You saw the possibility for something more than I did. I'm sorry I didn't realize that." He reached out and took Joey's hand. "Who knows what would have happened if I hadn't had the accident? Maybe we'd be an old married couple by now."

"Or bitter and divorced."

They sat in silence for a while, their hands still intertwined. Danny had the sense they were saying goodbye in some way.

"I'm applying for school in the fall," he said finally. "I think I want to study design."

Joey's face brightened. "I told you that you should study art. There are some great schools in the area."

Danny nodded. "I know, but I don't want to limit myself. I may end up here, but I also may end up someplace new." He looked around and took a deep breath. "I love it here, and it's always going to be part of me, but there's a lot more world out there. I want to experience some of it."

Some of the enthusiasm in Joey's eyes faded, but he nodded.

"Depending on what happens with Tim, you should sell the house when your dad dies," Danny said. "Make a fresh start. There are just too many bad memories here, and Amy's never going to be able to come back without her head spinning around." He smiled encouragingly. "Besides, the suburbs are for straight people with kids, and senior citizens."

"'And high school girls with clear-skinned smiles, who married young and then retired.'"

Danny smirked. "We're not that young anymore, Joey."

Made in the USA
San Bernardino, CA
07 March 2015